In memory of all the C r
]

and in memory of one

The truth is often stranger than any fiction that can be written.

Cover Design

The cover of this book was created by Hammad Khalid, who can be contacted at **https://www.fiverr.com/hmdgfx**

Author's Note On The Language Used In This Book

This is a story about soldiers and to maintain authenticity the language used reflects that. There is a use of swear words of the strongest kind. It is not my intention to cause offence, but only to reflect the language that was and still is used by soldiers. Apart from the swearing there is other language used that may cause offence. I don't condone the use of that language, but it reflects the period in which the story is set. While we may live in more enlightened times and would never consider using such words, the 1940s were different and the language used is contemporary for the period. We cannot change the past, we can only change the present and the future and I'm glad that our language has changed and become more sensitive to the feelings of others but we must never forget our past. We should, however, seek not to repeat it.

Abbreviations of rank used in this book (in descending order of seniority):

Lt Col – Lieutenant Colonel (often referred to simply as Colonel by their own subordinates)
Maj – Major
Capt – Captain
Lt – Lieutenant
2Lt – Second Lieutenant
RSM – Regimental Sergeant Major (Warrant Office Class 1)
CSM – Company Sergeant major (Warrant Officer Class 2)
TSM – Troop Sergeant Major (Warrant Officer Class 2) as used by the commandos.
SMjr – Sergeant Major (generic)
CSgt – Colour Sergeant
SSgt – Staff Sergeant
Sgt - Sergeant

LSgt – Lance Sergeant; a Brigade of Guards rank, but sometimes used by the commandos instead of Corporal.
Cpl – Corporal
LCpl – Lance Corporal
Pvt – Private
Tpr – Trooper, a cavalry rank equivalent to Private but used by the commandos.

Cdo – the abbreviation used when naming a specific commando, eg 15 Cdo.

Other military terminology is explained within the text where the narrative allows, or is explained in footnotes.

1 – Weymouth

The four men lay in the thick heather, waiting. They knew their target was out there, somewhere, but not yet visible. The cloud scudded across the sky, sometimes revealing the moon and providing so much light that it hurt the eyes. Sometimes it was hidden, leaving a blackness so deep it was almost impenetrable.

When the moon was at its brightest the commandos covered their eyes, protecting their night vision. Sound was their best friend. Noise would tell them when their quarry was near. Then they would fall on them like the furies.

Some distance away they could hear voices, but they weren't the voices of the men they were hunting. Their blundering and calling would send their quarry to ground, like a rabbit hearing the rustle of a fox through the undergrowth. The commandos smiled a grim smile to themselves. They would never make noise like that. They were masters of stealth, capable of moving through the night silently, like wraiths. It was how they had got to this position undetected.

While daylight had lasted, they had followed the trail of bent grass, footprints in the soft earth, stray fibres left on twigs. It had pointed in a straight line across the landscape. Leading them through the woods and fields of southern Dorset until they had been sure of their quarry's destination.

Their quarry had done well to get this far, Carter had to conceded, but he knew it was now only a matter of time. The commandos had used their fitness to get ahead of the two men, leaving the slower police officers to act as beaters, sending their quarry into their waiting arms.

They were heading for Taunton, that much was obvious. It was the only place on their route that made sense. What their plan was when they reached the town was another matter. Perhaps they would try to board a train. Twice they had tried to steal a car, but the black market in spare parts, caused by the wartime shortages, meant that most car owners removed a vital part each night before they went to bed, in order to prevent just such an act. Half the cars in the country were up on bricks to prevent the rubber of their tyres from perishing, because there was so little petrol available for private motoring.

A voice called and a whistle screeched, but it was from the wrong direction. Whatever had caused the alarm to be sounded, it wasn't the two men that Carter and his little group were waiting for. Not unless they had changed course for some reason.

There was a sound, the rustling of a bush as the branches were parted to allow passage through to the other side. It was slightly to Carter's left. That was no surprise. No one could keep to a straight line when their course was continually being blocked by buildings, hedges or trees. It didn't matter. When they were as close as they would get, Carter and his men would rise out of the ground and issue their challenge. If the men were sensible, they would stand still and surrender themselves. If they were stupid, they would try to run. They wouldn't get far. To either side the rest of Carter's troop were arrayed in a line. The fugitives couldn't hope get past such a barrier.

Feet scuffed through the heather, the stems swishing against the men's trouser legs. They would be tired by now, having been on the move nonstop for two days, trying to put as much distance between themselves and Portland prison as they could. They had managed to snatch a meal, food stolen from a shop in a village. That had been the act that had given Carter and his men the starting point for the trail that they had then followed.

The cloud parted once again and Carter covered one eye, while the other searched the night for a sight of the two men. They were to the south, as expected, perhaps fifty feet to Carter's left. Danny Glass was on that side. Beyond him was Prof Green.

"Stand still and you won't get hurt." Glass's voice broke the silence of the night.

The men failed to obey. They tried to make break for it to their left, directly towards Carter. As they thundered towards him he rose up and swung the handle of his trenching tool at the nearest man's thigh, making a solid contact. He howled with pain but tried to continue his run, stumbling as his injured leg threatened to give way under him. The other man continued, making it past Carter but not very far past. O'Driscoll rose from where he had been lying and took one mighty swipe at the fugitive, the trenching tool handle making a sickening thunk as it made contact with the man's head. He fell as though pole axed.

"Steady Paddy!" Prof Green admonished as he ran up. "You're supposed to be arresting him, not killing him."

"Sure, haven't I arrested him. In fact, I'd say I've never seen a man more arrested than this one."

The first man was still making feeble attempts to get away, his lurching gait keeping him a fraction ahead of Carter. But Carter was walking.

"You may as well stop now." Carter said quietly. "I've got other men out there and they'd just love have a crack at you as well."

The man stopped and turned to face his tormentor. He took a swing at Carter with his fist, more out of frustration at being caught than anything else. Carter swayed out of reach then used his trenching tool handle to jab the man in the stomach. There was a whoosh of escaping breath and the man went down on one knee.

Satisfied that his man wasn't going anywhere, Carter raised a whistle to his lips and blew three long blasts. The sound would summon his men to him, ending their night's exercise.

The police would also respond, coming to collect the two prisoners that had escaped from Portland Prison two days earlier.

The request to help the police had been an unusual one, but Lt Colonel Vernon recognised the training value for his men. Stalking prey was a useful skill for a commando, transferring to the battlefield in the need to locate the enemy and then creep up on them. It was also a useful diversion for men who had been cooped up in barracks for too long.

After the raid on Honfleur, 15 Cdo had been billeted in the Territorial Army Drill Hall in Worthing for a few weeks before transferring to Weymouth in October. They were replacing 1 Cdo there, who had last been seen heading off to Southampton to board troopships for pastures new. Rumours were rife that they were to take part in a big operation, but no one really knew. Other rumours said they had been sent to Egypt to bolster Montgomery's beleaguered 8th Army, but that might not be true either.

But 15 Cdo now occupied 1 Cdo's former barracks and it was a considerable improvement on the drill hall and the commando's previous accommodation, the platforms of Bishopstone railway station.

Work had already started to re-build the commando after its devastating losses at sea and on land in August. Several new intakes of commandos had arrived from the training school at Achnacarry, including one group made up almost entirely of former police officers. The police had just had their reserved occupation[1] status lifted and many had rushed to volunteer for the armed forces. The commandos in particular had attracted them. Perhaps they hankered after some excitement after spending so much of the war chasing black marketeers and pulling bodies out of the ruins of bombed out buildings.

But for Carter the excitement of the chase couldn't block out his own worries entirely. His wife, far away in Scotland, was heavily pregnant and their last parting hadn't been as fond as it might. Given the choice, he would far rather be in Troon than in Dorset.

[1] Reserved occupations – At the outbreak of the Second World war, several industries were considered vital for the war effort, so people employed in those were exempt from conscription and also weren't permitted to volunteer for military service. These industries included the more obvious ones such as coal mining, steel making, ship building, aircraft production, farming etc. But they also included some less obvious occupations such as the police. The inclusion of the police may have been a precaution against large scale outbreaks of civil unrest, but in 1942 the restriction on the police joining the armed forces was lifted and many hundreds of police officers rushed to join up. The physical requirements of policing made them attractive to commando units, as their stature was useful in the newly formed heavy weapons troops, where the

strength to carry a Vickers machine gun or a 3 inch mortar was welcomed. At that time, you had to be over five feet eight inches tall to join the police, which was above the average height of about five feet six inches at that time. Height restrictions on the police were removed in the 1990s as they were considered to be discriminatory.

* * *

Despite the warmth of her first hospital visit with Carter, the rest had not been nearly so comfortable. Fiona had seemed withdrawn, her anxiety clear. In some ways it had to be expected. Her father had just died and she had nearly lost Carter to the war. It was natural that she should be worried. But there was more to it than that, Carter felt sure.

His service with the commandos had been the cause of their relationship faltering back at the beginning of the year. Now, as the first leaves on the trees were turning to gold, he feared that it might tear them apart again, just as he was about to become a father.

The train journey back to Troon had been frosty. Some of that might have been attributed to the fatigue of a heavily pregnant woman travelling on Britain's wartime rail network, but Carter wasn't foolish enough to think that was the only problem. It was as though Fiona has detached herself from him in some way. She seemed to be keeping him at arm's length, perhaps frightened that she might be committed to someone who might soon be dead.

There was little Carter could do to allay her fears. At every railway station, newspaper hoardings shouted news of the latest German offensive at Stalingrad. The rumours were that the Germans had reached the Volga river north of the city and were threatening to surround it. Everyone was speculating on what that might mean for the British. The words "second front" were commonly heard.

Once at Home Farm, Carter took to turning the radio off when hews broadcasts started. Fiona knew what he was doing but didn't comment on it. Cutting his wife off from the war news wouldn't stop the war from happening. Besides, they both knew the date on which Carter was due to report back to 15 Cdo.

To keep himself busy, Carter occupied himself by helping around the farm. He met Fiona's new farm hand, Sandy MacGregor and had taken an instant liking to him. Despite his injury he had an indefatigable optimism about him.

"Ach, it's only a we scratch" he had said as he hobbled around the farmyard on his crutches. "I'll be getting a new foot afore long and then you'll be thinking they're both real."

He would have made a good commando, Carter thought. But then decided not to wish that on anyone. Had he been a commando he might now be dead. Instead he was doing good work around the farm on any task that only required him to use one foot. He was certainly still able to milk a cow twice as quickly as either of the two Land Girls.

"How did you lose your foot?" Carter asked him.

"Some stupid Sassenach drove a tank over it." he replied. "We were part of Operation Crusader, the force sent to relieve Tobruk. We were moving through some tanks that were holding the line when a shell blast knocked me off my feet. The damn tank drove straight over my left foot and crushed it. He didn't know he'd done it, of course, so I was just left lying there. I might have died if it hadn't been for a Royal Engineers demolition party who were coming back across No Man's Land after blowing a bridge. They found me more dead than alive and got me back to a dressing station."

"That was last November, wasn't it?"

"Aye. I've been in hospital pretty much ever since. They didn't want to let me out until my wound had fully healed. I was sent back to Blighty via a hospital in South Africa, then spent some time in a convalescent home. Then I got news I was being discharged, so they sent me home on leave until the paperwork was done. It just came through this week, so I'm no longer a sojer, so I don't have to call you Sir."

"I wouldn't want you to anyway. Call me Steven."

"I can't do that either. Oot o' respect for Mrs Carter. She's my employer, ye ken. If ye don't mind, I'll call you Mr Carter."

"If that's what you want. Now, have you any jobs you would like me to do while I'm here?"

In many ways Carter's leave of absence at Home Farm had been a pleasant interlude. He was able to immerse himself in physical labour, which kept his mind off his recent experiences, but always the distance between himself and Fiona had nagged at him.

It wasn't until the night before Carter was due to depart that he raised the subject of Fiona's pregnancy. "The chaps were telling me that you've agreed to name the babies after them. Paddy and Danny, or maybe Patricia and Danielle."

"I think they may have been pulling your leg. They did ask if we'd chosen any names, but I certainly didn't agree to any. I do rather like Patricia for a girl though."

"If you want. It is quite nice."

"No, not for the West of Scotland though. Anything that has a hint of Catholicism about it doesn't go down too well in some quarters."

"Even today?"

"I think you need to go to a Rangers versus Celtic match some time to understand how religion still works up here."

Thinking about it, Carter had to concede that in some parts of the country being a catholic didn't go down too well even in England. Indeed, the monarch still wasn't allowed to be a catholic, so until that changed nothing else could be expected to.

"So, what names would you like?" Carter asked.

"If you've no objection, I'd like a boy to be named John, after my father."

"That's a wonderful idea. I can't think of anything better. What about a girl? Mary, after your mother?"

"How about Katherine, after my grandmother?"

"That's nice too. But if its twins, we're going to need two more names."

"What about your father's name?"

"No disrespect to my father, but I'm not keen on Gerald. How about James? It's my father's middle name."

"Given that we've had six kings of that name, I think we could get away with it despite its catholic connections. So, what about another girl's name?"

"How about Elizabeth, after my mother."

"And the name of our future Queen, assuming no boy princes arrive in the meantime. Yes, why not."

The discussion seemed to have thawed relations between them, as Carter had hoped it would. Time for him to broach the subject of his real worries. "You've been a little bit distant for the last few days. Is anything bothering you? Are you regretting marrying me?"

She looked down at her hands, holding the sewing that she had been working on. "No. I love you Steven. I think I've always loved you. But …" she fell silent.

"You're afraid you might be left alone."

She nodded her head. He couldn't think what to say. To mention that she would soon have two children to remind her of him didn't seem appropriate. They would be a substitute, no more. The idea of having children was to make them a family and they wouldn't be that if he didn't come home.

"Would you like me to ask for a transfer to a line infantry battalion?"

"I know you'd do it if I asked, but no. You love what you do, I know that. And I know you're good at it. When I met your men, while you were in hospital, they told me how much you are admired in the commando. All the men want to be in your troop. You have a reputation for being lucky. They think that with you in charge they'll have a better chance of making it to the end of the war."

"It's nice of them to say that, but several of my men were killed on the last raid and others were wounded. And …" he touched the last remnants of the bruises on his face, "… my luck might not be that good. I only just made it back myself. If Prof hadn't come back for me …" he left the rest of the sentence unspoken. It would be too distressing a prospect for Fiona to consider.

"No. You must stay where you are needed most. I'm being selfish."

"No, you aren't. You're being a mother and a wife. There is a big difference."

"I've not been much of a wife while we've been together this past couple of weeks."

"I didn't want to tire you out."

She laughed. "So, you think you can tire me out? I'll put that to the test just as soon as I've finished this sewing."

Carter was pleased to hear her laughter once again. He hadn't heard it since the commando had left Troon at the end of June. But he knew that her better mood would only be short lived. They may have talked about her worries, but nothing he had said had taken them away.

* * *

Aside from the never-ending training, there was little excitement for 15 Cdo. With so many military personnel crowded along the south coast there were the inevitable rivalries. Some were resolved on the sports pitches, others outside the pubs after too much beer had been drunk.

Part of the problem for the commandos was their reputation. Every other soldier, sailor and airman seemed to think it necessary to try to take the commandos down a peg or two. Most of the time they lived to regret it, but from time to time a commando would be found unconscious in an alley, dumped after he had been set upon by a gang of drunken rivals. It didn't help that the single ladies, and a few married ones, found the commando badges on their uniforms something of an attraction. It took only the appearance of a group of commandos at the door of a dancehall for the local women to abandon their escorts and gravitate towards the new arrivals. It did nothing to ease tensions around Weymouth.

Carter was given the job of trying to prevent some of the conflict. The easiest answer seemed to be to limit the number of occasions on which the commandos would come into contact with the members of other units.

There was a NAAFI canteen in the barracks, but it didn't have enough space for real recreational facilities. The bar was tiny, as was the cafeteria. There was no room for a snooker table or a darts board.

But the barracks had been built to house a battalion of six hundred men and the commando was only three hundred and fifty strong. Carter organised working parties to convert some of the space to make it suitable for leisure activities.

The QM had requisitioned a film projector for use in showing training films, so Carter made sure that the room set aside for use as a training cinema was also put to good use for showing more entertaining films. An agreement was made with the projectionist at the local cinema for films to stop off at the barracks for a night when they were being sent to the next cinema on the circuit. By coincidence the projectionist seemed to always have a packet of strictly rationed cigarettes in his pocket and he was seen out in his car more often than the petrol ration should have allowed.

A barrack room capable of housing twenty men became home to a snooker table that had been discovered languishing in the cellar of a mansion that had been taken over by the Navy. As the house wasn't being used as a residence, the table had been in the way in the room set aside for it by its previous occupants. The officers clubbed together and bought darts boards and the Local British Legion club donated a mixture of old darts which were fitted with new flights. Lads from the local area found they could earn a ha'penny a pint taking orders from thirsty commandos and collecting beer from the bar to take across to what had been nicknamed the "Pool hall" after a W C Fields movie in which the game had featured[1].

But allowing the commandos to meet girls was a much harder task. Another spare barrack room served as a dance hall, but there was no money available to hire a band. There were a number of concert parties, groups of enthusiastic amateur performers drawn mainly from military units and they could be persuaded to perform providing transport could be arranged. Carter became adept at negotiating deals with local Service Corps units for the loan of trucks.

The music problem was solved by the commandos themselves. In any large enough group of people there are always a few musicians. All that was needed was the instruments. Carter arranged for the officers' mess piano to be moved across to the designated dancing area and contacted the local Salvation Army citadel to see if they could help. Some battered brass instruments were given on loan, along with well-worn tenor and snare drums and some cymbals. The sound wasn't as tuneful as it might have been, but it was recognisable as music. Letters were written home to ask family to send whatever sheet music they had. What arrived varied from Beethoven to Blues, but the commandos were able to pick out the best of it and turn it into something that could be played at a dance.

The first dance was held at the beginning of October. Nurses from the local hospitals were invited, as were teachers from the local schools. Transport was organised and assurances made to Matrons and head teachers that their charges would be well looked after. Just to make sure, chaperones were provided. The dance was a success and paved the way for several more before the commando moved on. Just as in Troon, weddings soon took place, some organised more urgently than others.

Carter soon found himself being referred to as Billy Butlin[2], a nickname he wasn't quite as happy with as "Lucky".

The concert parties were the biggest success. They varied in quality, but the men liked their informality. The first one was something of an experiment.

It started with a pianist playing the old favourites: Tipperary, Pack Up Your Troubles, Roll Out The Barrel and more in that vein. The men sang along and it got everyone in the right mood. Next up came a comedian, a corporal, who told the bluest of jokes, much to the men's delight. Carter had heard of comedians like him but had never actually witnessed an act like it. They were certainly jokes that he couldn't tell his mother; his father neither, come to think of it. though they'd have gone down well with some of his friends from his student days.

A rather inept magician came on and was badly booed and heckled.

"Shall I quiet the men down?" Carter asked the fresh faced Royal Signals Second Lieutenant that had brought the party along.

"Oh no. This happens every night and he loves it. In fact he deliberately makes some of the tricks go wrong just to get a laugh."

A male tenor came on and sang some lovely Scottish ballads, mainly on the theme of unrequited love, along with a couple of operatic arias, before the penultimate act of the evening.

A diminutive you ATS[3] woman came on, young, barely in her twenties. She couldn't have been five feet tall in her army issues shoes. The pianist played a few chords then she started to sing. It was the Skye Boat Song, which the men had become familiar with hearing in the theatres they had visited in Scotland. The woman didn't have the best voice in the world, Carter had to admit, but it had a sort of sweetness that caught the ear. The room fell silent, taken under the spell of her rendition.

The next song upped the tempo a bit, a cheerful rendition of the old Harry Lauder favourite, "I'll Tak' the High Road'. Then the final song of her set, 'The Wild Mountain Thyme'. Perhaps it was the mood of the song or perhaps it was the way the woman sang it, but Carter would have sworn he saw more than one of the commandos wipe a tear from his eye.

At the end of the piece the room went wild with applause and the compere, the blue comedian, had to calm the men down. "Thank you. Thank you, gentlemen. And thank you to young Kitty Sutherland from Edinburgh."

The compere introduced the final performance of the evening, which was the tenor and the young woman, Kitty, singing duets from pre-war musicals.

Afterwards the commandos surrounded the young woman, all trying to persuade her out on a date.

"Shouldn't you recue her?" Carter asked the signals officer.

"More likely I'll have to rescue the men." He laughed. "No, Kitty can look after herself. And we'll be leaving in a minute anyway."

As they left the large barrack room more than one man gave Carter a thumbs up in appreciation of the evening's entertainment.

[1] Pool Sharks – The first film made by American comedy actor W C Fields, for which he had written the screenplay. It was released in 1915 and lasted only ten minutes.

[2] Billy Butlin – Founder of the holiday camp empire that still bears his name. His first camp was opened at Skegness in 1936. A camp built for him at Dovercourt in Essex was requisitioned in 1938 to house Jewish children evacuated from Germany under the *Kindertransports* programme before the outbreak of the Second World War. His camps at Clacton and Skegness were both requisitioned by the War Office for use as training camps and he built other camps for the War Office on condition that he could purchase them for use as holiday camps after the war. Visitors to the camps who have a military background often remark on their military style architecture.

[3] ATS – Auxiliary Territorial Service. This was founded in 1938 as preparations for war started to be made behind the scenes. It was the women's branch of the British Army and provided female personnel to release men from support roles for service in the front line. Typical duties were clerical, logistics, transport, catering and communications. The ATS became the Women's Royal Army Corps in 1949. The women's branch was disbanded in 1992, along with the Women's Royal Naval Service (WRNS) and the Women's Royal Air Force (WRAF) when equalities legislation made it necessary to integrate women into the armed forces, rather than treating them differently. From 1992 onwards all women serving in the armed forces served on equal terms with their male counterparts, with the exception of eligibility for combat service.

* * *

As the clock ticked towards eleven hundred hours, the commando stood in their troops, in three ranks, forming three sides of the parade ground of their barracks. Two troops stood on each side of a square that was open on its fourth side. Having just returned from five days training on Dartmoor, where they had bivouacked in tents made from their gas capes, Carter had been surprised to see the order requiring them to parade the next day.

The chill of a late October wind had the men rubbing their hands together in an effort to keep warm. The voice of Sgt Maj Finch rang out across the parade ground, calling the soldiers to attention. This was followed by the arrival of the newly appointed 2IC, Maj Charlie Cousins. He had been posted in on promotion from 6 Cdo. The reputation of the unit and the ribbon of the Military Cross on Cousins' chest told the men of 15 Cdo all they needed to know about his suitability for the job.

The 2IC stood the parade at ease again but didn't allow them to stand easy[1]. Carter wondered about the presence of half a dozen thick cardboard packing cases that were dotted along the open end of the square. What could be in them? No doubt they would find out soon enough. They must be related to the unexpected calling of the parade.

On the front of the Napoleonic headquarters building the hands of the clock ticked around to exactly eleven o'clock. The 2IC called the parade to attention once again and the CO marched to the centre of the open end of the square, made a left turn and continued until he came to a halt five paces in front of the 2IC. They exchanged salutes, the 2IC going first, then the 2 IC marched to the centre of the closed end of the square where he took up a position in between 3 and 4 troops.

"Number 15 Commando!" The CO's voice rang out. "No 15 Cdo, stand at ease! Stand easy."

The CO stood himself at ease before speaking again. "No doubt you came back from Dartmoor last night hoping for a couple of easy days in which to clean your kit and get ready for the next training task." As he spoke he turned from side to side, making sure that all three sides of the square could hear at least some of what he was saying, though the wind whipped much of it away before the sound could reach those furthest from him. "I did have that in mind for you but changed my mind when these …" he indicated the large cardboard boxes "… turned up unexpectedly. I will tell you more about those in a minute.

But first, as you all know, the commandos have often been described as a rag-tag army. It has been said that we look like a bunch of misfits wandering around Piccadilly Circus on a Saturday night. This is because, between us, we wear several different types of head gear. And it's not just you men. I wear a peaked cap, as do some of your other officers. But some wear forage caps, some wear berets and Capt Fraser wears a Tam O'shanter which, as we all know, is a heathen form of headdress worn north of the border." Vernon paused to allow the men time to chuckle at his joke, which they dutifully did. "And I won't even deign to describe the abomination that Tpr O'Driscoll wears." This brought even more laughter. Paddy O'Driscoll's caubeen with its green feathered hackle had been the butt of many a joke.

"For some time now the commandos, with the support of HQ Combined Operations, have been trying to persuade the War Office to issue us with a single form of head dress. This campaign gained some additional impetus this summer when those upstarts in the Parachute Regiment were granted the right to wear a maroon beret." This brought some booing, which the CO tolerated for a few seconds.. "Well. We finally won the battle."

There was a ripple of voices around the parade ground as the commandos shared the news with those who hadn't quite heard it. The CO allowed it to continue for a few seconds, then raised his hands for silence.

"Sadly, we have still not been allowed to adopt a cap badge of our own. All the suggestions for a suitable design have been rejected. But, from today, all the commandos under my command will wear the same style of hat. In a moment, I will be the first to place one on my head. After that you will be called forward by troops to have yours issued to you, following which any member of this commando who wears any other form of head dress will be regarded as being improperly dressed. Do I make myself clear?"

The was a ragged chorus of 'Yes, Sir.' around the parade ground, which brought a mock stern look from the CO.

"I said 'Do I make myself clear?'" This time there was a wholehearted shout.

"Very well. I will now bring you to attention and the ceremony will commence. Parade! Parade 'shun!"

Three hundred and fifty left boots crashed into the tarmac of the parade square, alongside the commando's right boots. The CO did an about turn, so that he was facing towards the open side of the square.

Sgt Major Finch marched forward with something held in front of him in both hands. It was reminiscent of a Chamberlain bearing a monarch's crown. But this was no crown; this was a beret, but its colour wasn't the familiar black of the Royal Tank Regiment, it was bottle green. A black painted cap badge was visible at the front. The commandos had been painting their badges matt black ever since they had been founded, as a precaution against the enemy seeing them sparkle in the moonlight.

The Sgt Major came to a halt in front of the CO, who removed his peaked cap. Extending his left hand he offered the hat to the Sgt Major, while raising his right hand to take the beret. The exchange completed; he placed the beret on his head. A spontaneous cheer rang out around the parade square.

The CO did an about turn, so he was facing inwards again, and raised his hand in a salute. A second cheer rang out.

After the CO had marched off and the Sgt Major had once again taken charge of the parade ground, the troops were called forward in numerical order to collect their berets. It was a significant moment for them, the unique nature of their role finally being recognised. Finally, they felt as though they really were one family, one band of brothers[2]. A new badge to go with the berets would have been nice and they were aware that the Royal Marine commandos already had that distinction, of which they were envious, but the beret was a start.

[1] Stand easy – Standing at ease is a formal drill position, in which the men are more relaxed than they would be if they were stood to attention, but they are not allowed to move or talk. Stand easy is an informal position, the men can chat and fidget, so long as they stay in their ranks. The command "Stand at ease" would be used when the parade is waiting for a parade to start, or when in front of an officer for a formal interview. Stand easy would be used while the men were waiting for the start of a briefing, the arrival of a train or other routine activities where strict silence or immobility isn't required.

[2] In Shakespeare's Henry V Act IV, Scene 3, King Henry exhorts his men ahead of the Battle of Agincourt, saying "We few, we happy few, we band of brothers. For he today that sheds his blood with me shall be my brother."

* * *

It was in the first week in November that the CO called the officers together for an announcement. "We've just received orders that we're to move overseas." He announced. "I can't tell you where, that will be revealed once we're on our ship, but I think you will have some clue because before we leave we'll be issued with khaki drill uniforms."

This brought some mutterings between the assembled officers. Khaki drill clothing was only issued for hot weather areas, which probably meant that their destination was North Africa or India.

"Firstly, all the men will be given a week's embarkation leave, so they have time to go home and say goodbye to their families. After they report back here, we'll be moving up to Glasgow to board a troop ship. Now, Steven, seeing as you will be up there anyway, there's little point in you coming all the way back down here again. There are another half dozen men who also have wives in Troon or the area around it, so you will form a work party in Glasgow, receiving the kit we send up in advance and making sure that it all gets loaded onto the ship." Dockyards were notorious for 'losing' military equipment and units were often frustrated to find vital equipment missing when they got to their destinations.

There were a few more details about advance parties and rear parties, dates, times and the other logistical information that the officers would need to brief their men, but the main question on everyone's lips was 'where?'.

"There's been a move of commandos to the Mediterranean." Carter commented to Andrew Fraser. "Both 1 and 6 have gone out there. Something big's on the way."

"Maybe they've just been sent to bolster Monty's 8th Army. You know, to prevent Rommel reaching the Suez Canal."

"Could be. Maybe that's where we're going as well. But that would turn us into line infantry, which isn't what we're trained for."

"Not necessarily. We could be used to raid Rommel's supply lines. It would mean him having to commit more men to protesting them, which would weaken his front line."

Carter nodded his head. That would make sense, he thought. The commandos were raiders. Their job was to get in amongst the enemy, create mayhem and then get out again. They all dreaded the day when they might be used as ordinary infantrymen. It would come, of course. If you push the enemy away from the coastline there's fewer opportunities to attack from the sea and that would leave the commandos without a job. It would be inventible that elite troops such as themselves would be found a new job, at the forefront of the war effort.

* * *

Making the best of his short period of leave became Carter's main objective. With Fiona now very heavy with the twins, there was little he could do to distract her. He suggested another stay in Edinburgh, but with winter setting in she said she didn't fancy having to face the east wind that seemed to scour the city of all its warmth. He then suggested Norther Ireland, but the prospect of a sea crossing, however short, was also a cause for rejecting the idea.

So, instead, he settled for a few days of home comforts, fussing around his wife and causing her to get more annoyed with him. She was too independent to tolerate being treated like an invalid and, although she understood what Carter was trying to do, she spent more time snapping at him than smiling.

It was therefore almost with a sense of relief that Carter reported to the Port Liaison Officer at Port Glasgow to start supervising the assembly of the Commando's kit. The majority of the commandos would travel together by train, but individual consignments of stores and weaponry were to be escorted up by smaller detachments of men and held on the docks until their ship was available for loading. With merchant ships in short supply thanks to attentions of the U-Boat packs, the speed of their turnaround was vital and they wouldn't be held back in port waiting for stragglers or late arrivals of equipment.

The commando found that they weren't to be the only passengers on board the ship. Drafts of young conscripts were being sent out to join units weakened by combat losses. They stared in awe at the commando's shoulder flashes and medal ribbons. After work the commandos were stood pints in the local pubs to encourage them to tell their stories. More than one fresh faced conscript regretted asking the question 'What was it like?'.

Over the following days the rest of the commando arrived and the ship was loaded. It was an ancient coal powered rust bucket which would probably have been sent to the breakers' yard had it not been for the war. Even the crew didn't seem to know their destination, though someone must have. On the day before they were set to embark the BBC news carried the story of Operation Torch[1], as it would become known: the United States led invasion of Morocco and Algeria.

Was that where they were going? It only served to fuel more speculation.

In the small hours of the following day the old ship slipped its moorings and made its way down the Firth of Clyde to join up with a convoy that was assembling north of the isle of Arran. From there they steamed down the Irish Sea, across the western end of the English Channel and out into the Bay of Biscay, keeping well clear of the French coast for fear of encountering U-Boats either returning from Atlantic patrols or setting out on them.

After two weeks at sea the commandos leant on the port railings of the ship to take in the sight of the Rock of Gibraltar, shouting abuse. By this time the tiny British outpost was known to be the commando's destination, so they were frustrated that their ship was sailing right past and into the Mediterranean Sea, to the newly liberated port or Oran in Algeria. After disembarking they were told they were waiting the arrival of another ship, which would take them back to Gibraltar.

There was much discussion about why they hadn't disembarked there days earlier, when they had passed it by, but Carter had been in the Army long enough to know that such decisions were baffling and, often, arbitrary. Most of the ship's cargo was destined for General Eisenhauer's forces in Algeria, so that was where the ship was sent. For the conscripts it was worse. They had several more days to wait in a transit camp before being moved on to Alexandria through waters patrolled by both German and Italian submarines and all ships passing through that area risked being bombed by Luftwaffe aircraft operating out of Libya and Sicily.

The ship that took them back to Gibraltar was the Prince Leopold, a well-known and much loved commando landing ship. It had been one of the landing ships that had transported the men of Nos 1 and 6 Cdos, who had participated in the capture of Algiers. They soon discovered why it was necessary for them to be transported by landing ship. The port of Gibraltar was so packed with shipping. both merchant and naval, that the only way to get the commando ashore was in landing craft.

[1] Operation Torch was a significant event during World War 2 and gets very little mention in the history books. Firstly, it was a major logistical challenge, as the whole invasion force had to travel

either from Britain or directly from the USA. Such a long sea voyage prior to an invasion had never been attempted before and wouldn't be attempted again until the Falklands War of 1982. The force was split into three elements, spaced hundreds of miles apart. The western most element was to capture Morocco, thereby preventing the closure of the Straights of Gibraltar should Spain decide to intervene on the side of Germany. The other two elements landed at Oran and Algiers, the major ports of Algeria, facilitating the build-up of forces that would eventually meet the Germans in battle at Kasserine in Tunisia. The primary objectives were the capture of port and airfield facilities, which would finally end German and Italian air superiority in the Mediterranean and cut their supply lines to Libya. The Vichy French[2] forces in Morocco and Algeria put up only light resistance, which meant that allied casualties were small, the United States suffering 524 dead and the UK 576 dead with 756 wounded all told. Many of those casualties were actually inflicted at sea, by U-Boats. This was less than had been suffered in a single day at Dieppe the previous August. The immediate effect of the landings was to force Field Marshall Erwin Rommel, commander of the *Afrika Korps*, to split his forces in Libya to face both east and west, paving the way for the British victory at the Battle of El Alamein the following month.

[2] Vichy France – The name given to the puppet French government permitted by a treaty with the Germans to establish itself in the unoccupied part of central and southern France, in the town of Vichy. From there it ruled what remained of the French Empire until the Germans occupied the area after Operation Torch. Technically it was neutral, but in fact it did what it was told by the Germans. Some parts of the Empire, such as Indochina, remained loyal to the Free French government in London and fought on against the Germans and then the Japanese. The head of the Vichy government was Marshal Pétain, the Hero of Verdun in the First World War.

2 – Gibraltar

Since the start of the war the British had been paranoid about the possibility of Spain siding with Germany and snatching the Rock of Gibraltar back. That or the possibility that the Germans might do the job for the Spanish while they looked on. So Gibraltar had been turned into an armed camp, jammed with troops and ships in the hope that the Spanish might be dissuaded from trying to reclaim the colony. Not only that, it was a valuable repair base for ships that had been damaged on route from Britain to the Mediterranean theatre, a vital supply line used to support the colonies of Malta and Cyprus and the 8th Army in Libya and Egypt.

It was something of a mystery why the Spanish hadn't repaid the Germans for all the help that Hitler had given Franco during the Spanish Civil War, by allying themselves with the Axis powers. Without German aircraft it was possible that Franco's nationalists might not have prevailed. In the summer of 1941 Spain had sent the Blue Division to fight on the eastern Front and it was clear that Spain's neutrality was more than a little biased, but they had never gone so far as to declare war on the Allies.

But the threat was constant and, whenever possible, commandos had been based on the Rock to strengthen the already large garrison. They would mount ostentatious landing exercises on the beaches on the eastern side of the peninsula, carried out in the full knowledge that Spanish and also, probably, German eyes would be watching. The message was clear: if you don't behave, we'll send the boys in.

The potential targets for the commandos were various gun batteries sited on the Spanish mainland that would be needed to cover any advance of ground troops towards the narrow causeway that connected Gibraltar to Spain. Such an approach wouldn't really be necessary. With an effective sea and air blockade the Rock could soon be starved into submission. But still Franco sat on his hands.

Of course, the Royal Navy had a choke hold on food and oil supplies to Spain, controlling what went into Spanish ports. This helped to keep Franco on the fence despite his fascist sympathies and despite the thousands of Spanish that had volunteered for the Blue Division and its air equivalent, the Blue Squadron.

But the commandos weren't bothered with the politics. Gibraltar gave them time to acclimatise to the Mediterranean sun, to hone their climbing skills on the famous Rock and to enjoy a few weeks of rare relaxation, even though they continued with the landing exercises. They were even allowed the occasional daytrip across the land border into Spain. Because so many Spanish worked on the Rock and Gibraltarians worked in Spain, keeping the border closed wasn't practical. While the visits were officially barred, due to Spain's neutrality, the local economy benefited from them so local officials turned a blind eye, so long as the military personnel wore civilian clothes, behaved themselves and didn't stay overnight. Enterprising Spaniards set up businesses that only operated during daylight hours just to accommodate the British soldiers, sailors and airmen.

"Assume that you will be spied upon." Lt Col Vernon said on briefing the officers after their arrival in Gibraltar. "We don't know how many Spanish workers who work on the Rock are in the pay of their intelligence service or the *Abwehr*, it could be hundreds. They may even have managed to suborn some Gibraltarians. The only safe thing to assume if you cross the border is that every Spaniard is selling information to someone, so make sure you don't give them anything they can sell. You must drum that into your men. Those Spanish Senioritas may be very pretty and more than a little accommodating, but they are probably reporting everything that is said."

Carter had call to recall those words a couple of weeks later when he crossed the border to visit one of the local villages. It was more of a stroll than a visit, a chance to get away from the claustrophobic atmosphere of the Rock. He had told himself that he just wanted to buy some of the delicious Spanish oranges that were in season, a luxury not seen in England since 1939. But he could have bought some of those from a stall within yards of his billet. But he soon became aware that he was being followed.

The man was clumsy, not really taking enough care. Perhaps he wasn't worried whether or not he was seen. Every time Carter turned around, he was there tying a shoelace, examining a flower growing over a garden wall or just leaning against a building. He was Spanish, if his complexion was anything to go by, wearing a cheap suit, a rumpled white shirt with a greasy tie knotted around his neck. He hadn't shaved in a while. Like many commodities, razor blades were in short supply in Spain.

Carter felt like trying to shake him off, but that would make it appear that he was up to something, which he wasn't. That would probably just result in him being followed on his next visit.

He passed a hastily constructed shack, outside of which two women stood. The shack had been closed down by the police under their strict morality laws at least twice to Carter's knowledge but had always managed to re-open. The women's blouses had deeply plunging necklines and they held the hem of their skirts high up on their thighs on one side, showing the maximum amount of leg. The grinding poverty created by the civil war had forced many women into prostitution.

"You wan' buy me drink?" One of them said, making a little kissy pout at the same time.

"Not today." Carter replied with a smile. It wasn't the first time he had been accosted and it wouldn't be the last. The exchange rate between the pound and the peseta was sufficiently favourable to encourage soldiers into such establishments, though they rarely left with any money still in their wallets. "But that man behind me has just been paid. I'm sure he would love to have a drink with you."

The women's faces lit up and as the man approached Carter could hear the two women encouraging him inside. It took him several seconds to disentangle himself from them and by the time he reached the corner, Carter was lost to sight.

He smiled to himself. It had been fun to discomfort the man, but that was all he had done. He stepped into a shop and bought the oranges he wanted and by the time he returned to the street the man was outside, so close that they nearly collided.

“Sorry old chap.” Carter tilted his Panama hat in apology as he stepped aside. He stifled a grin and led the man all the way back to the border check point again. It only occurred to him later that he might have attracted undue attention to the shopkeeper who had sold him his oranges. That was the problem of living in a police state.

After returning to the British side of the border, Carter called in at the Royal Military Police station and reported his encounter with the Spaniard, in accordance with standing orders, provided a description and then thought no more about the incident.

* * *

Rubbing sweat from his face, Carter entered the yacht club which had been allocated to 15 Cdo as their HQ. It had the advantage of having showers and changing rooms on the ground floor. He was just returning from a rock-climbing exercise with his troop, ascending the Rock by one of its tougher climbs before jogging back down to the town using the service road that wound its way down the Rock’s flanks.

The CO was just coming down the stairs from the upper floor, where the bar had been turned into an office-come-briefing room during the day and an officer’s mess by night. “Ah, Steven, good timing. I have a visitor looking for some advice and I was looking for someone to sit in. I would appreciate the input of a troop commander, if you have the time.”

“I was just going for a shower, Sir.” Carter explained. “Can you indulge me for a few minutes? I don’t think I’m good company for anyone with a sensitive nose right now.”

“Of course. I’ll offer my guest a drink on the veranda while we wait.”

Not wishing to keep his CO waiting, Carter hurried his ablutions and made his way up to the first floor and out onto the balcony that ran around three sides of the building, providing views over the yachting marina. He stopped dead in the doorway when he saw the identity of the visitor. What was he doing here?

Vernon caught sight of Carter. "You know Major Warriner, don't you Steven?"

"Our paths have crossed before, Sir." Carter tried to keep his voice neutral but was struggling. Warriner's presence didn't bode well for someone and Carter suspected that the someone might be himself.

"Good to see you Steven." Warriner extended his hand to be shaken. Carter couldn't be so ill mannered as to refuse, even though the thought had crossed his mind.

"What brings you to Gib?" Carter refused to use Warriner's rank or to call him Sir, knowing well that the rank was assumed so that he could move easily through the world by adopting a military disguise.

"I had a bit of business here. Nothing that concerns you, you'll be pleased to hear." Warriner turned back to Vernon. "Young Steven here did me a great favour earlier in the year, when you were gracious enough to lend him to me."

"Ah, that was you, was it? Steven has been very closed lipped about the whole affair."

"As he should be. But I'm glad you've brought him in. I know how experienced he is and his advice on this other matter would be welcomed."

Carter had to admit he was intrigued. Anything that Warriner was involved in was bound to be dangerous and Carter was a danger junkie[1]. But he had to take care. One wrong word and Warriner would have him invading Spain on some spurious pretext.

"So what advice can we offer?" Carter asked.

"I must ask you to keep what I tell you strictly confidential. I can't go into details, but even the sketchy information I'm about to give you could endanger lives."

"We're well used to keeping secrets, Warriner." Vernon said, a slight edge to his voice.

"I know, but I just needed to make the sensitivity of this information clear. Although it isn't really my remit, I have offered to help a certain, shall we say, government department with a problem that has arisen. They have an agent in Algeciras who missed their scheduled contact with their handler yesterday. The protocol for such a lapse is to reschedule the contact for the same time the next day, today in fact. Again, they failed to make contact. It is assumed that the agent has been compromised and has either gone on the run or been arrested by the SIGC[2]. The thing is, we don't know for certain which it is and we need to find out. Our agent knows the identity of other agents in the region, which places their lives in danger. We have to try to find out what has happened to them."

"So, what does that have to do with us?" Carter asked, knowing that his CO would probably already have asked the same question.

"The people here in Gibraltar want to mount a mission to try to find out if our agent is still at liberty. We can't risk exposing any of our agents in Spain, so we want to mount an operation to go across and take a look. Where you come in, as the experts in this sort of thing, is to give us advice on how best to go about it."

"So, it's what we would call a reconnaissance mission."

"If you put it like that, then yes."

"Where is the objective?" Carter was on comfortable ground and didn't mind taking the lead. His CO would intervene if he thought Carter was going too far or making unwise suggestions.

"An apartment in central Algeciras. The agent lives there. However, they also frequent a night club in the town and also the flat of the German consul in the town."

"Is he really the consul?" Vernon asked.

"It's the title he uses." Warriner replied. "That will satisfy as far as this conversation is concerned."

It was interesting that Warriner had used the personal pronouns 'they' and 'them' to describe the agent, rather than 'he' or 'him'. It was deliberate. Was it possible that the agent was female, but Warriner didn't want to give away that level of detail? Carter thought so.

Instead he asked, "What size team would you be sending?"

"Probably four. One to do the actual … reconnaissance and the other three to cover his back."

"Have you thought about how you might do the job?"

"Not really. The simple way would be to send a team across the border during daylight. They can catch the bus into Algeciras and then walk when they get there. I could probably arrange for a car to be available if they had to leave in a hurry."

"If the agent is in danger, would they bring … them back?"

"Possibly. If they have been arrested, then that wouldn't be possible. We'd have to think about breaking them out of custody and that would be a whole different operation. It would be easier to withdraw our network of agents and start again from scratch. But, for obvious reasons, we don't want to do that if we don't have to. It would be very disruptive."

"OK. Well, in the first place I wouldn't try going across the border. I know from personal experience that it's too easy to be followed. In this case any Spanish agent wouldn't even have to board the bus. They would just arrange to have the bus station in Algeciras placed under observation. There would be plenty of time to make the telephone calls and make the arrangements. The bus takes nearly an hour to get there." Carter knew that much, having made the trip once before.

"How would you do it?"

"I'd go in somewhere where the Spanish are looking the other way. I'd take an MTB across the bay to one of the beaches on the far side of the town, then send the party ashore in a dinghy. It would have to be under cover of darkness, of course. I'd bring them out the same way as well, with maybe a plan B of them going east and being picked up from one of the beaches on the eastern side of the peninsula if that were necessary. It's too easy for the Spanish to swamp the border with police or army and cut off a retreat there."

"There aren't any MTBs in Gibraltar at the moment and we can't wait for one to get here." Warriner objected.

"The RAF has a rescue launch; I've seen it out in the harbour." Carter countered. "That could do the job."

Warriner went silent as he thought through what Carter had said. A thought struck him. "What about weapons."

"If they're supposed to be civilians, then nothing bigger than a handgun. They would need shoulder holsters to conceal them under a jacket. Perhaps take good quality knives with them, if they know how to use them without cutting their own wrists. A couple of grenades each might also be an idea, but they would have to be concealed in a bag of some sort. They'd be too obvious in a jacket pocket."

"You seem to have all the answers, Steven. You wouldn't like to do the job for us, would you?" Although the question had been posed in a slightly jocular manner, Carter had been half expecting it. While the intelligence services might be good at recruiting and handling agents, they weren't trained to mount the sort of covert incursions that were second nature to the commandos. On the other hand, commandos weren't trained to carry out spying missions of this sort.

"Thank you for offering." He replied, sending a 'help me' glance towards his CO, "But I've got my responsibilities with the commando to think of."

"Steven's right. I can't spare him right now." Vernon's tone of voice didn't allow for any sort of argument.

"Well, it was worth asking." Warriner seemed to take his rejection with good humour. "Thank you for your time. I won't take up any more of it."

He went back inside the club's bar and picked his peaked cap up from Vernon's desk. Carter watched his back as he headed out of the door and down the stairs.

"Why do I think we haven't seen the last of that man?" Vernon asked.

"Because we haven't, Sir. He's not the sort who takes 'no' for an answer."

"If we were to get orders to undertake the task he described, would you be willing to take it on?"

"If it was made an order, Sir. Otherwise I think I'd let someone else have the honour this time."

"Most of our officers are as green as grass. You know that Steven. I'm sure they'd jump at the chance to do it, but I wouldn't feel at all happy about asking any of them."

That was an argument Carter couldn't ignore. They had lost so many experienced officers during Operation Dagger and those that remained were needed to lead their troops, not undertake hair brained schemes across the border in Spain. That applied to Carter as well, of course, but he at least he had the advantage of having undertaken similar operations before.

[1] Junkie – although this might seem like a modern term it actually dates from 1920s America and the prohibition era. Junk was the slang name for heroin, perhaps because of its association with 19th century opium trafficking when junks were used in China to transport the raw opium. From the noun junk we get the adjective junkie.

[2] SIGC - Servicio de Información de la Guardia Civil, the intelligence and counter-intelligence arms of the Spanish Guardia Civil, the state police service.

* * *

It didn't come as much of a surprise when Carter was summoned to HMS Rooke later that day. Since the commando had arrived in Gibraltar it had adopted different working hours to avoid the heat of the afternoon. First parade was at oh six hundred hours, they stopped work for a mid-morning snack if it was convenient, then stood down for the day at fourteen hundred hours. That allowed the commandos to idle away the rest of the day swimming or taking a siesta, as they had learned that the traditional Spanish afternoon nap was called. Even though these winter months were a lot cooler, the commandos decided to continue with the summer working routine. For the leisure period to be interrupted by the CO's summons, it had to be of the highest priority.

They walked to HMS Rooke, a ‘stone frigate’ as shore establishments were known, that was the military headquarters of the Rock in more peaceful times. Now much of the military command structure operated from a warren of tunnels and caverns dug out of the Rock itself by the Royal Engineers. They were still digging and the local population joked that if much more rock and soil was removed the Rock would collapse inwards like a badly made souffle.

Their identification documents were checked by a military policeman, who then made a telephone call to arrange for them to be escorted through the building. This wasn’t a place where anyone was allowed to walk around unaccompanied. They were ushered into an office, were offered a seat and then left alone, but not for long. Carter and Vernon leapt to their feet once more as a Commodore entered the room, followed closely by Warriner. He just about managed to keep a triumphant look from forming on his face.

“Please sit down, Gentlemen,” The Commodore said in a brisk tone. “I’m Commodore Hislop. I’m afraid I can’t tell you what I do, but I’m sure you can probably work it out for yourselves. Warriner here I know you have met. You must be Lt Col Vernon of 15 Cdo.” He offered his hand to be shaken. “And you must be Lt Carter. No, I see I am mistaken, you are Captain Carter now.”

“Yes, Sir. I was still a Lieutenant the last time … Major Warriner and I worked to together.”

“Indeed. Major Warriner has been telling me something of that work, though of course not the details. He speaks very highly of you.”

I’m sure he does, Carter thought. Flattery is always a useful weapon when trying to persuade someone to do something they don’t want to do. Aloud he said “I’m very flattered. I just did my job.”

“But what a job, young man. What a job! But that isn’t why I have invited …” Carter noted the euphemism that replaced ‘ordered’ “… you here. Major Warriner, or at least some acquaintances of his, have a problem and it seems that you might be helpful in solving it for them.”

"Sir, Major Warriner has explained something of the problem." Vernon interjected when the Commodore stopped speaking for a second. "With respect, it isn't really a mission suitable for the military. If my men were to be caught doing covert operations in Spain, they would be arrested as spies."

"Whoever does this job, civilian or military, runs the same risk." The Commodore pointed out. "We all work for the same employer Vernon and that is His Majesty the King. While you are on Gibraltar your unit is seconded to the garrison, which comes under the command of the Commander in Chief, British Forces Gibraltar. He has determined that not only could you assist major Warriner in this matter, but that you will do so. I am only the messenger in this matter; however, it is a view I also hold." The words had been spoken in the mildest of tones, but the glint in the Commodore's eyes suggested that it would be unwise for Vernon to disagree.

"I understand, Sir. I just wished to point out that we may not be the best people to do the job. If we are ordered to do it, however, we will."

"There are no 'best people' in this case. There are only those who are the best from what we have available and that has been deemed to be 15 Cdo and Capt Carter in particular. Now, I have other matters to take care of, so I will leave you in Warriner's hands." The Commodore stood up and crossed the room to face Carter. Instinctively Carter and Vernon also rose. The Commodore extended his hand for Carter to shake. "I wish you luck, Captain. You are probably going to need it."

"I try to rely on good planning and preparation, Sir, but I know that luck always plays a part in military operations."

"Indeed it does. It was that bounder Napoleon who said, 'Give me lucky generals, not skilful ones[1].'"

The Commodore acknowledged Carter and Vernon's salutes and left the room.

"Sorry to have to pull rank like that." Warriner said once the door was closed. His tone suggested he was anything but sorry. "But we are in a terrible bind. We have to find out about our agent and, if possible, get her out."

The change of personal pronoun was immediately noted by Carter. "So, we're looking for a woman then."

"You are. Not that it makes any difference, we would be mounting this operation if our agent was a man. It just so happens that the agent is a Mata Hari[2] type, which is very useful when it comes to gathering information. It's amazing what some men will say when they're in bed with a beautiful woman."

He opened his briefcase and withdrew a folder. "I'd better start from the beginning, otherwise this will make no sense." He opened the folder and turned it so that Carter could see it. The topmost enclosure was a photograph of an attractive woman. It looked like the sort of photograph that would be used for publicity purposes.

"This is Emilia Morantes, code name Chaffinch, aged thirty two. She's a night club singer in Algeciras, though she doesn't do much work these days because of her … other activities. Seniorita Morantes was recruited by us when we discovered that she is the mistress of the local commander of the Guardia Civil. She is related by marriage to a Gibraltarian family and is pro-British. Well, pro-British for a price. Not only did we recruit her, but we also persuaded her to start a second affair with the head of the *Abwehr* in Andalucía, Colonel Max Grau. Since her recruitment Chaffinch has been accommodating both men, without either knowing about her relationship with the other. At least we didn't think they knew about each other, but that may no longer be the case.

She has been feeding us some very useful information both on Spanish police operations and on what the *Abwehr* are doing. It enabled us to identify two Gibraltarians who were about to carry out sabotage operations in the dockyard. It is far too risky for her to make contact with her handler direct, so she reports through other agents in the area, which is why we're so anxious to know if she has been captured. The lives of up to a dozen agents could be hanging by a thread."

"Earlier you said that she was due to make contact with her handler but failed to do so. Now you are saying that she didn't work directly with her handler." Vernon observed.

"Correct on both counts. By direct, I meant face to face. Once a week she dials a telephone number in Algeciras. It's better you don't know where that number is located. She uses a public telephone, a different one each time as far as is possible, but she may have become careless and used the same one more than once.

The sole purpose of the call is for her to say one of two code words. The first means that she is safe, the second tells her handler that she feels she may be unsafe, for whatever reason. The handler is then supposed to tell her what to do. In an emergency, of course, she can just make a run for the border and hand herself over to us, but the weekly contact is supposed to work as a sort of security blanket[3] for her. Just knowing that her handler is close by once a month is comforting. Anyway, as you already know, yesterday she failed to make contact and we want you, Steven, to go and find out why. The best possible scenario is that she has just fallen ill and is confined to her bed. The worst is that she has been arrested by the Spanish or captured by the Germans."

"And if she has?"

"Then it's up to you. If you think you can get her out, then give it a try. If not, just come back and report. I'll give you a telephone number you can ring to let us know."

Carter was just about to ask why they would need a telephone number if they were coming back, when he realised that there was a possibility of them not coming back either.

"What if we're captured?" He asked instead.

"If you're captured by the Spanish, you will be treated as spies and will be put on trial. As Spain is neutral, they are unlikely to risk executing you." Very comforting, Carter thought. Warriner continued. "It would create too many diplomatic problems. If, on the other hand, the *Abwehr* captures you they will surely interrogate you and they're unlikely to be subtle about it. Perhaps they'll then hand you over to the Spanish, or perhaps they'll just take you out into the hills of Campo di Gibraltar[4] and you'll never be seen again." Very much not so reassuring.

[1] In fact there is no evidence that Napoleon ever said that or anything like it. Cardinal Mazarin, who was Chief Minister of France (1642-1661) is known to have asked of a general not "EST-IL HABILE?" (Is he skilful?) but "EST-IL HEUREUX?" (IS HE LUCKY?).

[2] Mata Hari – Real name Margaretha Geertruida "Margreet" MacLeod, a Dutch exotic dancer (her maiden name was Zelle) and courtesan who was convicted of being a German spy and was executed in France on 25th October 1917. She was initially recruited by the French to spy for them but sold her allegiance to the Germans while on a visit to Spain in 1916. Following the execution by the Germans of a Belgian double agent, Mata Hari came under suspicion, was arrested by the French and put on trial. It was discovered that much of Mata Hari's identity was a fake, created by her to enhance her position in society, but it was evidence enough to get her convicted. In reality it is unlikely that her spying activities ever caused much real damage to either France or Britain, even though the charges against her alleged that spying activities had caused the death of 50,000 men. Today she would be regarded more as a Walter Mitty like character.

[3] It is often quoted that cartoonist Charles Shultz first used the term 'security blanket' in his 'Peanuts' comic strip in 1956. His character Linus is often seen holding a blanket up to his face while sucking his thumb. This is incorrect. Although Shultz did use the term for the first time in its popular form, it was actually coined much earlier to describe a type of blanket sold in America which was secured across the top of a child's cot to stop the child climbing or falling out. It first went on sale in 1925. I assume that Warriner would have heard the term from his American counterparts in London.

[4] Campo di Gibraltar - The administrative area of Andalucía that encompasses Algeciras and the border with the Rock of Gibraltar.

3 – Algeciras

One strong pull with the paddle sent the dinghy in to grind against the rocky shore. Carter and his men rolled over the side to stand in the knee-deep water. Green, the last man out, gave the dinghy a shove to send it back out into deeper water. The RAF crewman moved from one end to the other and started to paddle back out towards the air-sea rescue launch hidden in the darkness further out to sea. The boat would be back in Gibraltar, the crew eating an early breakfast, before Carter and his men were even in the town.

He had brought Prof Green and Danny Glass with him, more on the grounds that it was easier than trying to win an argument about leaving them behind. O'Driscoll had been banned from the operation. His coppery red hair was too distinctive for him to pass for a Spaniard. It was stretching things far enough for the other four to do so. O'Driscoll's place had been taken by another Danny from 4 Troop's Easy section; Danny Mitchell who had performed well at Honfleur during their last op.

Carter led them up the beach and into the scrubby brush that filled the gap between the sea and the narrow road that ran behind the beach. He raised his hand to halt them and they lowered themselves until they were kneeling, blending in amongst the low bushes. Carter gave two low whistles.

There was a moment's anxious silence, then the whistles were returned, two, then another two, the correct answering signal. There was the sound of movement in front of them then a darker shape appeared.

"Franco." Carter said.

"Churchill" the figure replied.

Carter stood up and stepped forward to greet their guide.

"Welcome Signor." He said in slightly accented English. "You can call me Felipe."

Whether that was the man's real name or not didn't matter. Code names were the norm in the sort of circles in which Warriner operated.

"Glad to meet you, Felipe." Carter replied, meaning it. If Felipe had gone to the wrong beach, or more likely Carter's dinghy had landed on the wrong beach, life would have become more difficult without their guide and translator. "Please, call me Lucky. These are my team, Prof, Danny and Mitch." The abbreviation of Mitchell's second name to form a nickname had been agreed only hours before, to counter the problem of the two matching forenames.

"I don' think I will know who is who until I see you in the daylight." Felipe said. "But welcome to Algeciras."

"Will it take long to get to the town."

"An hour, maybe a little more. We can walk the road, as we will see any patrols coming and have time to get into hiding." Unlike Gibraltar, as a neutral country Spain didn't have any blackout restrictions in place. At night Algeciras lit up the sky on the far side of the Bay of Gibraltar, serving only to make the colony seem even darker. Any patrol vehicles would have their headlights lit, making them easy to see at a distance. Fuel was in such short supply that any vehicle was unlikely to be driven by a civilian. "I think that it is in the town that we will have more chance of meeting with the police or army."

Even that was unlikely, Carter had been told. Landing at three in the morning meant that most people were in bed, so the police were hardly likely to be out in force. There would be some down by the docks, where the tabernas catered for the sailors from the merchant ships that stopped off in the port, but elsewhere the peaceful citizens of the town would attract little police attention.

"There were no signs of roadblocks." Felipe informed them. "But sometimes they mount them by surprise." With Spain so recently engulfed by civil war and Andalucía being one of the provinces that had stood against the Nationalists with tens of thousands dying at the siege of Malaga, which had been a Republican stronghold. There was still suspicion that the region might rise against Franco's government once more, so the authorities took no chances. Algeciras itself had been Franco's first beachhead on his return from Spanish Morocco, so the town was considered to be a bit safer for the Nationalists.

"We'll worry about them if we come up against any." Carter said. "Well, Felipe, we're in your hands. Lead on."

Felipe turned and led them the short distance to the road, turning right to head northwards along the bay. To describe the rutted dirt track as a road was to be generous, Carter thought, but it was marked on the map as such.

Their briefing had been as thorough as the time would allow. The RAF had flown many sorties along the three mile territorial limit, taking photographs of southern Spain from its border with Portugal in the west to Cartagena in the east, trying to identify military installations and possible preparations for an invasion of Gibraltar. This had given Carter a wealth of photographic information from which to identify a suitable landing beach. It had to be small, somewhere to which the Spanish authorities would pay little, if any, attention. It also had to be devoid of human habitation, which ruled out many of the beaches close to the small fishing villages dotted along the coast.

The beach he had chosen was about four miles from the edge of the town; a gentle stroll for the commandos. Carter was immediately impressed with Felipe's field craft. He moved as silently as the commandos. He also had no difficulty in keeping up with their pace. Carter wondered what he might have done for a living before he had been recruited by the British. There was still a lot of smuggling along the south coast of Spain, or so he had been led to believe.

The small group made good time getting to Algeciras, with no alarms along the way. The suburbs were quiet, even the dogs seemed to be asleep. As they approached the centre of the town the roads became narrower, the houses and apartment blocks close together as though seeking comfort from each other. A few lights started to show through the shutters as early starters stirred themselves to have their meagre breakfasts, or perhaps nursing mother rose to feed their babies.

Felipe brought them to a stop, drawing them into the entrance of a narrow alley between two shuttered shops. The men huddled close so they could hear. "The apartment block you are interested in is just around the corner." Felipe whispered. "I'll point it out to you when we get there. The apartment is on the first floor, facing the street."

"Is there a back way in?" Carter asked.

"There is an alley that goes to the rear. Only one door. It connects to the main entrance by a passageway."

"Prof, you and Mitch go to the back. Find somewhere to observe where you can't be seen. If you see any signs of anyone else, get out straight away and come back here. Danny, you and I will take a look at the front entrance. If it's all clear we'll go inside and take a look at the apartment."

"What you want me to do, Lucky?" Felipe asked.

"Does Chaffinch speak English?" Carter cursed himself for not asking the question before they had even set out. It was the penalty of having to make plans in a rush.

"Who is Chaffinch?" The Spaniard gave him a puzzled look. Then the answer dawned on him. "Ah, Chaffinch lives in that apartment. I'm sorry, I don't know. I was only given the address and told to bring you here, then to the safe house."

"In that case you come with us. If anyone challenges us you can answer for us."

"What you want me to say?"

"Depends what question is asked. Say you're looking for a friend who has promised us work. Make up a name. They'll say you have the wrong address, so just apologise and we'll leave. We can keep the place under observation and have another try later. But first show Prof and Mitch where the alley is, then come back for us."

"OK. You follow." Felipe said, leaving the alley.

He was back a few minutes later. At the entrance to the alley he waved his arm and they followed him along the street to the nearest corner. Peering around to the left he beckoned Carter forward. "There." He said. "The third door on the far side of the road."

Carter counted the doors set into the walls. The street was one long building with doors puncturing it at intervals. Shuttered windows could be seen in the dim street lights. On the first and second floors the windows also had iron railed balconies that reached out and almost touched the balconies of the block opposite. At the very top of the building Carter could see dormer windows piercing the roof line. Each house had probably started out as an individual town house, with rooms at the top for servants, but they had been divided up into apartments long ago.

Carter was just about to lead them into the street when a match flared in a doorway directly across the road from the one in which he was interested. He drew back. The flame flickered out, to be replaced by the glow of a cigarette. It brightened as the smoker drew more smoke into his lungs, before dimming again. So, he wasn't the only person interested in that apartment building. But were they just there to keep watch, or was it a trap, designed to capture whoever came to find out about Chaffinch?

Carter led them back to the alley. "Any chance you were seen when you took Prof and Mitch?"

"No. We didn't enter the street. We went across the road and down the side of the building."

"You still might have been seen."

In the darkness Felipe shrugged his shoulders. "Possible." He had to admit.

But no alarm had been raised, no police whistles sounded and the watcher was still at his post, not hurrying away to find a public telephone, so it was probable that Prof and Mitch hadn't been detected. But what did he do about whoever was watching the front? If he had been in France the answer would have been simple. He would have ended the man's life. But he was under strict orders not to do anything like that here. At best it might spark a major diplomatic incident if it was discovered that the British were involved, at worst it could result in Carter and his men being arrested not for spying, but for murder. And that could lead to nothing less than the death penalty.

Banging the man on the head - he assumed it was a man – was no better. The human skull is thin in places and a blow meant to render the victim unconscious could just as easily kill. It might be OK in the movies, but his unarmed combat instructors at Achnacarry had been in no doubt about the possibility of it causing death. They had only one option if they wanted to get into the apartment building. They had go in by the back door and hope that there wasn't anyone watching that as well.

Carter briefed them on the new plan. "Felipe, is there a way of getting round to the alley without being seen crossing the street?"

"We can go back the way we came, take a different route and cross the street much further down. Then circle around by the next street and come back from the other side."

"Ok, we'll do that. You lead the way."

It would be slower and Carter was acutely aware that time was marching on. They wanted to be in and out of the apartment block before daylight arrived. Felipe was supposed to provide them with a safe house for their use during the day then, when night arrived once more, they would recommence their search by going to the nightclub. Night-time made it much less obvious that they weren't Spanish. Felipe would ask some questions while Carter and his men made sure they weren't followed. Once the questions were answered, they might have some idea where else to search.

Although slow, the journey was uneventful. There was more noise to be heard through the shuttered windows they passed; a radio, voices raised in argument, the rattle of crockery. It all served to remind Carter that time was ticking away. He resisted the urge to check his watch. It wouldn't delay the rising of the sun and would only give away his nervousness.

Prof looked at them in surprise as they paused by his hiding place, a gap between two reeking dustbins. Carter raised his finger to forestall any questions. There would be time for those later. Carter motioned him to stay where he was, then followed Felipe further along the alley to the rear door of the house. It opened under his touch.

The long passageway was lit by a single dingy bulb halfway along the high ceiling, but it was enough to allow Carter to assess the ground floor layout. Two doors were positioned side by side about halfway along, matched by another pair on the opposite wall. So, four apartments on the ground floor, two facing the front and the other two facing the rear. The layout was probably the same on the upper floors. To Carter's left there was a stairway, which turned through one hundred and eighty degrees at a half landing above his head, before continuing upwards. Carter led the way silently up the concrete steps, staying close to the wall so that he could see further around the corner. The landing was empty save for a bicycle leaning against the wall outside the apartment immediately to his left. The one he was looking for was number five, which was at the front on his right as they approached cautiously.

Carter placed the flat of his hand on the door and pushed gently. It swung open under his palm. He could see why immediately. The doorframe was splintered where someone had forced their way in.

Indicating to Danny Glass that he should remain at the doorway to keep lookout, Carter led Felipe through and into the corridor of the apartment. He stopped and shrugged his small rucksack off his back. Reaching inside he removed a torch, aiming it downwards before he switched it on. If the beam accidentally hit the shutters of the windows, the watcher outside couldn't fail to see the light.

But the torch produced enough light for his night vision accustomed eyes to pick out some detail. To his left a door opened inwards. Further along there was a second door, then a third at the far end. Facing him at the end of the corridor was a large wardrobe made in dark wood. Immediately to his right was a coat stand with a couple of coats hanging from it, a straw hat hanging above them. Just past that was a tallboy with a telephone perched on top and a woman's handbag next to it, alongside a bunch of keys. That didn't look good. No woman left their apartment without their handbag and keys. At least, not voluntarily.

The first door on the left stood open and gave into a combined sitting room, dining room and kitchen. Closest to him was a pair of shabby, overstuffed armchairs with a coffee table in between. A small sideboard stood against a wall, supporting a radio and some framed photographs. Beyond that was a small dining table with two hard back chairs, one at either side. Under the left-hand window was a sink and draining board, then a cooker with a gas bottle beside it, then the second window, beneath which were cupboards. Standing against the wall on the right was what Mrs Hamilton referred to as a 'press'. A tall freestanding unit with cupboards and drawers for storing crockery, cutlery and food. The room was tidy, suggesting it hadn't been searched.

Carter moved along the corridor to the second room. The door was shut but opened easily when he turned the doorknob. It was a bedroom, the left-hand side dominated by a double bed. The sheets were rumpled and the pillows askew, as though someone had just got out of it. On the right was a dressing table with a free-standing vanity mirror. The surface of the dressing table was cluttered with pots of makeup and bottles of perfume. Small items of jewellery were scattered about as though dropped carelessly. In front of the dressing table was a padded stool on which some underwear was draped as though it had just been removed.

Behind the door stood a heavy wardrobe, the twin of the one at the end of the corridor, suggesting they were matched pair. Carter opened the door. It was split in two, dresses hanging on the left while shelves were on the right, loaded with neatly folded clothing. Carter was no fashion expert, but he recognised that half the dresses were plain frocks for everyday wear, while the remainder were more stylish, for evening wear.

Framed pictures adorned the walls and from their subject matter it would seem that they had been chosen with male visitors in mind.

The final room was the bathroom. Clean and tidy but unremarkable except for the male shaving equipment arranged on the glass shelf above the wash basin.

Carter returned to the hall to find Felipe rooting through the handbag. He held up a large purse, which he opened. It folded out to accommodate bank notes. From one of the folds he withdrew a piece of stiff card. Showing it to Carter, he saw the photograph of the woman, Chaffinch taking up one side, opposite close typed information.

"This is her?" Felipe whispered. "This is Chaffinch?"

Carter nodded his head. "Then the police have not taken her. They would take her identification documents with them. It is a crime to be on the streets without this card."

So, if not the police, then who? The obvious answer was the *Abwehr*. In which case Carter had a problem. He was about to lift the telephone to make his report when he had second thoughts. It was quite possible that someone may be listening in on the line. Better to use a public telephone.

"There's nothing more we can do here." He told Felipe. "Take us to the safe house. Also, I need to find a public telephone."

* * *

The safe house was a small family dwelling located in the northern suburbs of the town. They had passed through an area where small businesses plied their trade, workshops, small warehouses, a second-hand car dealership selling German and Italian cars and several other types of premises.

They had passed a man unlocking a building, but he barely gave the five passers by a glance. It was the time of the morning when people were going to work, which didn't require any curiosity to be satisfied.

Carter stopped at a public phone to make a call to the local number that he had memorised. It had rung for a long time before a sleepy voice had answered. "Si!"

"The bird has fallen from the nest." Carter said, feeling slightly foolish saying the phrase out loud.

"Please repeat." The voice said in cultured English.

Carter obliged.

"Understood." There was a click and the line went dead.

Chatty sort, thought Carter, before carrying on along the street in the wake of Felipe.

"The house belongs to a ship's officer." Felipe explained. "He is currently on a voyage to South America and won't be back for several weeks. A friend of a friend has the keys in case of an emergency. That friend of a friend has leant them to me. I think he thinks I am bringing a woman here. Please, don't show yourselves at the windows. This is a respectable neighbourhood and strangers will attract attention."

Felipe showed them around the house, which only consisted of five rooms. There was a kitchen, which Felipe had stocked with tinned food for them, a living room, two bedrooms and a bathroom. After a quick breakfast Carter organised a rota for them to keep watch through the front and rear shutters, then went into the larger bedroom, removed his heavy work shoes and lay down to try to get some sleep.

But sleep wouldn't come. Where was Chaffinch? Every time he tried to clear his mind in preparation for sleep the question returned. She had to be in the hands of the *Abwehr*. It was the only explanation that made any sense. And if she was being held by them, was it possible for Carter to do anything about it? Could he mount a rescue?

He had been shown photographs of the Consulate building currently being used by the Germans. It was far bigger than warranted for the size of the town. In fact, a town the size of Algeciras didn't really warrant a consulate at all. If diplomatic representation was needed, perhaps to assist German sailors passing through the port, then it would be more normal to appoint a local expatriate businessman to act as an honorary Consul, or even a Spanish businessman with links to Germany. But here in this town the Germans had a staff of six, five of whom were living in some comfort at the town's best hotel. Only the Consul, Max Grau, lived in the top floor of the Consulate building. Which meant that if Chaffinch was being held inside, then a raid might be possible.

But how to find out if she was there? She could be being held anywhere.

She had to be there. If they held her anywhere else the Spanish authorities could intervene to rescue her, because diplomatic immunity[1] wouldn't apply to any other building. The Consul and the Consulate building enjoyed diplomatic status, but that was limited to Consul's duties in that role. The kidnapping of Spanish nationals fell way outside that remit, Carter knew. That meant that if the Spanish found out, it could cause the Germans considerable embarrassment. While everyone knew that Spain's neutrality was biased towards Germany, it wouldn't do for Spain to be seen to stand by while its own citizens were abused by a foreign power. At least, that was Carter's reasoning.

Which meant that Carter had some leverage.

"Felipe!" Carter called. "I need to go somewhere, and I need the right clothes to dress in."

All the commandos had been dressed as Spanish workers, in heavy dark trousers, plain white shirts and hard-wearing jackets. The jackets were especially important. For reasons Carter couldn't understand, the Nationalist government insisted that all males wore jackets when outdoors. For what Carter had planned he needed something more business-like. A search of the wardrobes produced a smart suit which just about fitted Carter, so long as he kept the trousers well belted. The Spanish sailor obviously enjoyed his food. He also had smaller feet, which meant that Carter could do nothing about his heavy work shoes. But his shirt would pass muster with one of the Spaniard's ties to adorn it.

Danny Glass and Mitch Mitchell were left at the safe house. Five men walking together would look out of place. As it was, Carter and Green would trail Felipe at some distance, as though they weren't with him.

The sun was quite high when they reached the smart street on which the Consulate building stood. It was a sturdy two storey house standing in its own small patch of ground, with iron railings separating it from both the street and its neighbours. Flower beds and narrow strips of well-manicured lawn completed the picture. On a flagstaff jutting from the wall above the door hung the red and white Nazi flag with its swastika emblem in the middle.

Along the street a café was open, business suited people sitting drinking coffee and reading the morning newspapers. "You and Felipe watch the front from there. If I'm not out in an hour, go to the police. Felipe, you must insist on seeing the commanding officer of the Guardia Civil and tell him that Emilia Morantes has been kidnapped by the *Abwehr*. Take her handbag and identification card with you, so they know you have tried to find her at her flat."

"How do I explain that?" Felipe asked, a frown wrinkling his brow.

"Tell them you're a friend of her mother. She's been trying to telephone Emilia and not been able to get an answer, so she asked you to visit."

"And how do I know the *Abwehr* has her?"

Do I have to think of everything? Carter asked himself, before realising that he did. "A neighbour heard the door being broken in. When she looked out, she saw four big men dragging Emilia out of the apartment three days ago. When she protested, they spoke to her with German accents and told her to mind her own business."

It wasn't the best cover story, but it was the best that Carter could come up with at short notice. It would stir the Guardia Civil into action. Felipe then had to get out of the police station as quickly as possible and disappear before the Police started to take too much of an interest in him and his connection to Emilia, because the cover story wouldn't withstand close scrutiny.

What the Guardia Civil might do with that information, Carter didn't know. It was unlikely that they would try to enter the Consulate building in strength, but it was possible that one officer might seek a meeting with the Consul to make it clear they knew what was happening. Whether or not the Spanish would actually escalate the crime into a full-blown diplomatic incident was another matter and would be decided in Madrid, not Algeciras. But Emilia was the girlfriend of the Chief of Police, so he was bound to react to the kidnapping of his beloved in some way.

[1] The Vienna Convention on Diplomatic Relations wasn't created until 1961. Until then the conduct of diplomatic relations and the status of diplomats and their embassies and Consulates was mainly the matter of tradition, rather than legality. A convention had been signed in Havana in 1928 but only covered the countries of the American continents and was therefore not binding on any others, though its principles were being followed in many other countries. Therefore, Carter is making assumptions about what might or might not happen in Spain.

4 – The Consulate

Carter strode up to the Consulate's solid looking front door looking far more confident than he felt. It was possible that he was being watched, so looking as though he had nothing to fear was important. He was about to bluff the local head of one of the most feared intelligence services in the world and you don't do that by looking shifty or fearful.

He pulled on the metal rod that sounded a bell deep within the building. He heard the sound of feet approaching before the door swung open to reveal a Spanish man, dressed in a butler's livery.

"I'd like to see Herr Grau, the Consul." Carter said, trying to sound as imperious as he could.

The man stood to one side, opening the door wider to allow Carter to enter. "May I tell Herr Grau your name and the purpose of your visit?" The man asked in faultless English.

"My name is Steven Carter and I wish to discuss the whereabouts of Senorita Emilia Morantes." Carter replied. If the name was familiar to the Spaniard, he didn't allow it to show on his face.

"Please wait here." He said, indicating a row of hard back chairs that were positioned along the wall of the spacious entrance lobby. He knocked on the door opposite the chairs, waited for an answer then entered the room beyond. Carter caught only a glimpse, a large portrait of Kaiser Wilhelm II hanging on the wall above an opulent carpet before the door was shut.

Carter took the time to study the ground floor layout. At the far end of the lobby a polished wooden staircase led upwards. Halfway up, the staircase split, turning through ninety degrees on both sides to continue upwards to the first floor. On the half landing a bust of Adolf Hitler stood on a black marble column.

On the ground floor, other doors led off to more rooms to the left, the right and beneath the stairs. Behind one of them a telephone rang and then immediately fell silent as someone answered it.

The door opened and the Spanish butler reappeared. "Herr Grau will see you now." He announced, stepping out into the hall to make room for Carter to enter. As he did so the butler pulled the door closed behind him. It shut with a solid sounding thunk.

The room was modelled on the library of a wealthy man. The wall opposite the window was lined with books, but too far away for Carter to read any of the titles. The shelves followed the wall around behind Carter until they reached the doorway. Beyond the window, mirroring the painting of Kaiser Bill, was a similar sized one of Otto Von Bismarck, the architect of modern state of Germany. The wall facing Carter was also lined with books on either side of a marble fireplace, the space above it dominated by a giant painting of Adolf Hitler, a studio portrait, no doubt a copy of the one already hanging in the *Nationalgalerie* in Berlin.

In front and beneath the portrait was a large desk, empty of anything other than a telephone and a desk lamp. Sitting behind the desk was a middle aged man that Carter assumed was Colonel Max Grau, though in his persona as Consul he wouldn't use the military honorific.

Grau stood and reached over the table, offering his hand, before sitting down again after Carter had shaken it. He waved Carter towards a comfortable chair that stood at an angle to the desk.

"You are a brave man, *Mr* Carter, walking onto German territory." He stressed the 'mister', letting Carter know that he suspected that he would normally use a different title. He was roughly the same height as Carter, stocky but not overweight. He wore a pale coloured suit with a Nazi badge in the lapel buttonhole, a simple white shirt and a tie that bore military style stripes.

"I may be on German soil, but you are surrounded by Spain. If you wanted to imprison me it wouldn't be easy to get me all the way to the nearest airport to fly me out." Carter was by no means sure of that. Besides, they didn't have to get him out of Spain to kill him and dump his body.

"But we could do it, you know."

"I wasn't so stupid as to come here without telling anyone. If I don't return within the hour, my colleagues will go to the police and tell them everything we know about the disappearance of Srta Morantes."

"Which is what, precisely, Mr Carter."

"That she is, or was, your mistress. That your men were seen dragging her from her apartment three days ago." That second part was a bluff, but Grau wouldn't know that.

"I and my men have diplomatic immunity. The Spanish can't touch me."

"As a Consul your immunity only stretches as far as the conduct of your duties here in Algeciras. It doesn't cover you for the committing of crimes unconnected with those duties, such as kidnapping. While I must admit that the local police are unlikely to enter these premises to search for Srta Morantes, they can make enough of a fuss for your Embassy in Madrid to take exception to the fact that you have been sleeping with a British agent and have now had her kidnapped. I'm not sure that your employers in the *Bendlerstraße*[1] would approve of that part. They also wouldn't like to have to admit that the *Abwehr* is operating in Spain. It could be very embarrassing in international terms."

That wiped the smug expression from Grau's face. It would be very embarrassing for him personally if such an accusation were to be made. It would make him look foolish, which was what Carter had bargained on.

He tried to shrug off the accusation. "I have no idea what you are talking about, Mr Carter."

"I think you do, Herr Grau. So here is what I propose. You hand over Srta Morantes and we'll say no more about it."

The German sneered at Carter. "You really think I would do that?"

"So, you do have her then." A statement of fact, not a question.

"We do, Mr Carter. And when we have found out all that she knows, we will kill her." He stood up abruptly. "Come with me."

He led Carter out into the lobby and then towards the stairs at the rear, before diverting to the door that stood under the overhang. He pulled it open, revealing another flight of stairs leading downwards. The stairs were narrow concrete, lit by bulbs screened by glass bowls set into the side wall. Grau led the way down the stairs to the bottom.

There was a short corridor ending in a blank wall. To one side a door hung open. Inside Carter could see a metal framed bed with a stained mattress, a chamber pot underneath. The door opposite to the cell was closed, but Carter could hear shouting from inside. The language was Spanish. The rooms had probably been a wine cellar at one time, or perhaps for the storage of food in cooler conditions than could be arranged on the ground floor.

Set into the closed door was a small panel, which Grau flipped open. He indicated that Carter should look through.

A large man stood bent over a woman tied to a chair by her hands and feet. The woman didn't look up at the sound of the viewing panel being opened, but the man did. His expression was blank, incurious. He turned back to the prisoner and started shouting at her again in Spanish.

The woman was naked, Carter realised. What he could see of her face was a mass of bruises, her lips swollen to twice their normal size. Blood matted her hair and was streaked down her breasts and thighs. The man paused in his shouting, obviously giving the woman an opportunity to reply, but she just shook her head, resigned to whatever was going to happen next.

What happened next was that the man drew back his arm and gave her a roundhouse punch to the side of the head. She cried out in pain as the blow knocked her sideways, almost toppling both her and the chair. The man reached and grabbed her shoulder, pushing her upright once again.

The woman shook her head, clearly stunned by the blow. But she said nothing. Carter was stunned. He had never witnessed such violence being used against a woman before.

"You are shocked, Mr Carter?" Grau's smug tone was back.

"You are brutes." Was all Carter could find to say. The German just laughed.

"You British will never win the war while you shy away from doing what must sometimes be done."

"Is it necessary for her to be naked?"

"People feel vulnerable when they are naked; women even more so. It helps in the interrogation that the subject feels vulnerable."

"Has she been …" he didn't even want to say the word.

"No. At least, not with my permission. It is counterproductive. Once a woman has been raped, the threat of rape can no longer be used as part of the interrogation. For most women the threat is sufficient to get them to talk though not, seemingly, for this one."

Grau leant into the viewing panel and called through. "*Genug, Gustav. Sie hat keinen Sinn für uns Tote*."

The man stood back, looking a little disappointed. He went out of sight for a moment and returned with a bucket. He threw the contents, water Carter assumed, over the woman. Then he untied her.

The woman was led into the corridor between Carter and Grau and pushed roughly into the cell. The door was slammed behind her then the key turned in the lock. The man went back up the stairs, his work done for the present.

"Your arrival served a purpose in the end. It has granted poor Emilia a reprieve, if only a short one. If I had left Gustav to his work he would doubtless have knocked the woman senseless. There is a fine line between torture and execution, you know, Mr Carter." As he led the way back up the stairs Carter could hear the sound of sobbing coming from behind the cell door.

Back once more in the office, such civilised surroundings after the barbarity that Carter had just witnessed, Grau sat behind his desk once more.

"How did you find out about her?" Carter asked, not really expecting an answer.

"An agent of ours was arrested in Gibraltar. He had only recently been recruited. I remembered that I had mentioned the man's name in the presence of Emilia. It made me start thinking about other …

issues we had recently suffered. Emilia seemed to be the one common factor. I set a trap for her. I let her hear me tell one of my men that an agent was due to meet his handler in a café near Cathedral Square, then I had the café watched. Sure enough, British counterintelligence agents appeared. It was all the proof I needed of Emilia's perfidy. It is a great pity. I was quite fond of her."

"Not fond enough of her to prevent your man from torturing her." Carter observed.

"When love flies away, it leaves nothing behind, not even pity." Grau replied with a shrug. "Well, I have things I must be doing, Mr Carter, so I'll bid you good day." He rose and offered Carter his hand, which Carter ignored.

"You aren't bothered about me going to the police about Srta Morantes?"

"No. I must admit the thought did worry me a little for a few minutes, but not anymore. You see she was also betraying the head of the Guardia Civil in Algeciras. I knew she was sleeping with him, but I didn't mind. I used her to find out what the Spanish were up to and she was happy to tell me. When he finds out about that, he will be even more merciless than me. The Spanish are much less sophisticated in their interrogation techniques. So, go to them if you wish, Mr Carter. They will not be of any help and you will only make matters worse for Emilia. With me she will get a quick death at least."

Carter realised that his bluff had failed. Keeping his face as impassive as he could, Carter left the Consulate, just glad that the Germans hadn't decided to take him prisoner as well.

[1] The *Bendlerblock* in *Bendelerstraße*, Berlin, was the home of the *Oberkommando des Heeres* (Army High Command) and the *Abwehr* until the end of World War 2. Bendlerstraße has now been renamed *Stauffenbergstraße* in memory of Claus Von Stauffenberg, the German army Colonel who tried to assassinate Hitler in July 1944.

* * *

"Of all the crazy schemes you've ever come up with, that has got the be the craziest, the maddest …" Prof Green ran out of words to describe what he thought of Carter's plan. "Come on, Lucky. Even you've got to admit that we've got pretty much no chance of pulling this off."

Carter wasn't about to admit anything of the sort. "What about you, Danny. What do you think?"

"I do what I'm told, Lucky, so if you give the order and I'll follow it. But I have to admit that I'm with the Prof on this one."

"Mitch?"

"I'm the new boy here, but I've heard the stories of the sort of things you've done in the past. I'm like Danny, you give the order and I'll be right with you, but if you really want my opinion, I'm with the other two."

Carter turned to the last of the small group assembled around the kitchen table in the safe house. "I can't give you orders, Felipe. I have no idea who you work for and I don't want to know, but what do you think of the plan?"

"Like the others said, is crazy. But sometimes crazy plans work."

After leaving the Consulate Carter had taken Green and Felipe around the block to survey the area, taking care to make sure that Grau hadn't had him followed. On either side of the Consulate building were others like it; the homes of prosperous businesspeople or the offices of equally prosperous companies. They offered a line of approach, but also the risk of discovery if they tried to cross through the gardens.

But at the rear there was the bulk of a church, standing in its own grounds and reached by a parallel road. The church had a new roof and there were still patches of soot, evidence of a fire. Felipe told them that it had been burnt by Republicans before the civil war. The more extreme elements of the Republic had no time for religion or its practitioners. The likelihood was that the church's priest had died at the same time as his church was destroyed.

They walked around the side of the ancient building to find a courtyard set between the solid walls of the church and the rear walls of the houses. Carter was able to pick out the Consulate from the black painted shutters. The other houses used white. Along the wall, benefiting from the shade thrown by the church, wrought iron benches were spaced at intervals. The wall itself was painted with scenes taken from the Bible, some of the paint looking very fresh, signs of recent renovation. Small shrubs stood in tubs dotted along the wall and the outside of the church. It was a place of calm and contemplation.

Checking to make sure they weren't being observed, Carter climbed onto one of the benches, grasped the tiles that topped the wall and heaved himself upwards far enough to see what was on the others side.

There was a small garden area, shaded by trees. It was as neatly trimmed as the one at the front, not a single weed allowed to disturb the carefully laid out flower beds, not a single blade of grass allowed to grow longer than its neighbours. In the centre stood a wooden table surrounded by wooden folding chairs. A place to enjoy an evening drink before dinner, perhaps. To the left of the rear of the house was a single window with shutters folded back against the walls, it was flanked by a doorway. Carter suspected that the kitchen was on the other side of the door. To the right was a large French window. Carter at once let go of the top of the wall and dropped back onto the bench as he realised he was looking directly at a man sitting behind a desk, working on some sort of document. That had been close. It would only have needed the man to look up for Carter to have been seen.

"OK, I've seen enough. Let's go back to the safe house. Felipe, I'll need another public telephone."

He had relayed the message "The bird is in an iron cage." Iron meant *Abwehr*, 'metal cage' would have signified the SIGC.

"Is it possible to let the bird out of the cage?" the reply came.

"I don't know, but I'm thinking about it."

"Do you need the seagull?" meaning the air-sea rescue launch. Carter had wanted to use 'albatross' as the code word until it was pointed out that it was the nickname the RAF gave to the eagle badges they wore on the shoulders of their uniform jackets. It would be a giveaway if it was overheard.

"Not tonight. Tomorrow night unless you hear otherwise." Carter replied.

Now they were back at the safe house and Carter had outlined the plan to try to break Chaffinch out of her prison.

"We know that all the other Germans are living in a hotel. Only Grau will be inside. If we're as quiet as we know we can be, there's almost no risk."

Which is what had led to the disagreement. Everyone except Carter thought that the plan was bound to fail.

"They may have alarms fitted to the doors and windows.[1]" Prof pointed out. Carter hadn't thought of that. He knew that banks used burglar alarm systems, but they weren't common in private houses. Not for the first time Carter wondered how Green knew so much about the world of crime.

"I didn't see any signs of sensors on the front door." He countered, not adding that he hadn't really been looking for any.

"How would we know that all five of the other Germans were out of the building?" Glass asked. "If they've got a prisoner, that Gustav you told us about may stay behind to guard her."

"I don't think that's likely. She's a woman who has been badly beaten and who is locked in a cell in a cellar. She isn't in any position to free herself. But we can watch the building and count them out at the end of the day."

"But now that you've called on them, they may think you might come back for her." Green pointed out.

"As you pointed out yourself, Prof, I'd have to be mad to do that. Which is why I think the plan will work. They won't think I'm mad enough to attempt a break in."

"How would you get it?"

"The French window looks like it might be weak enough to force. But I can always cut a hole in it. Felipe, can you get me a glass cutter?"

"I think I know where one can be bought."

"Good. I'll also need you to go back to Chaffinch's apartment. She'll need clothing and shoes."

"It may still be being watched."

"If the watcher was from SIGC, then maybe. But not if Grau had sent him. They know we know Chaffinch is no longer there, so there's no point in keeping watch on an empty apartment. But you can always go in the back way, like last time."

"Si. I can do that." Felipe didn't sound too enthusiastic about the idea, but then again, he was running a considerable risk.

"You don't have to if you don't think it's safe. Just guide one of my men there."

"No. Is OK. I'll do it." Carter suspected that Felipe's pride had been injured by the suggestion that he was afraid. Misplaced pride had killed more than one man, Carter knew.

"It sounds like you're going ahead with this plan anyway, Lucky." Green said with a resigned tone.

"I am. You aren't. I'm not going to ask you to get yourselves killed because I'm mad enough to attempt this."

"That's never stopped you before." Danny Glass chuckled.

"Things were different. Then you always had the chance of being taken prisoner. I don't think that applies in this case. The Germans won't be worried about the niceties of the Geneva Convention if they catch us inside the Consulate. They'll shoot us out of hand."

"Besides, the Commando Order[2] gives them Hitler's direct authority to shoot us anyway." Green said.

Carter couldn't argue with that logic. The rules of war, at least those made by the Nazis, had changed in recent months. Not that it bothered the commandos. They took the Commando Order as a compliment. It meant that their raids were having the desired effect.

"Well, if you're going then I'm going." Mitchell said, surprising Carter. While he was a good solider, he wasn't known for taking the lead, which is why he still hadn't been rewarded with promotion.

"You're as mad as he is." Prof grunted.

"No, I'm not. We came here to do a job and the job isn't finished. Our orders were to bring Chaffinch back if we could. The boss thinks we can, so I think we have to give it a go, mad idea or not; Commando Order or not."

"Well, when you put it like that ..." Danny Glass said.

"What? You as well?" Green threw up his hands in despair. "Oh, fuck it. Count me in as well. You'll only get yourselves killed if I'm not there."

It was blatant manipulation, of course. Carter had to admit that to himself. But once he had one of them agreeing to go with him, the other two had been bound to follow.

"What about you, Felipe?"

"I go with you, but I will not go inside the Consulate. If they catch me then I will be handed over to the SIGC and what they will do to me ..." he didn't need to say it out loud. "I keep watch outside."

"Good man. If it looks like it's all gone wrong, it will be very man for himself anyway."

"Now I will go and get the things you have asked for. Is there anything else you need?"

Carter listed a few other tools that might be useful to a burglar then handed over a wad of pesetas. Felipe counted them out then handed half of them back.

"You will leave straight after? In your boat?" Felipe asked.

"No. It's too risky. If the alarm is raised the Guardia Civil will seal the town. I hope the alarm won't be raised, of course, but accidents happen and we have to be ready for those. No. I'll plant the idea that we're heading for Gibraltar, then we'll come back here and hide out for the day. We'll leave tomorrow night, all being well."

[1] The first burglar alarm system was patented by American clergyman Augustus Russell Pope in 1853. In 1857 his patent was purchased by Edwin Holmes, an entrepreneur, who started to manufacture and sell the alarm system commercially in New York, at that time a crime troubled city. He later linked his alarms to the newly created telephone system. Most of the alarm systems used sent a signal along telephone lines to alert the police or fire services, but they could also trigger an audible signal on the protected premises. The majority of modern alarm systems are based on innovations made during the Second World War and afterwards.

[2] The infamous Commando Order or *Kommandobefehl* was issued on the instructions of Adolf Hitler on 18th October 1942 and stated that all commandos/special forces personnel who were captured, even those in uniform, were to be executed without trial. This followed a raid on Sark (Operation Basalt) which resulted in four out of five German prisoners being killed by commandos, allegedly while trying to escape to raise the alarm. The fifth prisoner was taken back to England. There is a school of thought that suggests that Hitler gave the order because he had become enraged by the effect that the commando raids were having on his forces. He is known to have described the commandos and other special forces as nothing more than thugs and gangsters. It is suggested, therefore, that the Sark raid was only a pretext for an order that would have been issued anyway. Even if this view is not correct, ordering the execution of enemy personnel without benefit of trial is regarded as a war crime (just one of many on a very long list that could have been levelled against Hitler). Over a hundred Allied servicemen and women are known to have died as a consequence of the Commando order.

* * *

The appraoch to the church had been straight forward. Leaving the safe house just after midnight, they had checked to make sure they weren't being followed, which was easy to do in the deserted night-time streets. Felipe led them by a circuitous route, avoiding main roads that might be patrolled by the police.

Danny Glass had been in position at the front of the Consulate since the late afternoon, first in the cafe and later,when the cafe had shut, in the darkened doorway of a commercial premises that had closed for the night. It was his job to count the Germans out of the building then make sure that none returned later. He was also supposed to warn of any lights on in the house after midnight. After delivering the commandos to the church, Felipe went around to the front to collect Glass and bring him back around to join the main group. Even if soemone were now to turn up, there was no way for him to pass a message back to Carter.

"All quiet, Lucky." Glass gave his report. "All five Germans left at about six o'clock. I recognised that Gustav from your description. The downstairs lights went off at about eight, then the last upstairs one that I could see went off at ten."

"Good. There're no lights on at the back of the building, so Grau must be asleep by now."

He hefted the small backpack onto his shoulders, now containing the clothing and shoes that Felipe had collected from the house. He checked to make sure his Webley was snugly in its shoulder holster under his heavy workman's jacket, then stepped up onto the same bench he had used earlier in the day.

No lights were visible in the upper storey, but he hadn't yet checked out the ground floor. Pulling himself up by the arms, he raised his head above the red terracotta tiles that topped the wall. As his eyes cleared the barrier he could see that the lower half of the building was also in darkness. He lowered himself down again.

"All clear." He whispered. Green stepped up beside him and joined his hands to make a step. Carter pit his foot in, Green hoisted him upwards and Carter grabbed the top of the wall to take more of his weight on his arms. As his body rose, he bent himself across the wall, and Green let go of his foot, allowing Carter to swing his legs up so that he was lying along the top of the wall. It was a standard manoeuvre, learnt on the assault course at Achnacarry. He wriggled around so that his legs were hanging on the garden side, then lowered himself down, letting go to drop the final few feet to the ground, landing with no more than a soft thud.

Danny Glass and Mitch Mitchell followed behind, moving silently ahead of Carter to take up posts to the sides of both the kitchen door and the French window. Glass tried the kitchen door handle but shook his head to indicate that it was securely locked. Mitchell grabbed the handles of the French doors and pushed downwards. He also shook his head. Carter wasn't surprised. If it had been his own home back in sleepy Ayrshire, he would have checked that all the doors were secure before joining his wife in bed. Why should the Germans be less security conscious in Spain, just a few miles from where their enemies plotted and planned?

He shrugged out of the rucksack and opened one of the side pockets to remove the diamond tipped glass cutter that Felipe had bought that afternoon. With it he carved a neat circle in the glass to the left of the door handle, the side that held the door lock. The sound of the cutter grating on the glass was deafening to him, but he doubted it could actually be heard more than a few feet away.

He pressed his fingertips to the edge of the engraved area and pushed gently. Nothing happened. He pushed a little harder. Still nothing. In desperation he placed the palm of his hand against the circle of glass and leant on it. The glass disc popped out and fell to the floor. Carter cringed, expecting to hear the crash and tinkle of it smashing, but it just made a gentle thump on the carpet inside the doors.

He waited, just in case any sound had been heard. Looking upwards he checked the windows for lights hastily switched on, but there was nothing. He reached inside, feeling for the key. If it had been removed there would be a problem. He'd have to fall back on the second tool that Felipe had bought for him, the two foot long crow bar, which Green had described as a 'jemmy'.

His fingers encountered cold metal sticking out of the lock's face plate; he turned it and heard the snick of the lock being released. Withdrawing his hand he pushed down on the door handle and pulled gently. The door left hand door swung open, but the right hand one stayed in place, held shut by sliding bolts at the top and bottom.

Mitchell stepped inside and checked the room to make sure it really was empty, then returned to the door. His job was to keep their escape route open. Outside, Glass would do the same in the garden.

Switching on a torch, making sure to keep the beam pointing groundward, Carter moved silently across the room to the door on the far side. He turned the handle slowly and the door swung inwards. Whoever was responsible for maintenance in the building was doing a good job preventing the hinges from squeaking.

The hall was empty and silent, lit from the outside by a street lamp, its light streaming through a stained glass panel above the double doors that Carter had used only the previous morning. Coloured patterns ornamented the floor where the light reached.

He stopped, listening intently for any sound. He could hear nothing but the silence and the pounding of his own heartbeat in his ears. The floor here was tiled, the sort of surface that would make a lot of noise when he walked across it in his leather soled workman's shoes. He bent over and undid the laces, slipping the shoes from his feet one at a time. Holding them in his free hand, he started the slow but careful crossing to the doorway under the stairs. Halfway across he realised that he didn't have a free hand with which to draw his gun if he needed to. He remedied that by placing his shoes next to the bottom of the stairs as he passed them. The cellar steps were concrete and would create the same sound problem as the tiled floor; as would the concrete floor of the cellar itself.

In his stocking feet, leaving moist footprints across the pristine tiles, Carter tip-toed his way to the cellar door. Like all the others, it opened easily to his touch. The lights were on, but that didn't worry Carter. There was probably no reason for them to be switched off and it saved having to fumble for the switch in the dark.

Carter made his way slowly down until he could see the length of the corridor. Empty.

He moved more quickly. With an extra layer insulating sound from the upstairs rooms, it meant he no longer had to exercise so much caution. The door to the interrogation room stood slightly ajar, but the room was dark. To his right stood the door to the cell, where he very much hoped that Emilia Morantes, agent Chaffinch, was still confined. Otherwise this whole operation had been a waste of time.

The lock still held the key. Why would it not? He turned it. There was a scraping sound, as though the mechanism wasn't quite so well maintained as the rest of the house. He pulled on the door handle and it opened with a squeal of protest. The room was brightly lit, normal for a prisoner under interrogations. The more deprived of sleep the victim was, the more disoriented they became and the easier it became to confuse them and extract information.

The woman was lying on her side, her back towards him, still naked. She didn't react to his arrival and she was whimpering slightly, her body twitching. Carter thought she was probably asleep, her dreams haunted by her recent experiences.

Carefully he slid his hand over her mouth, preventing her from crying out. She woke instantly, her eyes wide with fear. Carter raise a finger to his lips. "*He venido a ayudarte.*" he said, hoping he had remembered the phrase correctly. I have come to help you.

"*Quien eres tu*?" she replied. Carter didn't understand the question but hazarded a guess that she was asking who he was.

"*Inglés.*" It would have to do as an explanation for the moment. He put his finger to his lips again, silencing further questions. He took the rucksack from his back again and started pulling the folded clothing out. Laying the items of underwear and a dress on the bed beside her. She grabbed at a pair of pants as though her life depended on them and started to pull them on.

While she did that, Carter pulled the last item from the rucksack, the pair of shoes and laid them on the floor at the foot of the bed. They didn't look like they were suitable for walking, but they would have to do. He turned his back as she rose from the bed and started to put on the rest of the clothing.

Which is why he didn't see the door of the interrogation room open and Max Grau emerge from it, a Luger pistol held in his hand. He crossed the corridor with two long strides.

"How very gallant, Carter." He said. "And how totally predictable."

Shocked at the sound of the voice, Carter turned. He was reaching for his gun when Grau spoke again.

"I wouldn't do that if I were you. Mind you, it won't matter if you do. I'm going to shoot you anyway."

"I'm more use to you alive." Carter said, stalling, hoping to find some opening he could exploit. But Grau was keeping his distance. He'd have plenty of time to kill Carter if he tried to rush him.

"Possibly. But you provide a legal way for me to get rid of the girl when I'm finished with her. Your gun will be the murder weapon and it will appear that I have shot you in self-defence. Not down here, of course. I wouldn't be entertaining my mistress down here."

"You'd have to explain the bruises."

"But of course. You inflicted them when you were trying to beat information out of her. So near the truth and yet so far. The Guardia Civil will see things the way they want to see them. It will save them a lot of time and effort having to come up with an alternative explanation."

The woman had stopped dressing, half in and half out of the dress that Felipe had chosen. Out of the corner of his eye Carter could see the look of fear and loathing on her face. Her hopes had been raised, only to be dashed once again.

She let go of the dress and it fell to crumple around her ankles. Then she snapped.

Launching herself at Grau she raked his face with her fingernails, sending him backwards as he tried to get away from her. he raised the hand holding the Luger and tried to beat it down on her head, but the angle was wrong and it just hit her shoulder instead. With his free hand Grau tried to punch the woman, then to push her away, but she was fighting him with an unhuman fury. But Carter knew that she was severely weakened. The adrenalin which she had harnessed wouldn't keep her going for long.

Carter grabbed Grau's gun, raising it so that if the weapon fired it would do no harm. Grau resisted, pulling the hand way from Carter, at the same time squeezing the trigger. In the small cell the report was thunderous and left Carter's ears ringing. But he didn't allow himself to become distracted. With his left hand he drove a fist hard into Grau's ribs, driving the breath from his lungs. Grau's reflexes made him release the Luger so that he could better defend himself. But he couldn't tackle two attackers at once and Emilia was still intent on trying to scratch his eyes from his head. He placed his hands around her neck and started to squeeze, which gave Carter time to slam the gun into the side of Grau's head. He reeled backwards, colliding with the wall. Carter kicked his knee, which buckled under him. Emilia stepped backwards a pace, about to launch a fresh assault, but Carter got there first. He smashed his fist into Grau's face, feeling the blood from his ravaged face slick under his knuckles. Grau's head snapped backwards, hit the wall and he slid downwards, too dazed to support his own weight.

Carter stepped in front of Grau, preventing the woman from attacking again. He raised his hands to fend her off, but the fight had gone from her. Satisfied that she wouldn't attack again, he pointed to the dress that was still around her ankles. She nodded and stepped away to finish dressing.

Carter had a new problem to deal with, how to secure Grau and prevent him raising the alarm. There were restraints in the interrogation room. They would have to do. The woman was now fully clothed, sitting on the bed pulling on the shoes, muttering to herself. Carter suspected that she was criticising Felipe's fashion choices, but she could have been saying anything.

He attracted her attention and mimed tying Grau up, then pointed across the corridor to the interrogation room. She nodded her understanding and crossed the corridor.

Grau was starting to come to his senses, rubbing at his head with one hand and touching his face to try to assess the damage that

Emilia's finger had inflicted. He looked at his fingertips to see how much blood had come away. There was quite a lot, even though the wounds were actually superficial.

"You won't get away, Carter. I'll tear this town apart looking for you."

"We'll be long gone before you even get out of this room." Carter bluffed, implementing his plan to plant misinformation and lay a false trail. "By car we'll be back at the border before it opens for the day." It was far too risky a route for them to take, but Carter hoped that Grau wouldn't consider that.

The woman returned and handed Carter the lengths of rope that had been used to secure her.

"On the bed." Carter ordered. Grau complied readily enough. He wouldn't want to risk further injury if Carter had to do things the hard way. He lay on his belly and placed his hands behind his back, ready to be secured. But that wasn't the way Carter was going to do it. He took one hand and started to tie it to the bedhead, before doing the same with the other, leaving Grau unable to get off the bed and unable to bang on the cell door to raise the alarm.

"You probably aren't very familiar with the work of William Congreve." Carter chatted amicably as he started to secure Grau's feet to the bed frame. "He was a 17th century playwright and he wrote the line 'Hell hath no fury like a woman scorned.' It's one you would do well to remember." Carter chided. "Now, how are we going to keep you quiet?" he mused aloud.

Carter mimed tying something around his mouth and Emilia nodded her understanding again. She went back into the interrogation room. When she returned, she was holding a single stocking and a pair of pants, which Carter assumed were the ones she had been wearing when she had been kidnapped. He nodded and grinned his approval, before stuffing the pants into Grau's mouth and securing them with the stocking.

As Carter lifted his backpack once more, Emilia let off a stream of Spanish in the direction of Grau's face, then spat on him.

"Toodle pip, old chap." Carter said as they left the cell, his apparent nonchalance only skin deep. Inside, his stomach was still churning from the narrow escape.

He closed the door behind them, wincing as it squealed once again before clunking into place. He turned the key, but this time removed it and dropped it into the pocket of his jacket. It would provide a further delay as whoever discovered Grau's whereabouts had to force the solid looking door.

He led the way back up the stairs, realising too late that there was now a light on in the entrance hall. He came to an abrupt halt at the top of the stairs as he found himself staring into the barrel of another gun. This one was being held by the butler, though he was in less butler like clothing of a dressing gown over a pair of striped pyjamas, with tartan slippers on his feet.

"Senor Carter." He looked beyond Carter to identify the figure behind him, still obscured by the wall. "And Srta Morantes. So, the noise I heard was a consequence of you trying to rescue her."

"You're a neutral." Carter said desperately. "You don't have to get involved."

"But I am also a falangist[1], which is why I am employed here." The butler countered. Seeing the Luger in Carter's hand, he spoke again. "Do not let my humble position in this household fool you. I fought in the Civil War. You would not be the first man I have killed. Where is *Oberst* Grau?"

The use of the military title told Carter that the butler knew his employer's real profession. Which probably meant he was also prepared to protect his employer's secrets.

"Herr Grau is in the cellar." Carter admitted. Out of the corner of his eye he spotted movement in the doorway on the far side of the lobby. Mitchell would have stayed hidden when the light came on, but the voices talking in English could only mean trouble, so he had approached the door to see what was going on. Carter had to keep talking to keep the butler focused on himself, giving Mitchell time to creep up from behind.

"I'm afraid that Herr Grau has been keeping your compatriot, Srta Morantes, prisoner here."

"That slut. I don't care about …"

It was Mitchell's shoes on the tiles that gave him away. The hard leather sole clattered as he stepped forward. The butler whirled towards the sound.

"Shoot and you're dead!" Carter warned him, raising the Luger to reinforce his threat. The butler hesitated, alternating his aim between Carter and Mitchell, realising that if he shot one then the other would kill him. In the end he did the sensible thing. He raised his hands in surrender. Mitchell completed his journey across the hall and relieved the butler of his weapon.

Carter stepped fully into the lobby, allowing Emilia to move to the top of the cellar steps. She looked nervously at the second armed Englishman, not sure whether to be frightened. She gave the butler a deathly glare, making Carter suspect that there was some history between the two.

"Well done, Mitch. Take Srta Morantes outside and get her over the wall. I'll take care of Jeeves here."

Carter made a shooing motion to Emilia, encouraging her to go with Mitchell. Once they had disappeared into the backroom, Carter stepped aside and used the barrel of his Luger to indicate that he wanted the butler to descend the cellar steps.

"I hadn't realised you slept on the premises." Carter admitted his mistake.

"Servants usually do." The butler reminded him. Carter told himself that he didn't know that. In the house he grew up in, a woman came in three times a week to help with the cleaning and the laundry and, if his parents threw a dinner party, she would come to help in the kitchen, especially with the washing up, so that his mother could play hostess. All of that had stopped with the war, of course, when the woman left to replace a man in a factory who had been conscripted. But he knew that in the big houses, the ones that took ten minutes or more to walk along the drive, they did have servants who slept in the house.

Carter made sure that he kept some distance between himself and the Spaniard. If he had fought in the Civil War then it was possible that he had picked up some unarmed combat skills along the way. He had no intention of allowing the man to turn the tables on him. At the place where the doors of the cell and the interrogation room faced each other, the Spaniard stopped and gave Carter a quizzical look. Using the Luger's barrel, Carter pointed to the left; the interrogation room.

"Sit!" Carter commanded.

He looked around for something with which to restrain the man. Emilia had taken all the rope to use to bind Max Grau. There was a cupboard standing against the wall and Carter opened the doors, taking care to keep his gun levelled at the Spaniard's chest. Inside he found a cornucopia of torture instruments. The interrogator, Gustav, hadn't got around to using them on Emilia. Or maybe he just preferred to use his fists. But inside he found what he needed. They were the jump leads normally used to start a car by connecting it to the battery of another vehicle. In the bottom of the cupboard stood the battery they might have been connected to if Carter hadn't arrived when he had. It might only be twelve volts, but the current it was capable of delivering would burn the flesh, without the added danger of causing death by electric shock. But the jump leads would serve a purpose by restraining the butler.

Heaped in the corner were Emilia's discarded clothes. Carter found the other stocking and tore a length of cloth from her dress. The cloth he stuffed into the Spaniard's mouth, then secured it with the stocking.

At last he was ready to leave.

He made his way back up the stairs and through the office that led to the French windows. Cursing his forgetfulness, he returned to the hall to retrieve his shoes, put them on and went out into the garden, pushing the French door shut behind him. He had no idea why he had done that, it just seemed like the thing to do.

Lying along the top of the wall were Mitchell and Glass, a gap in between them. Carter took a run and leapt upwards, throwing his hands up. The two commandos grabbed an arm each and hauled Carter up until they could grasp the straps of his rucksack, which they then used to pull him the rest of the way, until he was half hanging over the garden and half hanging over the courtyard. Mitchell and Glass twisted their bodies, lowering their legs and landing softly on the bench beneath. With the top of the wall clear, Carter was able to swing his legs over and drop down beside them.

All that remained to be done was to make their way back through the town to the safe house.

On the way back, Carter stopped at another public telephone and said just one sentence to the sleepy sounding voice on the other end of the line. "The bird is out of the cage." Then he hung up.

[1] Falange – the informal name of the *Falange Española Tradicionalista y de las Juntas de Ofensiva Nacional Sindicalista*, which was the largest fascist political party that backed Franco during the Spanish Civil War. They were founded in 1934 from the merger of two other fascist leaning parties. While not adhering to all the tenets of German or Italian fascism, they were closely enough aligned to both to gain the support of both Hitler and Mussolini. Falangism all but died out following the death of Franco, but in 1979 a new Falange party was founded in Spain and in recent years has seen an increase in support.

5 – The Seagull

Rubbing at his stiff neck, caused by sleeping in an uncomfortable chair, Carter came awake. He checked the time, cursing silently as he realised he should have started his turn on watch almost an hour before. It was a problem he could never overcome. Soldiers don't like waking their officers and telling them that it's their turn to do anything and being in the commandos didn't change that.

Sleeping in the chair had been the only option after he had finished his earlier shift, after they had returned from the Consulate just as the first light of dawn was breaking over the Campo di Gibraltar. Emilia had been given the main bedroom to herself and the other bedroom was shared by whichever of the men wasn't on watch, which just left the overstuffed armchair for Carter.

Rubbing the sleep from his face he saw that it was Felipe who was peering through the slats of the shutters, on the lookout for any impending danger.

"You should have woken me." Carter complained, but not too harshly. It probably hadn't been Felipe's decision to let him sleep on.

"You were tired. You push yourself very hard." The Spaniard offered by way of explanation.

"That's what we do." Carter replied mildly. "I can't ask my men to do anything I'm not prepared to do myself."

"I don't think that would work in the Spanish army. Privilege counts for everything there. Rulers rule and everyone else does as they are told."

"Did you fight in the Civil War?"

"No. My family has a business in Spanish Morocco[1]. I was sent there, out of harm's way."

"Your English is very good. Where did you learn to speak it?"

"The benefits of having a wealthy family. I was sent to school in Gibraltar."

"And now you …" Carter hunted for the right word to use. "…serve the British."

"Our interests overlap. I hate Franco and all that he stands for. He oppresses the people of Andalucía because we stood against him during the Civil War. There can be no peace in Spain until he is defeated.[2] I may be from a wealthy family, but I am a Republican at heart."

Carter was taken by surprise by Felipe's vehemence, but he had met plenty of his type at university; young men from wealthy families who felt guilty for their privileged birth and who sought to assuage their guilt by supporting radical parties. Not just the socialists or communists, but the fascists as well.

"While Spain is officially neutral, he sides with Hitler and Mussolini whenever he can, so he can be sure of their support if he ever needs it again. So, if they are defeated, Spain can rise again and depose Franco. So, I assist you in any way I can."

"I have to say; we would have struggled without your help and knowledge of the town. We're trained to operate in open country where we don't encounter the civilian population except by accident. Trying to navigate around a town where we are strangers and don't speak the language, would have been very difficult without your help." Felipe gave an embarrassed smile.

"I do what I can. Speaking of which, while you were sleeping I went out and tried to find out what had happened after we left the Consulate. I went to a couple of cafes that I know, where people gossip a lot." He gave a knowing smile. "Apparently British commandos broke into the German Consulate last night and locked up the Consul and his butler. The Spanish authorities are very angry that such a thing should happen. Roadblocks have been set up on the road south, towards Cadiz and north towards Malaga and Sevilla. But the gossip is that the British are already back in Gibraltar."

"Did the gossip say why the British attacked the Consulate?"

"No. Nothing was said about any … other person who might or might not have been there. Most people think that the commandos were breaking in to find secrets, such as the names of German agents in Gibraltar."

It was natural conclusion to draw if you didn't know about the Consul's mistress, Carter had to agree. It also meant that the local population were well aware of the presence of the *Abwehr* in their midst.

"But the roadblocks have been mounted anyway, even though everyone thinks we're back safely in Gibraltar." Carter said. It had been his hope that everyone would think just that, so they wouldn't start looking for them in the town.

"Yes. It shows the Germans that the Spanish are taking the matter seriously. No doubt there will be protests made to the British Ambassador by our *Ministerio de Asuntos Exteriores*, the Ministry of Foreign Affairs. but I don't think we have to worry too much about the roadblocks. Many of my friends are … I shall say they make regular trips to Morocco, but they don't depart from the port here in Algeciras. So they know the roads that the Guardia Civil usually close and which are left unguarded. We'll find a way back to the beach tonight."

"I'm glad you feel so confident."

[1] Spanish Morocco – Created by a treaty in 1912 between France and Spain, it consisted of two strips of land extracted from the greater territory of the historic Kingdom of Morocco. One strip was on the southern border, around Cape Juby, adjacent to the modern-day territory of Western Sahara, which was under Spanish control from the 1700s to the 1970s. The northern strip centred on Ceuta, 9 miles south of Cadiz Province in mainland Spain, some of which still remains under Spanish control. The existence of the Spanish territory of Ceuta is sometimes used to justify the British possession of Gibraltar.

[2] General Francisco Franco Bahamonde became leader, or Caudillo, of Spain in 1939 and remained in power until his death from natural causes on 20th November 1975.

* * *

They left the safe house shortly after midnight, the time when the working population could be expected to be in bed. Felipe would return later to put the house back in order so that the ship's officer wouldn't notice when he returned from his sea voyage.

They followed Felipe south through the town, towards the port area. Green went in front with their guide, Carter escorted Emilia and Mitchell and Glass brought up the rear, monitoring the street behind them to make sure they weren't attracting any attention. After about half an hour of walking they reached the warehouses that surrounded the docks, used to store goods waiting for export or to hold imports until their owners paid the customs dues and arranged transport. Behind the warehouses was the cluster of streets housing the dock workers, along with the businesses that kept them fed and entertained.

Algeciras wasn't a big port, certainly nowhere near the size of Cadiz, further west along the coast. But it was only a short voyage across the Straights of Gibraltar to the Spanish enclave at Ceuta and Morocco beyond it, which made it popular with the coastal traffic that plied its trade back and forth. Not only was there a ferry, but the Spanish Navy also kept boats there, monitoring the movements of the British and their allies, making sure that they didn't stray into Spanish territorial waters and also reporting back to whoever was interested in such things.

There were pools of sparse street lighting along the road, which Felipe took care to avoid. The sounds of their feet might be heard, but if anyone looked out through their shutters they might not see anything in the shadows beyond. The houses were small, interspersed with larger blocks, the apartments of which Carter suspected wouldn't be any bigger. Shops and closed up cafes were dotted among the residential properties and one corner was taken up by a cinema, garish posters advertising that week's offerings. Those businesses were all in darkness. Few of the houses had lights behind their shutters. Hard working people went to bed early.

The buildings stopped abruptly as they reached the edge of the town. One moment there was a tarmacked road flanked on both side with buildings, the whitewash flaking and some of the plaster crumbling. Then there was an earth track through open fields cloaked in darkness. The commandos liked darkness; it gave them an edge.

They had gone about a hundred yards when Green held his hand up at shoulder height; the stop signal.

Taking Emilia's hand Carter pulled her down and closer to the verge at the edge of the field. Instinctively he drew his hand gun from its shoulder holster. There was a delay of several minutes, then Felipe crept back towards them, getting close to Carter so that he could whisper.

"Voices, two as far as we can tell. Muffled slightly, as though they're in a vehicle. It's too dark to see. They are speaking Spanish."

"Guardia Civil?"

"I don't think so. Their roadblocks are usually well lit. They like everyone to know they're in charge of the situation. This could be *Guardia Urbana*, the local police, sent by the Guardia Civil to watch this track. It might also be army or even customs officers looking for smugglers."

"OK. Go back to Green and ask him to try to get a closer look, then both of you come back here."

There was an agonising wait while Green crept forward to carry out his reconnaissance. Carter was glad he had left the safe house so early, allowing plenty of time to accommodate delays such as this.

After about twenty minutes, by Carter's watch, Felipe and Green appeared silently next to Carter, so quietly that they almost caused Emilia to call out in surprise.

"They're local police." Green reported. "Only two in the vehicle as far as I can see. It's some sort of van, closed at the back so we can't see inside. They're about a hundred feet in front, measured from here. No sign of any others. If there's more, they're doing a better job of keeping themselves concealed."

It was a thorough report; just what Carter would expect of a commando as experienced as Green.

"How close did you get?"

"Close enough to touch the side of the vehicle." Close enough. Carter couldn't have asked for more.

He signalled to Mitchell and Glass to close on him. They were only a few yards away, just visible in the starlight. There were so many factors to consider. They had to remain quiet, as any noise might attract attention. Carter could actually see the nearest *Guardia Civil* check point, no more than half a kilometre distant on the Cadiz road, lit up like daylight. They had to have a generator with them to provide that much electricity; probably mounted on the back of a lorry.

His men were capable of killing the two police officers so silently and quickly that they wouldn't even know they were dead. But that would make matters much worse in diplomatic terms. The two officers weren't involved in the war. They were just obeying their orders, protecting the lives of innocent Spanish civilians. He would do it if he had to, but he didn't want to.

Finally, he had Felipe to consider. He had to live in the area. If they left any clue to his identity behind, it could result in his capture. That would include any memories of his voice. Carter wasn't sure but he thought criminals had been caught because their voice had been recognised. Carter couldn't risk that. He could go with them, but Felipe hadn't expressed any wish to do so and he probably wanted to continue his covert war against Franco. His sudden disappearance would be noted, preventing a return at a later date.

Then there was the woman, Emilia. She couldn't move quietly, the way the rest of them had been trained to do. Even Felipe seemed to be capable of moving with considerable stealth.

But they couldn't just sit there hoping the police would become bored and move on. It left him few options.

He made his decision. If it went wrong, he'd have two dead police officers on his conscience, but it was the best he could come up with. "Prof, Danny, I want you two to creep up on either side of the van. I'll go around the back with Mitch, just in case there's anyone inside. On my word, stick your guns through the van windows and Prof, you tell them not to move. Felipe, what's Spanish for 'Don't move or we'll kill you?'"

"*No te muevas o te matamos*." He replied.

Prof tried the phrase out and Felipe corrected his pronunciation until he was close enough for his words not to be misunderstood.

"Felipe, I want you to tell Emilia what to say to the police for us. When we call you forward, she has to speak, not you."

"I understand. She goes with you to Gibraltar, so it doesn't matter of the police know about her."

"Correct. Tell her she must tell them to hand over their weapons. Then she must tell them to get out of the van." In careful whispers Felipe relayed the instructions and Emilia nodded her head in understanding. Even in the darkness Carter could see her eyes were wide with fear, but she was holding up well.

"Felipe, you stay here with Emilia and when I give two whistles, bring her forward to do the talking. We'll secure the two police with their own handcuffs and stick them in the back. Then we'll use their van to take us to the beach." He paused, examining their faces in the dark. "How does that sound, chaps?"

"No worse than any of your other plans." Green said. Carter was glad that O'Driscoll wasn't with them. He'd have probably been far more scathing. Carter spat on his hands and rubbed them in the dirt, picking up soil and using more spit to mix it into a thick paste. He streaked it across his face and neck, breaking up the outline, making it harder for the eye to recognise them as being human. Emilia was about to do the same when Carter stopped her. By the time she was close enough for the police to see her, they would already be restrained; or, at least, Carter hoped they would. Rubbing soil into the damaged skin of her face would hurt and might also poison her wounds and Carter didn't want that to happen. It would be a vicious irony for her to get to Spain only to die of blood poisoning.

"*Ve con Dios*" Felipe whispered, as they set out. Go with God. So, Felipe wasn't that much of a Republican. Or was it just evidence of the phrase that he had heard only recently, that there were no atheists in foxholes?[1]

Green guided them along the left-hand side of the road, while Glass took the right, so that he didn't have to cross over when they reached the police van. They moved painfully slowly, taking care that each foot was placed silently on the ground before placing their weight on it; making sure that no twig would snap, no stone would rattle. It was a skill they had practiced many times before and they knew that patience was the key. Speed meant mistakes and mistakes cost lives. They kept their bodies as low as they could, almost duck walking, so that the darkness of the ground concealed them. All it needed was for one of them to pass in front of one of the lights shining from Algeciras for the two Spanish police to know there was someone in front of them. All four had buttoned their dark jackets up to their necks so that no hint of white shirt showed to give them away.

The van was parked facing the town, the direction from which any threat was expected to approach. Presumably the police officers thought that they would hear anyone approaching and would be able to light up their targets with the van's headlights before ordering them to halt and give themselves up. But their bored chatter had given them away and Green would now be the one giving the order for them to give themselves up.

They were only halfway to their destination when Carter heard the first sounds of their voices. He couldn't make out individual words, but it wouldn't be any use even if he could, as he wouldn't be able to understand what they were saying. But the sound told him where the van was, still hidden by the night.

Step by slow step, they continued forward until the van was no more than ten yards in front of them. They froze as the vehicle's engine cranked over, the noise splitting the night. It backfired twice, then rattled into silence again.

"*Madre de Dios*!" Carter made out above some other words. That, he knew, meant 'Mother of God' a common Spanish epithet. Carter would have liked to have said the same.

A door squealed open on ungreased hinges and feet ground into the dust of the road. There was some more swearing; at least, that was what Carter presumed was being said. Some banging was followed by another squeak of hinges.

A torch beam flared into life, revealing the open side bonnet of the van, a uniformed police officer silhouetted by the light's backwash as he peered inside, trying to unravel the mysteries of the internal combustion engine.

Some instructions were shouted from beneath the vehicle's bonnet and the engine cranked again. The result was the same, some groaning and backfiring, followed by a rattle until silence reigned once more.

More squealing hinges and a second police officer followed the first, leaning into the van's engine compartment, looking for goodness knew what. An argument ensued, with a lot of pointing and shrugging of shoulders. Finally a decision must have been reached.

The two figures returned to either side of the vehicle and searched inside, pulling out objects and arranging them about their persons. That much Carter could see by the torchlight on his side. He had clearly made out the shape of some sort of sub-machine gun being slung around the police officer's neck.

The two figures met up again at the front of the vehicle, then started to walk down the road towards the town, the torch's beam guiding them.

If the beam deviated by so much as a couple of feet from the centre of the road, it couldn't help but pick out the commandos crouching by the verges.

Out of the darkness a figure stepped, a gun held up, pointing unwaveringly at the two police officers. Glass had decided to end matters. Carter silently applauded his initiative but wished he hadn't done it. The policemen were leaving, they could have been allowed to pass unmolested, resolving the problem for the commandos without them having to do anything risky.

Green was quick to react. "*No te muevas o te matamos*." He called from the darkness, moving forward as he did so, revealing himself to the two police officers. More importantly, he revealed the gun he was holding, backing up his words.

The two officers stopped dead, raising their hands above their heads, looks of shock visible on their faces as the torch beam passed across them, before it was pointing vertically upwards.

Carter let go the two whistles. Any verbal command could have been confusing, with no one being too sure who it was meant for. He heard the approach of feet, not quite running, but not walking either.

Felipe took Emilia behind the two prisoners, so they could hear her voice but not see him whispering instruction into her ear. She fired off some rapid Spanish and the police officers started to divest themselves of their weapons and other equipment. When they dropped their police issue hand cuffs, Carter scooped them up and grabbed the arm of one of the officers to attach the cuff, dragging the arm around behind his back before repeating the movement with the other arm. He then did the same with the other two police.

The two were bundled into the back of the van and the door slammed shut behind them. Emilia's last translated instruction to the prisoners was to stay quiet, because they were being watched and if they made any noise, they'd be killed.

"We can't use the van to get to the beach now." Carter said. "We haven't got time to try to fix it."

There was a quick exchange of Spanish between Emilia and Felipe, before he translated. "She says she can't walk much further in the shoes she has."

Carter could understand that. He hadn't thought them suitable for walking when he had given them to her in the Consulate; dancing, maybe; walking, no. It was a problem he should have resolved the previous afternoon. Felipe could have gone out to buy her something more suitable for walking. Too late to think of that now!

"Tell her to keep going for as long as she can. After that we'll have to take turns to carry her."

Her expression showed what Emilia thought of that idea but she, also, had no choice.

They set off into the darkness once again.

[1] This phrase was probably coined at the Battle of Bataan (Philippines), fought between January and April 1942. There are several possible originators of the phrase, including a US Army chaplain, two different officers and a civilian war correspondent. But it is undoubtedly American.

* * *

The second hand of Carter's watch ticked around to oh three hundred precisely. Raising his torch, he pointed it out to sea, as close to the bearing on which the RAF rescue launch should be as it was possible to estimate, then sent the signal. Three flashes, followed by two flashes then a final single flash; a five second gap between each group.

A single flash was returned. Nothing more complicated was needed and if an enemy had tried to replicate the original, trying to guess at the correct response, it would mean that they were in a trap.

There was a risk of discovery in using a light signal. There might be other boats out in the dark, waiting for them. The signal might even be seen by people in the town. No doubt the Spanish had their own equivalent to the Coastguard and they might well be on the lookout for unusual activity out at sea.

The rest of the journey had been slow but uneventful. After about half a mile Emilia had to admit that her feet were in too much pain to allow her to walk any further. Each man, Felipe included, had taken it in turns to carry her, piggyback style, for about half a mile. She wasn't very heavy and the commandos had endured worse. Even Felipe didn't seem to mind the weight, though Carter had arranged the rota so that he would be last to take his turn, which meant that he was least likely to have to carry her more than twice.

Carter's calculation was right. He, Green and Glass had each taken three turns, Mitchell and Felipe just two by the time they reached the narrow, almost invisible path that led to the beach. How Felipe had identified it in the darkness Carter didn't know, but he stopped exactly where the path started without seeming to examine any landmarks.

Even with the interruption caused by the presence of the police and the reduced pace caused by carrying Emilia, they had arrived on the beach with almost half an hour to spare. The parting at the top of the path had been brief. The commandos each shook Felipe's hand and wished him well, then Emilia had given him a peck on the cheek. Within seconds he was swallowed up by the night and they turned their back on the track and made their way down to the beach.

They sat silently in the scrubby bushes just behind the beach, waiting for the appointed hour. It had grown cold and Carter had to lend Emilia his thick jacket, as her thin dress was no match for the cutting edge of the sea breeze and she had started to shiver. Or perhaps it was just fear.

They heard the approach of the dinghy, or dinghies as it turned out, long before they saw them. Two small inflatable craft, tied together by a rope to prevent them becoming separated in the dark, one khaki clad airman in each, paddling from the rear until the fronts ground their blunt snouts against the coarse sand.

The commandos crept forward, three getting into one dinghy while Carter helped Emilia into the other. He pushed the dinghy out until he was knee deep in the gentle waves, before he climbed into the little craft and grabbed the spare paddle to help with the propulsion.

They didn't try to rush. The splashing of paddles would have run as much risk of attracting attention as showing a light. It took nearly twenty minutes to reach the launch, untying the rope so that one dinghy could go to each side so they could all board at the same time.

Carter asked one of the crew to escort Emilia below, while he climbed the short ladder to the small bridge, where he found the boat's skipper. He was a pink faced young officer who, Carter thought, would probably have looked more at home wearing a boy scout's uniform. On both epaulettes a single thin pale blue line, sandwiched between two darker ones, denoted that he was a Pilot Officer. That was the lowest commissioned rank in the RAF, which meant the lad was probably fresh out of the training school. Carter would have preferred someone a little more experienced to be in charge of the boat, but it was too late to do anything about that now. At least the boat had reached the correct location.

"Slow ahead." The young officer said, his voice low but steady. Sound carried a long way across water.

The engine's revs had hardly started to build when a lance of brilliant white light pinned them in its glare. There was no mistaking the powerful marine spotlight.

"Enemy patrol boat!" The Pilot Officer barked. "Full ahead together. Evading action."

At least the young man was decisive, Carter thought.

"He must have been waiting out there for us." The young man observed, a slight break in his voice betraying his nervousness. "Probably heard us arriving and was waiting to see what we're up to before showing his hand. He won't be alone. There are probably others strung out across the bay."

Dots of tracer fire streamed from close beside the spotlight and stitched their way across the bay towards the launch. The Cox'n span the wheel and the launch leaned hard over as it went into a high-speed turn. The deck canted alarmingly and Carter was worried that they might capsize completely, but the man on the wheel knew what he was doing. As the tracers streamed away from them on the port side he immediately reversed the turn of the wheel, cutting beneath the arc as it swung back towards them.

There was the clatter of bullets striking something metal, then the tracer stream was passing them on the starboard side.

"Aren't you going to fire back?" Carter shouted above the howl of the wind created by the boat's speed.

"We aren't at war with Spain, Captain Carter." He shouted back. "And I'm not going to be the one to start one. When we get to international waters, I'll be within my rights to fire back."

"Such fine points of law don't seem to be bothering the Spanish." Carter retorted.

"We are intruding on Spanish territorial waters, Captain Carter. They're entitled to stop us. Strictly speaking they should order us to stand too, but such niceties will be forgotten if they manage to capture us and take us to Algeciras. We can protest as much as we like, but we'll still be interned."

"Can you arm my men? With rifles they can take out that spotlight and the machine gunners will be firing blind."

"I'll arm them if you agree not to open fire until I give the word."

"You have my word on that. How long till we're in international waters?"

"At this speed, about ten minutes. It would be less if we could steer a straight course." He went over to a voice pipe mounted on the forward bulkhead and bent over it, just as one of the bridge widows shattered. If he hadn't bent over, he would probably now be dead. He gave some instructions then returned to Carter's side, fighting the wind that now blew through the missing window. He made no comment about his narrow escape and Carter had to admire his outward calmness "My master-at-arms will issue your men with rifles. Can they really hit the spotlight at this range?"

The Spanish boat was about three hundred yards behind. "It may take them a few goes, but they only need one shot on target. What are our chances of outrunning the Spaniard?"

"Pretty good. I could get thirty six knots out of this boat in a straight line and I'm pretty sure they haven't got any patrol boats that are faster."

Carter left the wheelhouse and dropped down to the aft deck. His men were huddled in the lee of the bridge superstructure, trying to stay out of the wind.

"The penguins[1] are going to issue you with rifles. Hold your fire until I give the order, then try to take out the spotlight. Once you've done that, aim for the machine gunners."

There was another clatter of bullets striking the boat and it lurched suddenly, seemingly out of control. Carter hurried back up the ladder to the bridge. Inside he found the Pilot Officer was now at the wheel, struggling to turn it back on course, while the Cox'n sat slumped in the corner, blood flowing from a wound in his skull.

"Deal with him, will you Captain." The RAF man made it sound like a request, but it was in fact an order. Despite their difference in rank it was the RAF officer who was in command. It was an authority that even a General couldn't overturn.

Carter bent over the airman, checking to see if he was still alive. He was still breathing, his breath coming in shallow gasps, but he was unconscious. That was probably for the best as it protected him from the pain from his wound. Carter located the first aid box, mounted on the side wall of the bridge, opening it up and pulling out some swabs. He started cleaning blood from the wound. It was quite a deep gash, but Carter couldn't tell if it had damaged the bone of the skull. All he could do was bandage the man's head and hope for the best.

"You see that light over there?" The Pilot Officer asked, pointing westwards towards the Spanish coastline.

Carter straightened up and peered through the side window, which was also now devoid of any glass. "Yes, I see it."

"When we come abeam of it, we're leaving the three mile limit and your men can open fire."

"Can you give me that in plain English. I don't know what 'abeam' means."

"It means at right angles to our direction of travel. That is if we were sailing in a straight line, of course, rather than dodging around like we are."

Carter checked the angle of the light coming from some building sitting on the coast. It was still a degree or two in front of them, as far as he could work out, but the angle was changing quickly.

Carter finished bandaging the injured crewman's head. "What shall I do with him?" He asked.

"Probably best to leave him where he is. You could do more damage by moving him. He's no safer below decks than he is above anyway. There's only half an inch of marine plywood separating the lower decks from the Mediterranean Sea. Nothing that would stop a bullet."

"Do you want me to steer, so you can take care of other matters." Carter offered.

"What does a soldier know of our seafaring ways." The officer chuckled.

"You'd be surprised." Carter answered enigmatically, remembering his voyage back to Scotland after Operation Absolom.

"Thanks, but as soon as we're out of harm's way I'll get one of my men to take over."

As the officer swept the boat into another turn, Carter guessed when they crossed the true course and checked the position of the light again. If it wasn't abeam yet then the difference in angle was too small to be visible to the naked eye, which was good enough for Carter. He scrambled down the ladder and scuttled across the deck to his men, lying prone at the aft railings. He saw the RAF crew preparing to fire the Oerlikon gun that was mounted half way along the aft deck. At last they would be able to fight back.

"OK, guys. See if you can, hit that spotlight. If not, then go for the machine guns. A bottle of Scotch to whoever gets the light."

The three commandos started firing, slow, carefully aimed shots. As each one cracked away across the water they pulled back on the bolts of the rifles to propel the spent cartridge over their shoulder and push another round from the magazine into the barrel.

Danny Glass fired a shot and a fraction of a second later the spotlight went dark. He let out a whoop of victory. The machine gun was still firing however and every time it did, a few more rounds drilled into the launch. The spotlight might be out, but the fluorescence of the launch's wake would still be visible across the water, guiding the gunners.

Help came unexpectedly. At least it was unexpected by Carter and his men. Another spotlight cut through the darkness. This one was far more powerful and it originated from in front of the RAF launch. At first Carter's spirits fell, thinking that there was another Spanish vessel cutting them off from their destination. But he was quickly proved wrong. There was a gout of flame from the mystery vessel and the rushing sound of an artillery shell arcing above their heads. The shell missed the Spanish vessel, but it was probably meant to; a literal shot across the bows.

Pinioned by the spotlight, the Spanish boat broke off the chase and made a high-speed turn back towards the safety of its own port.

Carter returned to the bridge. "You didn't tell me you had company." He said, slightly accusingly.

"I didn't know we had, not really. I was told that the Navy would provide support if they could, but no one said in what form. I knew there weren't any MTBs in the harbour.

The spotlight was still tracking the Spanish launch as it made its way homeward. By it's light Carter could make out the sturdy lines of a corvette.

"There'll be trouble over that." The Pilot Officer predicted.

"How so. The Spaniard fired on us in international waters."

"He'll claim we were still in Spanish territorial waters, even if we weren't." He turned the wheel, Pointing the bows back towards the Rock of Gibraltar, a looming black bulk on the horizon.

"We'll be docking in about twenty minutes." He added.

[1] Penguins – One of several derogatory terms used by soldiers to describe members of the RAF. It was particularly mocking because penguins can't fly. The term may have been coined to mock the RAF's marine branch: birds that can't fly but which float on the water.

* * *

The launch nudged against the quay and hidden hands grasped the ropes thrown by the crew members, holding the boat hard against the concrete so that a gangway could be slid across. Carter sent his men ashore first, then Emilia, while he said his farewells and expressed his thanks to the young RAF officer.

"Think nothing of it." The young man replied. "It made a change to have some excitement. Now, if you wouldn't mind, we've got a couple of hours before daylight to make it look as though this boat has never left port. We don't want the Spanish to have any photographic evidence of our misdemeanours."

"That'll be a bit of a job." Carter commented, looking at the splintered woodwork of the rails and decking and the missing glass from the wheelhouse.

"Nothing a bit of paint and some new glass can't fix. Putty will fill the bullet holes well enough to prevent them being spotted by anyone at a distance. We'll leave it a couple of days and then go into drydock to get the proper repairs done. We've got a couple of holes below the waterline that will have to be fixed before we can put to sea again."

Carter could hear the chug of the pumps, sending gallon after gallon of bilge water over the side and into the harbour.

He saluted the young man and made his way along the gang plank, just as the ambulance carrying the injured crewman drove away, it's bell clattering. His feet were hardly on the quayside before the gangplank was removed and he heard the power of the launch's engines increase, to take her out to her anchorage.

A Naval rating saluted Carter and invited him to follow. He was taken to a low building at the end of the quay, guarded by an armed sailor. Carter was shown in, then the door was shut behind him.

"Well done, Carter." Carter's eyes hadn't adjusted to the bright light before Warriner had grabbed his hand and shook it like he was trying to pump water. "Do you mind if we have a debrief before we let you go back to your normal duties?"

"Some sleep would be welcome." Carter protested.

"We won't keep you long. Better to get it written down while it's still fresh in your mind."

Carter knew when to admit defeat. He could see his three men, each sat at a desk opposite uniformed NCOs. Intelligence Corps, Carter presumed. One chair sat empty, a bespectacled officer sitting behind the desk, looking across at Carter with a curious expression. There was no sign of Emilia. It was as though she had never existed.

“What will happen to the corvette skipper, opening fire on the Spanish like he did?” Carter asked. Warriner would know.

“He’ll have some lengthy reports to write, complete with all his navigation calculations to prove where he was, not that it will make any difference. The Spanish will accuse him of faking them. Then it will all be down to the politicians and diplomats in Madrid and London. The Spanish will claim they were fired on while still inside their own territorial waters, while pursuing a launch that had entered their waters illegally. We’ll claim that there was never any launch and that the Spanish fired on the corvette in international waters. The Spanish will know that we’re lying and we’ll know that the Spanish are lying; at least lying about where they were when the corvette opened fire. In the end it will all blow over, especially when the Ambassador reminds the Foreign Minister that there is a Spanish oil tanker anchored off Cadiz still waiting for British certificates to be signed before the Royal Navy will allow it to dock. Now, if you want some sleep, you’d better get over and talk to the intelligence people.”

* * *

Carter could have done with another hour’s sleep, but he had found a note on his bed telling him to report to the yacht club at fifteen hundred hours. He made his way through a light drizzle, welcoming the feel of it on his skin.

The yacht club was alive with officers, who crowded around Carter, asking him questions about where he had been and if the previous night’s gunfire had anything to do with him. He declined to answer and the officers stopped asking as soon as they realised they would find nothing out from him. The 2IC was the last to greet him.

“This arrived for you two days ago.” He handed Carter a thin envelope with the lozenge shaped GPO[1] logo with a crown above it; a telegram.

Carter’s heart skipped a beat. This had to be personal and it could only mean one thing. He tore the envelope open and quickly scanned the contents.

"TWINS BORN TODAY STOP BOY AND GIRL JOHN AND KATHERINE STOP MOTHER AND BABIES FINE"[2]

Seeing Carter's face go pale, the 2IC asked "Everything all right, old chap? Not bad news, is it?"

"No … no. It's good news. Great news in fact. I'm a father. Twins, a boy and a girl."

Officers suddenly reappeared around Carter, slapping him on the back and congratulating him.

"I think this calls for the bar to be opened. I'm sure the CO won't mind." The 2IC announced.

"What won't the CO mind?" Lt Col Vernon's voice came from behind them.

"Young Carter here's just become a Daddy." A voice came from the back of the crowd.

"In that case, then yes, the CO doesn't mind the bar being opened. But business first, I'm afraid."

The officers fell silent, turning to face their commanding officer.

"We have been given fresh orders." He announced. "We're to prepare to depart for pastures new. You'll be told the destination once we've boarded our ship, but I can tell you that we leave in three day's time."

There was a buzz of fresh excitement. Despite the constant training and exercises, the commandos had started to feel confined by the Rock. It would be good to go somewhere that held the possibility of walking more than two miles in a straight line without being halted by a border fence or the sea.

"I'll give you a more through briefing in the morning." The CO continued. "Now, I officially declare the bar open and the first round is on Captain Carter."

[1] GPO – General Post Office. The name given to the combined postal and telecommunications service in the UK before the telecoms arm was renamed British Telecommunications (BT for short) in 1969, then privatised in 1984. The remaining part of the organisation was renamed The Post Office and split into three

business, Post Office Ltd, which ran the high street retail and sub post office network, Royal Mail and Parcelforce. Royal Mail and Parcelforce were privatised as a combined business in 2013 with the government retaining a minority shareholding.

[2] Punctuation in telegrams was always spelt out, as the original Morse code used to transmit them didn't contain punctuation. Even when punctuation was added to the code it was felt that the need for clear punctuation, to remove ambiguity, was best served by continuing to spell out the words. Only the final "stop" is omitted from telegrams.

6 - Algeria

The port of Algiers appeared to be one solid mass of ships and soldiers. Liberty ships were tied up in trots of 3 or 4, merchants ships discharged into lighters because there was no space on the quayside and there were half a dozen more craft waiting in the approaches for their turn to dock. One of them, The SS Lough Neagh, was the temporary home of 15 Cdo.

The quayside itself was swarming with soldiers and sailors, mainly American. They wore their M1 helmets and carried their Garand M1 rifles, they swore and they jostled and none of them seemed to know whether they were coming or going. Lorries forced their way through the ranks, trying to get to a ship to load or away from a ship having been loaded. Huge crates, containing goodness knows what, swung from cranes and derricks, looking as though they would fall at any moment onto the heads of the masses below. A landing ship was discharging Sherman tanks through its clam shell bow doors, directly onto the quayside across a folding ramp.

Christmas had come and gone before 15 Cdo had been able to board ship. Their original transport had limped into Gibraltar, listing badly after sustaining a hit from a torpedo fired from a U-Boat. Had she been farther from the Rock she might not have made it at all. But she wouldn't go beyond Gibraltar until she'd had major surgery in the port's dry dock. That meant 15 Cdo lost their berths and had to wait until new transport could be found.

The Lough Neagh was a ship that no one wanted to travel in. She'd been built sometime during the First World War and hadn't been modernised since. She'd ploughed a furrow between Dublin or Belfast and Liverpool for year after year, carrying mainly cattle, the smell of which had permeated every layer of her chipped and scarred paintwork. Pressed into war service she'd slowed down every convoy that she had ever been part of. Convoy commanders secretly hoped she'd be sunk by a U-Boat, but it was always some other, faster ship that got it.

Now the commandos sat on board and suffered. Being winter it still wasn't that warm, but beneath the cramped decks of the old steamer, the men grew hot and peevish. Carter didn't like the ship for a different reason. Its smell of cattle reminded him of Home Farm and his distant wife, Fiona. It made him feel homesick.

The CO had tried to persuade the Captain, an obdurate Ulsterman, to take them along the coast and allow them to go ashore in the lifeboats. Their future accommodation could be seen from the beach, he had discovered when he and the QM had gone ashore to inspect it. But the Captain wouldn't be persuaded. If he left his position off the harbour mouth, he'd lose his place in the queue, he said and he wasn't risking that.

All things come to an end, even the commandos' forced incarceration aboard the ship and at last the Lough Neagh was allocated a space at the quayside. The soldiers stumbled down the gangway, their kitbags over one shoulder and their rifles over the other. Technically they were in a combat zone and should have been wearing steel helmets, just like the Americans, but they weren't about to give up their green berets.

Assembling on the dockside they looked for the transport that should be waiting to take them to their new home, but they looked in vain.

"Don't just stand there like a bunch of street walkers on a slow Monday night." The Sergeant Major shouted. "Pile up your kitbags and form a chain. We've kit to unload."

It should have been unloaded by one of the ship's own derricks, but keeping his men occupied was more important to the NCO than using the tools provided. If he let them loose on the quayside it wouldn't be long before some of them started to drift off in search of beer.

Eventually two trucks did arrive, American two and half ton trucks, or 'deuce and a halfs'[1] as they were nicknamed. They were the work horses of the American Army, their equivalent to the Bedford QL 3 ton trucks, affectionately known as Queen Lizzie's, used by the British.

The men groaned when they saw them. Complaining wasn't common amongst commandos, but after being cooped up on board the Lough Neagh they weren't happy about having to march to their barracks.

Even the two trucks wouldn't be enough to carry all their equipment. It would require several round trips and would probably take the rest of the day and half the night.

The Sgt Major organised the men into three groups: one troop would leave at once so they could greet the two lorries and unload them, the main body of four troops would follow on behind once the unloading of the ship was complete and the final troop would act as a rear party and load up the lorries when they returned to the docks.

The route to the barracks led them past the Great Mosque, which was reputed to be a thousand years old. Not that the commandos were interested in that. The road then skirted around the Casbah, the oldest part of a very old city, before heading north west along the coast. As they left the teeming city behind them, the houses started to become more prosperous looking. Walled gardens were topped with brightly coloured flowers and the shouts of children could be heard from some. Carter recognised the language as being French. To their right the commandos could see the beaches, with sunbathers dotted along at intervals. If it had been Blackpool, Carter thought, the beach would have been jammed on a day such as this, but for the Algerians it was probably quite cool.

They marched in silence, which was unusual and gave an indication of the state of morale. In normal circumstances the commandos would always sing one of the old marching songs brought home by their fathers from the Great War.

Fort-de-l'Eau had been a barracks for native troops under the Vichy French. Now that the Allies had arrived the native units had been disbanded or moved further away from the supply lines. It spoke badly of the Allies that they didn't trust their new comrades. The barracks itself was built on an old colonial style, a square walled compound with the barrack rooms built against the outer wall, leaving a large square parade ground in the middle. Some outbuildings had been added to cater for the mechanisation that followed the Great War, mainly garages and workshops for cars and lorries, which replaced the stables used by French colonial officers for their horses.

Every soldier thinks he has left his barracks clean and ready for the next occupants and every soldier curses the previous occupants for leaving their accommodation in such poor order. Carter heard his men grumbling, but he knew they had endured worse, not least having to live on Bishopstone railway station the previous summer. He heard Fred Chalk, his Troop Sergeant Major balling at the men to stop moaning and get on with it.

The main problem was the lack of beds. While there were metal bedframes, there were no mattresses. The QM had asked for them, but so far they hadn't been delivered. They would have to sleep on the floor, which didn't improve the mood.

A guard roster had been posted on the Orderly Room notice board and Carter noted that his men were the designated troop for that night. How that had been arrived at he didn't ask. Someone had to be first and it wasn't fair that it should always be 1 Troop, so 4 Troop it was on this occasion.

It had sounded bigoted, but Lt Col Vernon had briefed the officers that they could expect attempts to steal anything that wasn't nailed down. On the march to the barracks they had seen evidence of that with small items of American military equipment being visible inside doorways or being worn by people in the street. It wasn't that they needed whatever they stole, it was the fact that it was owned by the British or the Americans. The ethnic Algerians didn't see the Allies as liberators, just as another occupying army, just like the French before them. The Vichy French governor had been replaced by one sympathetic to the Allies and supported by the Free French authorities in London, but everyone knew who was really in charge. As such, their supplies and property was fair game for theft. Carter's challenge, as the officer in charge of the inaugural guard force, was to try and thwart that ambition.

Taking a walk outside the walls Carter soon realised that the external buildings wouldn't keep anyone out. The doors were flimsy and the hasps even flimsier. It would take days to find the stock of padlocks amongst all their equipment and even then the doors would need reinforcing, so there was no way of securing them short of mounting a strong guard. Equipment had already been piled inside by the advance party, mainly boxes of ammunition. Carter couldn't contemplate that being spirited away during the night, so the first thing he had to do was get it moved inside the walls.

He assigned a section of men to that task and then climbed up onto the walls, using the walkway built above the roofs of the accommodation blocks. They had a clear view all around the area, over the tops of the bungalows that had been built along the coast road to the sea in one direction and away towards the Atlas Mountains that ran from east to west behind the city. But the town had encroached quite close to the walls on all sides. Not the nice neat bungalows of the French, which were on the side closest to the sea, but the meaner buildings that housed their servants or the unemployed. The fort had probably stood in open countryside when it had been built, but the city had expanded to surround it.

There wasn't much that could be done about that. Carter wasn't about to start evicting people from their homes so he could demolish the buildings. They'd have to live with it. His guard would have to prevent people from getting too close, which meant foot patrols outside the walls as well as sentries above.

The main gate was the weak point. It was high, made of wood and, when closed, secured a gap in the walls. At the moment it stood open, a sentry box stood just outside, adjacent to a striped pole lying across two supports, a lump of concrete fixed at one end to allow it to be raised without too much effort. The pole was metal, not that it made any difference. It was a token barrier to stop vehicles. A pedestrian could just walk through the gap between the pole and the wall. The gate would have to be kept closed at night, with two sentries outside to prevent anyone attempting to open it.

A group of boys had gathered by the gate where a couple of members of the advance party had been positioned to prevent entry. None of the boys was more than twelve years of age, Carter thought. They were all dressed in the long, hooded qashabiya favoured by the ethnic Algerians. The thought crossed Carter's mind that they might have been sent to spy out the land, then he chided himself for such an uncharitable thought. They were probably just curious about the new arrivals.

"What's the plan, Lucky?" A voice came from behind him. Carter turned to see his two section commanders, Lieutenants Murray and Barraclough, approaching.

"Just looking to see how we should place the guards." He replied. He explained the problems with the storage buildings and the need to keep the exterior of the walls patrolled during the night.

"What about sending patrols further out, through the local streets and houses."

Was that really necessary? Carter thought. "What's your thinking?" he asked aloud. Commando leaders always encouraged the input of ideas from their subordinates, to reject the suggestion out of hand was unthinkable.

"If the locals can see we're on the lookout for trouble, they're less likely to try to encroach on the walls of the fort. It'll also discourage anyone from spying on us from the shadows."

It made sense, Carter had to admit, though it would stretch their resources a little. "OK, we'll do it. But they can't carry firearms. They can carry trenching tool handles but they're to be used only for self-defence."

The British army-issue trenching tool handle served as a handy club. It wasn't as long as a pick axe handle, but was much bigger than a police issue truncheon. It also had an iron collar wrapped around one end. It made a formidable weapon in the right hands. "I don't want to start a war with our neighbours. Right, it will be two hours on and four off. Able and Baker sections will take the first watch, followed by Charlie and Dog, then Easy and Fox. Pool George and How sections and split them into three groups to mount the patrols. We're on duty for two days. When we come back on duty again in twelve days' time, we rotate the shifts so that George and How take on sentry duties and Easy and Fox mount the patrols, then we keep the rotation going."

"What about the officers and the senior NCOs, Lucky?" Ernest Barraclough asked.

"I'm just getting to us. We each take charge of one watch. I'll take first shift, then you Ernest and finally Arthur. Fred Chalk will be my deputy, and your own sergeants will be yours. I want them to lead some of the patrols. They can draw sketch maps of the surrounding area and take note of anything they see. There's no harm in knowing who our neighbours are and what they're up to. All sentries are to carry rifles with loaded magazines and fixed bayonets but make it very clear to them that these people are not our enemy. Rifles are not to have bullets up the spout and are not be cocked. Our neighbours are to be treated with respect and consideration. On the other hand, they aren't allowed inside the fort unless they have a legitimate reason."

"We'll need some rules of engagement to give to the men." Barraclough suggested.

"Good idea, Ernie. You can draw them up while I brief the CO on what we're doing. Arthur, you can start posting the sentries and get the first foot patrols out. I shouldn't be long."

Carter turned on his heel and headed towards the building that had been designated both the officer's mess and their headquarters. In an outer office he found the Sergeant Major sitting beside a desk next to the fort's only telephone.

"Is the CO in?" Carter asked.

"In conference with the 2IC and the QM, Sir." He answered. "I'll let him know you're here."

The Sgt Major went through the door behind him. As it opened Carter heard the sound of subdued voices but couldn't make out any words. The Sgt Major returned a few seconds later. "Please go through, Sir."

Carter did, entering the room and saluting. The three senior officers were arranged around a battered old desk, sitting on rickety looking chairs. All of them were normally cheerful men, but the expressions on their faces suggested anything but cheer right at that moment. Carter wouldn't have been surprised if a coffin had been present, so funereal was the atmosphere.

"What can I do for you, Steven?" The CO asked.

Carter filled him in on the arrangements that had been made with regard to the guarding of the fort.

"Patrols? Are you sure they're necessary? The natives are supposed to be friendly, you know."

"I think Steven might be right." The QM interjected. "One of the Service Corps drivers who's bringing our kit from the docks told my Sergeant that three lorries have gone missing from the lorry park in recent days and no one has a clue where they've gone. The Y … Americans are also reporting a lot of equipment losses. It does no harm to lay down a marker and keep our perimeter pushed out as far as is practicable."

"Very well. OK, Steven. Write all that up as a set of Guard Orders and I'll sign them." Apparently dismissed, Carter saluted and left. He had just reached the sunlight of the parade square when he heard a voice calling on him to stop. It was the 2IC, Major Cousins.

"Steven, a quick word if I may."

"Of course, Sir."

"You have a reputation, may I say, for unconventional thinking when it comes to rules and regulations." It was said with a smile, so Carter knew he wasn't in trouble. At least, not yet.

"I'll confess to stretching rules to their limit on occasion, Sir, though I try to make sure that they don't stretch so far that they get broken."

The 2IC gave a knowing smile, recognising the careful turn of phrase for what it was. "Then you may be able to help. We have a bit of a problem with transport. In fact, we haven't got anything other than a battered Jeep we've scrounged off the Americans. We only got that because they've got plenty that don't have dents in them.

Those two trucks we've got aren't permanent. Once all our kit has been delivered they'll be off back to wherever they're based. The trouble is, without transport we've no way of getting to any sort of decent area for training. We can march far enough from here to set up a safe rifle range and we can play sports on the beach, but that's about all. We haven't got any landing craft so we won't be doing any beach landings, though we've brought Goatleys[2] and can do some training with them. So, using that fertile mind of yours, do you have any suggestions as to how we might solve the problem."

Carter's brow furrowed as he considered the matter. If they had enough money, they might be able to hire some trucks from local sources, perhaps. But getting fuel for them would be a difficulty. With official vehicles came access to official fuel dumps. In the local economy fuel was in very short supply.

"Can I ask you, Sir. What is our mission here?"

"That's part of the problem. We haven't got one. Officially we are assigned to the British Division here in Algiers. But we haven't been assigned to a Brigade. That means that, as yet, no one knows what to do with us. The CO asked the divisional Chief of Staff if there were any plans for us to carry out any raids and all he got was a shrug of the shoulders. It seems we've been sent here in case we're needed, but no one seems to need us. That means we're tail end Charlie when it comes to getting supplies."

"Hence no mattresses for our beds."

"Precisely. All we have here is what the last occupants left behind."

"But if we had a job to do, we'd presumably get the equipment we needed to do the job, including transport to take us to suitable training areas." Carter let the suggestion hang in the air.

"Out with it, Steven. What are you suggesting? We can't lie to the Chief of Staff; he would know that we haven't been assigned to any operational tasks."

"He might, Sir. But he isn't the only person with access to transport."

[1] Pronounced 'doose' to rhyme with loose, not deuce to rhyme with juice.

[2] Goatley boats were collapsible boats propelled with wooden paddles, or, in an emergency, rifle butts. They had a wooden floor and the sides were made of canvass supported by moveable iron rods. Each boat could carry eight men and their fighting equipment. In the film A Bridge Too Far, they were the boats seen being used by Major Julian Cook (played by Robert Redford) and his men of the US 82nd Airborne Division, to cross the Waal River at Nijmegan.

* * *

The following day found Carter and the 2IC driving the dented Jeep into the palatial courtyard of General Eisenhower's headquarters in Algeria. It might once have been an actual palace, but more recently it had been the HQ of the army of the Vichy government in France. They had now been consigned to other offices in the city to make room for the Allies.

At the outer gate their identities were checked by guards, ordinary infantrymen and directed to a parking area. Before being allowed to enter the building their identities were checked again before they were confronted by a pair of burly MPs in white helmets and webbing, stationed inside the door.

One of the MPs checked a clipboard. "Your names aren't on a list to visit Col Styvant today, Sir." The MP objected.

"I'm afraid it's all a bit last minute." Maj Cousins explained. "Orders from the top, not time to put names on lists."

The second MP lifted a telephone and dialled a number before muttering a few words. He hung up. "OK. Sir, you can go up. Second floor, turn right and it's the room at the far end." He pointed the way to the ornate staircase.

At the top of the first flight, Carter had to call Cousins back before he started up the second flight. "When the Americans say 'second floor', they mean the first floor." Carter reminded his senior officer. Following the rest of the directions they found themselves in a large office occupied by a dozen men at desks. Phones were ringing, typewriters clattered and everybody seemed to be talking at once. Directly inside the door a Private First Class leapt to his feet and saluted, despite being indoors and not wearing a hat.

"We're here to see Col Styvant." Cousins announced. The PFC remained rigidly at attention, his right arm raised to his forehead. "I … I'm sorry Sir. I can't end my salute until you return it." The soldier stuttered. Different army, different rules, Carter told himself silently.

Cousins wafted his hand up near the area of his cap and the soldier visibly relaxed. "Maj Cousins and Capt Carter, 15 Cdo, here to see Col Styvant." Cousins repeated, trying not to sound tetchy. "And no, we don't have an appointment."

"The Colonel's very busy, Sir." The PFC pleaded.

"We're here on the very highest authority." Cousins said. It wasn't quite a lie. They were there on the authority of Lt Col Vernon, which was the highest authority they could get at that moment.

"I'll see if he'll see you." The PFC decided to let his boss make the decision.

He was back a few moments later and led them through a door at the rear of the office. Behind a desk stacked with papers sat an aged Colonel, probably recalled from retirement to take this job.

"PFC Gleeson tells me you're here on General Eisenhower's orders." The Colonel said after Carter and Cousins had saluted.

"We didn't actually use his name, Sir." Cousins replied. That detail might be important later, if they were ever called to account. The Colonel eyed them up, taking in their commando shoulder patches and medal ribbons.

"But you are here on high authority?"

"We are, Sir." Still not a lie, for the same reason as before.

"OK, what can I do for your 'high authority'?

"We've been detailed for a special mission, Sir." That was a lie, but anything the commandos did could be regarded as 'special', so they could justify that. "The matter is totally secret, only known to us and … our higher authority." Making it sound mysterious, they had decided, would excite fewer questions. If they made it sound as though the operation had to be deniable it would attract none at all. No one would want to know anything at all in case they had to answer for their part in it. "But we need to train in the sort of terrain in which we'll be operating. That means we need transport, but we haven't got any. You're the G4[1], Sir, so you're the person we have to talk to."

"What are you looking for?"

Cousins looked at Carter. "Twenty trucks," Carter said without hesitation. "With a fuel allowance for four hundred miles per truck per day."

"I can give you ten and fuel for two hundred miles a day." The Colonel countered.

That wasn't as many as they had hoped for, but it was better than nothing, Carter thought. They knew they wouldn't get twenty; that figure was just to open negotiations. On the other hand, he could bluff a little. "We were told we could have twenty, Sir."

"Well I don't have twenty to give you. Some people think I can pull trucks out of my ass at will!". Styvant shouted and thumped the table. In the outer office a brief silence fell at the outburst, with the exception of the ringing of the phones. Realising he may have overstepped the mark, Styvant forced himself to calm down. "Look, I can go to fifteen if you don't mind a few dents and scratches."

"They don't have to look pretty, Sir." Cousins conceded.

"Sgt Tulloch, get in here!" The Colonel shouted. Appearing like a pantomime genie through a trapdoor, a Sgt stood in the doorway to the office.

"Cut some orders for me to sign, for the release of fifteen deuce and halfs to …?"

"15 Cdo, Sir."

"To 15 Cdo. Five of those to be out of the base workshop. Also, authority to draw fuel for two hundred miles, per truck, per day. You can do the math on that."

“Yessir” The Sgt shouted, disappearing as suddenly as he had appeared.

“I take it you have your own drivers?” The Colonel said it as though he was expecting a negative reply.

“We do, Sir.”

“Just remember, the steering wheel is on the left, the gear shift on the right and over here they drive on the right hand side of the road.”

“I’ll try to remember that, Sir.” Cousins replied. If Styvant noticed the sarcasm, he decided to ignore it.

“Is that all?”

“It is, Sir.” Cousins and Carter snapped up parade ground salutes and made their escape.

They found their way along the corridor to the toilets and pushed their way inside. Cousins collapsed against the inside of the door in a theatrical fashion. “I can’t believe we got away with that, Steven.”

“We haven’t yet, Sir. We haven’t got the paperwork. I can’t believe we got fifteen. I was expecting twelve at the most.”

“Remind me not to play cards against you, Steven.”

“You did most of the talking, Sir.”

“But you put up the final bluff that forced him to fold.” Cousins went to one of the wash hand basins and splashed water over his face. “I think I’d rather face a Jerry machine gun nest than go through that again.”

“Let’s hope Col Styvant doesn’t decide to check our story with Eisenhower’s office.” Carter replied, as he led then back to the office to collect the paperwork.

[1] G4 – American military staff structures are standardised so that at each level of command everyone knows who is responsible for what. Staff officers at Brigade, Division and Corps level are designated S (staff officer), then a number. At levels above Corps they are designated G (general staff) and the corresponding number. S/G1 is responsible for personnel, S/G2 for intelligence and security,

etc. G4 is responsible for Logistics. The numbers go to 9 – civil/military co-operation. At lower levels of command the staff officer may be as junior as a Captain and may work alone. At higher levels the officer will probably be of Colonel rank or higher and will have a team to make things happen for him. Each staff organisation is headed by the Chief of Staff, who is answerable directly to the Brigade, Division or Corps commander or, as in the case of the HQ of the US Army in Algiers, to the Army commander, General Eisenhower. This staff structure has since been adopted across NATO.

* * *

The arrival of the trucks the following day was greeted with some level of awe by the commandos. It was as if they had never seen a truck before. Even the battered and bullet scarred victims drawn from the base workshop were admired as devotedly as a movie star.

For the officers it was a welcome relief to be able to get the men out on training exercises. The commandos were always happiest when doing something constructive. The officers were introduced to Sgt Etienne Dubois.

"Sgt Dubois was born here in Algeria." Colonel Vernon told the assembled officers and NCOs. "He speaks fluent Arabic and knows the Atlas Mountains as well as any man alive. At least, in the area of the mountains within a hundred miles of here, which is about as far as we'll be venturing for the time being. He will act as our liaison with the civil authorities, our guide during exercises and also as a translator should we need one."

Sgt Dubois was an unprepossessing figure. Small and wiry, he was scruffily dressed in a pair of loose-fitting trousers that looked more like some sort of bedroom attire. On his head was a floppy red hat. He also had a layer of stubble on his face that no commando NCO would permit while in barracks. Close up he smelled of the horrible cigarettes that were smoked by the local population. The rumour going the rounds was that the cigarettes were bulked out with camel dung, helped along by the fact that children were seen collecting camel dung in buckets. The rumour was also supported by the fact that one of the most popular American brands of cigarettes was called Camel and empty cartons had been seen littering the streets.

Seeing the looks of disdain on the faces of his officers, the CO continued. "Sgt Dubois's uniform may look a little unconventional, but it is the attire of the Zouaves[1], locally recruited French light infantry who have been protecting the French Empire for over a hundred years. I'm sure your fathers who fought in the First World War would recognise his style." Vernon concluded. "His local knowledge will be invaluable."

The commandos soon found that looks were deceiving. In terms of his field craft the Frenchman was a match for any commando and he was also capable of carrying just as heavy loads.

With transport at their disposal the commandos were able to learn the rudiments of working in arid conditions where sandstorms could blow up at a moment's notice. They learned to navigate without maps, which were scarce and inaccurate, just working on compass bearings, factoring in that they were unable to go in straight lines for more than few hundred yards because of the mountainous terrain. One of the key things they learned was how to find water and, if it couldn't be found, how to dig a pit and condense it out of the ground during the night. Such small lessons might, one day, save their lives.

Most of all they learned to recognise the dangerous wildlife that was abundant in the mountains. While looking like the wouldn't support anything more dangerous than ants, the mountains were actually home to a wide range of poisonous snakes and scorpions, including the deadly horned viper, which often hid buried in the sand, only its eyes visible, waiting for its prey. Dubois taught the commandos to look out for the rippled patterns left in sand and grit by the snake's side to side motion.

Scorpions were the main threat, however. The commandos learned to give their boots a brisk shake each morning before putting them on. Even in barracks it was a wise precaution. Not all breeds of scorpion were deadly, but even the mildest sting left the victim feeling nauseous.

They also saw several troops of Barbary apes, similar to the ones they had encountered in Gibraltar. But unlike their cousins, the apes in Algeria tended to keep their distance from humans, gathering their infants onto their backs and heading off to safer ground when the commandos approached.

On19th February the Commando was ordered to cancel all its training and remain in barracks. It took no great stretch of the imagination for them to work out that something big was happening. But still they hadn't been assigned to a brigade. They were just told to be ready to move at an hour's notice. News filtered through that the Germans had launched an attack at a place called Kasserine, which threatened the American armies moving along the coast road towards Tunis. Big tank battles were being rumoured, but back in Algiers real news was hard to come by. The commando's officers gathered maps together and tried to fathom out what was happening. Tunisia was the country immediately to the east of Algeria and everyone understood that the current Allied objective was to capture its ports and cities, cutting the Germans off from the sea and then continue the advance to link up with Montgomery's 8th Army, which was moving quickly through Libya. If successful, the strategy would end the war in North Africa.

But understanding this from the map and trying to work out what sort of contribution 15 Cdo might make were two different things. A sea landing probably wasn't on the cards. There were no landing craft available. The Americans had them all, keeping them safe in case they needed to make landings of their own.

"We might be asked to reinforce an American division." Andrew Fraser suggested.

Heads nodded. It seemed the most likely task. As tanks advanced they needed infantry on their flanks to prevent a counter attack. The faster the tanks moved, the more infantry they needed. But it was just speculation. Lt Col Vernon returned from the British HQ later that day, shaking his head, knowing little more than his men.

“There’s heavy fighting south of Kasserine, which is a town at the eastern end of a pass that bears the same name.” Was all he could say. “The pass gives access north and west to the flatter country along the coast, which is why the Germans wanted to capture it. From there they could cut the American supply lines and even threaten Algiers. The Americans have counter attacked, but it’s broken down into a bit of a slugging match. There’s a mixed force of French and American troops defending the pass, including a battalion of Rangers. The force is under the command of a Colonel Stark, who’s American. There’s an American Armoured Division to the north of them, but they were in the process of reforming after earlier fights and aren’t fully combat capable. So far, they’ve held the Germans and Italians at bay, but it’s touch and go.”

Their curiosity was satisfied the following morning. Through the fort’s gates a dusty Jeep was driven, a Sgt at the wheel. In the back was a British Brigadier, so smartly dressed that he could only be from HQ. Alongside him was an American Major, his soiled uniform matching the dust on his vehicle.

The CO was summoned and hurried from his breakfast to greet his visitors. They followed him towards his office, the Sgt tagging along behind carrying cardboard tubes of the type used to store maps.

The officers gathered in the centre of the parade ground, not knowing what else to do. The troops were cannier and stayed in their barrack rooms unless they had been detailed for duties. They had simple rules: Never stand when you can sit and never sit when you can lie down. Never miss an opportunity to eat or drink and never miss an opportunity to sleep; you don’t know the next time you’ll be able to do any of those things.

Half an hour later the officers and NCO’s were summoned into the general office, where maps had been hastily pinned to the walls. Reconnaissance photographs were scattered on the Sgt Major’s desk. The CO made the introductions.

“Gentlemen, may I introduce Brigadier Duncan, who is on the British staff in Algiers.” The Brigadier nodded. “And Major Riddick from the American 1st Armoured Division, who are engaged at Kasserine. The Major has come here at top speed to brief us on a mission in person. It's called Operation Carthage. Major."

Vernon stepped back, allowing the American to take centre stage.

"As you know, we're having a bit of bother, as you Brits are likely to call it, in the Kasserine Pass area. We are holding our own, but the main threat to us is tanks. We have anti-tank artillery and we have tanks of our own, but the easiest way to stop the Germans would be to cut off their access to fuel. We're bombing the hell out of any fuel dumps we can find and also attacking their supply lines, but still they're getting fuel from somewhere. Later yesterday we found out where." He pointed to a spot on a map.

"That's a place called El Kurum. There's nothing there as such, it's just a dot someone marked on the map back in the 1800s. Maybe there was once a fort there or something. But at the moment it is home to a very large Kraut fuel dump. Normally, we'd just send a squadron of B-24s to bomb the crap out of it, but there's a complication. Right next to the fuel dump the Krauts have put a field hospital. We were notified via the Red Cross about the location of the hospital a couple of weeks back, but no one mentioned the fuel dump of course. But it means that the hospital is protected by the Geneva Convention. If we bomb the fuel dump and anything happens to the hospital, then all hell will break loose. It might even nudge some of those countries that are sitting on the fence to side with the Axis."

The commandos knew he meant Spain and possibly Portugal, but it might even include Turkey, which had signed a Treaty of Friendship with the Germans in 1941 when German troops had entered neighbouring Bulgaria. Turkey entering the war on the Axis side could cause problems for both the British and the Russians.

"Would it really come to that, Sir?" A voice from the rear asked.

"There are fascist factions is all the neutral capitals of Europe who use every excuse to try to persuade their governments to side with the Nazis." The Brigadier replied, sweeping the room with a baleful look. "Let's face it, the commandos haven't got a squeaky-clean reputation in some quarters[2]. Personally, I don't think that reputation is justified, but the enemy turns every incident into a potent propaganda message. We cannot afford to gift the enemy anything that could be turned into another of those messages which will be whispered into the ears of Franco and his ilk." He turned his attention back to the briefing and nodded to Riddick to continue.

"So, gentlemen, to destroy that fuel dump requires a surgical strike, not a sledgehammer. I've been told by Brigadier Duncan that you are the surgeons we need."

The assembled commandos allowed themselves a small chuckle at the American's compliment. They normally saw themselves as the sledgehammer.

"Sir, surely the Jerries have broken the Geneva convention by siting the fuel dump there." One of the newer officers spoke up. "It makes it a legitimate target."

The Brigadier fielded that question. "That's probably one for the lawyers to argue about. But our understanding is that so long as they aren't using the hospital itself to store warlike materials, or as a refuge for combatants, then we can't touch it. To be honest, we wouldn't want to, apart from the humanitarian grounds, there's also the matter of self-interest. We wouldn't want to give the Jerries an excuse to start attacking our own medical facilities in retaliation."

"Any idea of how strong the defences are?" The 2IC asked.

Being more familiar with the problem, Major Riddick took up the question once again. "From the aerial shots we calculate it can't be more than a company strength. The perimeter doesn't include the hospital. If they armed it they would be in breach of the Geneva Convention themselves. You can't even approach the fuel dump from the hospital side. Any exchange of gunfire would risk hitting the hospital and we would take just as much of the blame as the Krauts. Everything you do has to make sure that not a scrap of damage is done to the hospital, not even so much as a splinter in the pinkie."

The information on the size of the defence force brought a sigh of relief. Operational doctrine dictated that you needed three times as many soldiers in attack than you did in defence if you wanted to achieve your objective. With three hundred and fifty men in the commando they would be strong enough to overcome a company with a strength of about one hundred and twenty. On the other hand, attacking the fuel dump without any stray bullets hitting the hospital tents was going to be a considerable challenge.

"What about approach routes?" Someone else asked. "We're going to have to get there without anyone seeing us, if it's behind Jerry lines."

"There's a route through the mountains." The Brigadier replied. "It's another reason we've chosen you for the task. You're the only troops available that have done any training on that sort of terrain. There's no way through for vehicles though. You go in on foot."

"What about getting back?" Andrew Fraser asked.

"Same way as you went in. We'll get you to your jumping off point by midday tomorrow, so you still have daylight to get through the pass. It's about ten miles long. Then you have a few more miles to cover in the dark before you attack. You blow up the fuel dump and then withdraw. It depends how quickly you can do that, but if you have to withdraw over open country by day, we're already arranging air cover to try and give you some protection on the way back."

"The key issue," Riddick continued, "is how you're going to destroy the fuel dump without burning down the hospital. There will be bits of red hot metal flying about, as well as burning camouflage netting and who knows what else. It's highly likely that something will land on the hospital tents and set them on fire."

"We're open to suggestions." Vernon added.

Heads were scratched, chins were rubbed and muttered conversation took place as the commandos considered the matter. It was Carter that thought he saw a solution.

"Sir, a hospital isn't really a place. It's more of a system. It might be in a building, or in this case, some tents. But mainly it's a collection of doctors and medical orderlies, their equipment and the people they're treating. Would I be correct in saying that?"

“I suppose you might. But is this really the time for such philosophising, Captain?” The Brigadier asked somewhat scathingly.

“Bear with me, Sir. If we were to force the medical staff to evacuate the patients from the hospital tents and take them to a safer location, we wouldn’t be destroying a hospital, we’d only be destroying some empty tents.”

“That’s a bit of a fine hair to split, young man. And what happens afterwards? We can’t just leave badly wounded men lying in the desert, even if they are the enemy. The Geneva Convention requires us to protect those wounded soldiers, so we’d still be in breach of the Convention.”

That was the flaw in Carter’s plan. But he was quickly rescued by the QM. “We could give the Jerries another field hospital. They come packed up and ready to load onto lorries. All we have to do is get it there.”

“What about an air drop?” Someone else said, as their brains followed the logic of the suggestion.

“Or a landing, if the ground’s smooth enough.” A voice added.

“We’ve got a complete field hospital in the stores depot,” The Brigadier admitted. “and the people who know how to put it together.”

“And we’ve got C47s sitting at airfields across Algeria.” The Major added, looking questioningly at the Brigadier.

“It would have to be a landing operation, though.” The Brigadier said “The hospital team doesn’t know how to parachute and there’s no time for them to train. Which means they’d have to come out with your men, Col Vernon. We couldn’t risk keeping the aircraft on the ground waiting for them to finish the job.”

“I don’t want to rain on anyone’s parade.” Maj Riddick intervened, “But there’s no airfield; at least, not that we know of. That means no landings.”

“In that case we parachute the equipment in.” Vernon interjected. “My men can put up the tents if someone can sketch the layout of them and the bundles and poles are all clearly marked. The rest, the unpacking of the medical equipment, will be down to the Jerries to sort out after we've gone."

There was a moment's silence while everyone tried to find any loopholes. The main problem with the plan was that it delayed the commando's withdrawal from the fuel dump. Burning fuel would send a thick plume of smoke high into the sky above the dump. It would be clear to the Germans from miles away that something was wrong, even if the guard force hadn't managed to get a call for help out over the radio. The very minimum that could be expected by way of reaction was for a strong reconnaissance force to be sent to find out what had happened and to assess the damage.

On the other hand, cutting off the German fuel supplies would vastly reduce the ability of the enemy to win the battle. It could save hundreds, even thousands of lives. It didn't take a mathematical genius to work out what had to be done.

"Very well." The Brigadier made the decision for them. "Be ready to move out at midnight tonight. I'll arrange transport … more transport, to get you to your jumping off point. Major Riddick will stay and help you to plan your route in and out and to act as liaison with the 1st Armoured Division. If you need anything from me, other than the field hospital, telephone me and I'll do what I can." He looked at the commandos, silently asking if there were any final objections. He saw only determined looks and the occasional excited smile from those officers that hadn't yet seen combat. "Now, can I get a lift back to HQ?"

"We can offer you the use of our Jeep, Sir." The 2IC said, escorting the Brigadier from the room.

The officers visibly relaxed as soon as the brass[3] was through the door.

[1] Zouaves – pronounced zwav. Light infantry recruited predominantly from the colonial French community in North Africa. They served in the French colonies across the globe and saw considerable service on the Western Front during World War I. As described, they did wear trousers that looked very like 'harem pants',

but which were the original pyjamas as worn in many eastern countries. The red floppy hat referred to above was a Fez, which could look a bit floppy when badly battered. The Algerian Zouaves were disbanded in 1962 when Algeria gained its independence, though they did form a sort of interim 'peace keeping' force for a while as they were trusted by both the French and the Algerians.

[2] From the very first, the Germans accused the commandos of committing war crimes. Most of the accusations were false, but the odd couple of incidents did appear to have some foundation. Five German prisoners were killed while trying to escape during Operation Basalt, a raid on Sark on 3rd October 1942, their hands having been tied. As mentioned in an earlier footnote, Hitler used it as an excuse to issue his *Kommandobefehl* authorising the summary execution of all British and American special forces personnel when captured. In 1945, in his recordings of his wartime memories, my father recalls that German prisoners of war received some "rough handling" after the discovery of the concentration camp at Belsen. Quite what he meant by that I'm not sure, but we can assume that it didn't involve tea and biscuits.

[3] Brass – From 'brass hat', a mocking reference to the gold oak leaf pattern braiding that officers of the rank of full Colonel and upwards wear on the peaks of their caps. Also the origin of 'top brass', to refer to senior commanders.

* * *

In the darkness the commandos lined up and passed ammunition boxes from hand to hand, loading them onto the trucks that had arrived earlier in the evening. After that would come the food and water, then they would be ready to leave.

In the general office, Sgt Etienne Dubois was acting as interpreter between the 2IC and the officer commanding a company of Tiralleurs[1] who had arrived to guard the barracks until the commandos returned. Although most of the military equipment would be going with them, the commandos would be leaving most of their personal kit behind. The men eyed the Algerian troops with some suspicion, unused to seeing brown faces wearing uniforms. They were even more unused to seeing brown faced soldiers carrying MAS-36 rifles topped with seventeen-inch spike bayonets.

Apart from the weapons the sight wasn't so unusual for the young men raised in the East End of London, Bristol or Liverpool and other cities with major ports, but for those from the back streets of Manchester, Birmingham, and a dozen other cities, or from the green hills of Devon and the flat fens of Lincolnshire, the close proximity with the native troops suddenly made them feel a long way from home. Some even realised, perhaps for the first time, that it was they who were the foreigners, not the Algerian soldiers.

"Do you think our kit's going to be OK here?" One of the newer recruit's to Carter's troop asked, suspicion heavy in his question. All the soldiers knew that despite their rigorous attention to guard duties, equipment had gone missing from the fort.

Carter gave a non-committal shrug. "Probably as safe here as it would be in the Ordinance Corps[2] compound." He understood his men's mistrust of foreigners, it was as British as warm beer, but he believed in giving everyone the benefit of the doubt. "Why, what have you got in your pack, the Crown Jewels?" Carter said with a grin, just to show he was teasing.

"No, Sir. But my Mum's photo is in there."

Such small things were talismans that the soldiers clung to; their one remaining contact with the homes they had left far behind them. He could understand the soldier's anxiety, while also acknowledging to himself that it was unlikely that an Algerian infantryman would have any interest in Pvt Cornrow's mother.

"I'm sure your Mum's photo is as safe here as it is anywhere." Carter tried to reassure the man. "Now, get these trucks loaded before we get too old to do any fighting."

At last all the kit was loaded and the convoy of trucks, now mixed between British and American models, trundled off into the night following Major Riddick's Jeep. At first the roads were good, well maintained concrete or hard packed earth. Tarmac was no use here. It melted too easily. But as they got closer to their objective, they turned off onto mountain roads so as to avoid the combat area around the Kasserine Pass. These were hardly more than goat tracks, full of potholes and ruts. As dawn broke, the convoy stopped to refuel from cans they had brought with them and the commandos took the opportunity to brew up and grab a bite to eat, consuming the food cold from the cans as there was no time to heat both the food and the tea.

As the sun reached its zenith they drew up at a point along the road that looked no different from any other spot. Lt Col Vernon joined Major Riddick at the front of the column and they consulted a map, laid flat on the bonnet of the Jeep with a stone at each corner to stop it from blowing away.

Carter watched from the back of his truck as they pointed, consulted the map and then pointed again. Riddick and the CO walked a little further along the road, passing an outcropping of rock and must have found what they were looking for.

With a shout from the Sgt Major the troops started to clamber from the back of their vehicles, throwing their webbing and packs down ahead of them. Unlike their previous raids, all the commandos were in 'marching order', complete with their big packs, rather than their less cumbersome 'fighting order'. But their previous raids had been lighting in-and-out raids. They had only needed to carry enough food and ammunition to sustain them for a day. This operation might be a lot longer, so they had to carry more to sustain them. Not just food and ammunition, but also spare items of uniform. It was no use finding you needed a fresh pair of socks if your spare ones were back in Algiers.

The ammunition was broken out and spare magazines were loaded. Each man would carry a hundred rounds for his own use, plus as much as he could squeeze into his ammunition pouches and backpack for use by the Bren guns. In addition, each man would carry two bombs for the two inch mortars, one in each side pocket of their large pack.

They were allowed thirty minutes to heat up some lunch and make another cup of tea, then they were ready to march.

While everyone else was eating lunch, Vernon and the officers of 1 Troop had gone ahead to carry out a reconnaissance of the first part of their route. 1 Troop were the designated reconnaissance troop and would lead the way along the pass, along with Sgt Dubois. Dubois had to admit his ignorance of the area. They were now in Tunisia and he had never crossed the border into the neighbouring French territory. But in the land of the blind the one-eyed man is King and at least Dubois had the experience of working in the sort of terrain they were about to deal with.

With a section of 1 Troop in the lead, the commando made their way into the mouth of the narrow pass. It was more of a ravine, carved out over the millennia by rainwater and snow melt. Even in Africa it sometimes snowed, Carter had discovered. Today the clouds were thick and low, threatening rain. Carter thought he heard the rumble of thunder, then realised he was hearing artillery fire from the fighting to their north.

"I always though Africa was hot and sunny." Paddy O'Driscoll observed as he clumped along behind Carter.

"We're less than a hundred miles from the coast." Carter replied. "That's close enough for rain to reach us. Besides, even deserts get some rain.

"And here was me thinking I'd be getting a bit of a suntan."

"With that red hair of yours, if the sun came out, you'd spontaneously combust." Carter replied with a chuckle. O'Driscoll had already had to be treated for sunburn caused by too much time on the beach without a shirt on. It had affected most of the fairer skinned men to some degree, Carter included.

There wasn't much for the commandos to do other than follow the pack of the man in front of them. Occasionally the ravine would widen to allow several men to walk side by side, but more often they were in single file. The route twisted and turned as the water that had formed it sought out the easiest path. Fissures split the sides where water had tumbled in from the flanks, increasing the flow along the bottom. Very occasionally they found a pool, formed in a hollow in the rocks, but for the most part the ravine was dry. For the moment they were heading up hill, but the slope was gentle enough for it not to cause the commandos any problem.

Even in the rocky terrain, life clung on. Anywhere that a little soil could gather scraps of vegetation dug in a toenail. There was coarse grass and skinny shrubs, protecting itself with vicious thorns to prevent itself being eaten. Thick leaves stored water until the rains came once more.

From time to time they would stop and scouts were sent scrambling up the steeply sloping sides to try to see ahead. They weren't expecting any trouble, but there was always the possibility of an enemy patrol having been dispatched to make sure that the route wasn't being used to infiltrate behind the lines; the very purpose for which the commando was now using it. For the same reason a section of 1 Troop had been sent ahead of the main column. It wouldn't do for the commando to stumble into an ambush.

In the middle of the afternoon they reached the summit, the ravine getting shallower and shallower until it hardly existed. They had lost all sense of direction with the twisting and turning. Vernon checked his compass and consulted Ronnie Pickering, 1 Troop's CO.

According to their briefing they should now go slightly south of east and another pass should start to develop, cut by water just as the first had been, but this time heading towards the Gulf of Gabes instead of north into the Mediterranean Sea. It seemed sensible to send out scouts to see where the pass recommenced.

They were nowhere near the highest point of the mountains. On both sides, peaks soared above them until they disappeared into the low cloud base. A pall of smoke drifted round the flank of the ones to their north, more evidence of the fighting that was taking place. Carter shivered as his body cooled after the climb. It was colder up here than he had expected and colder than the thin khaki drill of his uniform could cope with.

A scout returned, reported and the order was passed down the line for the commando to get back to its feet and be ready to move. They had to wait for the other scouts to return. It wouldn't do to lose any up here.

The route down was similar to the route up, a little wider and steeper, perhaps, but just as twisted. The base of the clouds was lit up from within by lightning then thunder, the real thing this time, rumbled overhead and rain started to fall, droplets big enough to sting when they hit naked flesh. The men scrabbled for their ponchos and draped them over both their equipment and their bodies.

Water soon started to trickle past their feet as the storm lashed the peaks. The soil was churned to mud by the commandos' feet, but as the soil itself was so thin they didn't become bogged down. The main risk was slipping on the wet rocks. The deluge continued for about thirty minutes then stopped as suddenly as it started, and the clouds started to break up behind it. Ahead of them, in the direction of travel, the rain still fell but the storm was moving away at a faster rate than the commandos could travel.

The sun was setting behind the commandos as the ravine eventually opened out to form a valley between the rolling foothills of the eastern extent of the Atlas Mountains. Vegetation was more plentiful and there were signs that goats or sheep were brought here to feed, though there was no sign of any at that time. The noise of the distant battle would be keeping the shepherds close to home.

What had been a ravine now carved its way across the valley in the form of a wadi, about five yards wide and no more than the height of a man in depth. The rain water that had fallen was already soaking into the sand at the bottom. Lt Col Vernon brought the column to a halt and announced a thirty minute meal break. No sooner had the words left his lips than hexamine stoves were being unpacked to heat mess tins of water. By opening the tins and standing them in the hot water, the same quantity could be used for two purposes, tea and heating food. There was always the risk of a drop of gravy bubbling over the side of a can, but that was of small concern to the commandos.

The CO made his way back along the column towards 4 Troop. "All OK, Stevem?" he asked as he arrived. He unslung his map case from around his neck.

"Fine, Sir. The men are in good heart." That was true. There was nothing like the prospect of a mug of tea to cheer up even the most miserable soldier and the commandos were rarely miserable.

Vernon stood close to Carter so that they could both see the map. "We're here." He pointed to a spot on the map where the contours started to broaden to form a V. The wadi was clearly marked on the map. "There's your objective, right there." He pointed. A road crossed the Wadi at a distance of about five miles. "Shouldn't take you more than an hour to get there."

"No, Sir. But we won't rush. It'll be dark in a few minutes and we don't want to suffer any injuries."

"That's fine. I don't expect you to be there before twenty hundred, so any earlier will be a bonus. The main thing is that you don't get to the fuel dump before we do. I've expect our ETA to be twenty hundred as well. We'll be waiting for you. We go in at twenty one hundred if you haven't arrived by then."

"4 Troop won't let you down, Sir."

"I know, Steven. You're my most experienced troop commander, that's why I've given you this job." He gave Carter a pat on the shoulder and headed back along the wadi to the front of the column. When the men had finished eating and stowed their equipment once again, he called them to their feet and they set off on a compass bearing that took them away from the wadi at an angle of about forty five degrees. Carter watched them recede into the dusk, then called his own men to their feet.

"OK, chaps. Five miles to go, but we can't get lost if we follow the wadi. Able, Baker, Charlie and Dog sections, get yourselves to the other side of the wadi. The other four stay on this side with me."

In single files they started out towards the distant bridge along both sides of the wadi.

[1] Tirailleurs – Originally Napoleonic light infantry, they were later recruited from the indigenous populations of French North Africa for service in the French colonies worldwide. Tirailleur battalions saw extensive action on the Western Front and Gallipoli during World War I. The Algerian Tirailleurs were disbanded in 1962 when Algeria gained its independence from France, but the majority of their ranks transferred directly into the army of the newly independent nation.

[2] Royal Army Ordnance Corps (RAOC) – the branch of the army responsible for keeping it supplied with its essential equipment. They also ran storage depots where the equipment was held until needed and where soldiers' personal kit could be held until their return to their barracks, if no other safe storage facilities were available. In 1996 they merged with the Royal Corps of Transport (formerly the Royal Army Service Corps) and the Army Catering Corps to form the Royal Logistics Corps.

7 – Tunisia

Although the stars lit up the heavens with a million pinpricks of light, it wasn't enough to see by, at least, not more than a few feet in front of them. The moon still hadn't risen. The briefing had told them it was a quarter moon, but that didn't help this early in the evening. Without the ability to take compass bearings on the nearest peaks Carter couldn't judge how far they had travelled. The hills were lower now. To the north they could clearly make out the flashes of individual guns as they fired artillery salvos at each other. The sound was clearer also, no longer being bounced off the sides of the hills.

Using that information and the elapsed time, Carter estimated when they were about a mile from their objective. The bridge across the wadi. He blew a single low whistle and the two columns stopped, the commandos sinking to one knee and turning outwards to watch for any enemy, not that they expected any. Not here.

Moving quietly, Carter went to the front of the column and located Prof Green, now leading Easy section. "OK, Prof, you know what to do. I'll give you a five minute head start, then we move out.

Green didn't bother to reply. He just signalled his section to move forward. On the far side of the wadi the vague shapes moved as Able section also led the way. Carter wondered if Fred Chalk, his Troop Sergeant major, had got over his huff yet. He had wanted to lead the reconnaissance on the bridge but Carter had refused him. He wasn't about to lose his trusted right arm in a firefight if the two leading sections ran into trouble. Carter would need him to lead any counterattack on the left side of the wadi. The troopers would be far more scared of Fred Chalk than they were of any German or Italian patrol. True, he had Ernie Barraclough on that side of the wadi as well, but he was as green as grass. If he had any sense he'd let Fred Chalk do the leading.

They weren't expecting any sort of guard force on the bridge. An aerial reconnaissance photo had shown no pre-prepared weapons pits or other defensive positions. But that photograph had been a week old; ancient in terms of what was now happening further north. It was entirely feasible that a commander, seeing a weak point in his supply lines, might decide to guard it.

The five minutes ticked past painfully slowly, but eventually the time elapsed and Carter was able to lead the rest of his Troop forward. They did their best to maintain silence, but the terrain along the side of the wadi was broken, rocks left there by water as it raced towards the lower ground, roots spreading from scrubby bushes. Even the most sure footed of the commandos were likely to stumble on something.

A figure loomed out of the darkness ahead of him. Carter stopped. "Wolverhampton!" he hissed into the darkness, gripping his Tommy gun more firmly, just in case. Once again the challenge and it's reply had been chosen because of the Germans' perceived difficulty in pronouncing the letter W. It also second guessed an attempted reply. The most obvious response was 'wanderers', but if that word was given Carter would fire without hesitation. It didn't occur to anyone at the briefing that if the enemy were Italian, the choice of password didn't make so much difference. But a password was still a password.

"West Bromwich" The correct reply came back.

"Who is it?" Carter asked.

"Cornrow. The bridge is all clear." So, not for the first time, complacency had led to the enemy making an error. The bridge was several miles behind the enemy's front line, so they had decided it wasn't at risk from a ground attack. And if it had been attacked by air, no amount of guards could have protected it. An anti-aircraft battery would have been needed and, presumably, there wasn't one of those available.

Carter led the troop onwards, moving faster now that they knew there was no enemy between themselves and their objective. They arrived at the bridge and Prof Green briefed him, pointing out where he had put his section to defend the bridge.

"No movement?" Carter asked,

“Not since we’ve been here.” Carter checked his watch. Nineteen thirty hours. It had taken them just over an hour to reach the bridge.

The ground on either side of the bridge was flat, giving a clear view along the road in both directions. If … when … the enemy came, they would see them in plenty of time. They’d hear them first, even above the rumbling of the artillery. The battle for Kasserine Pass must still be in full flow. Or perhaps it had just been reduced to an artillery duel. It was difficult to tell from that distance

Not knowing from which direction a threat may emerge, Carter split his force on both sides of the bridge and also on both sides of the road. They melted into the darkness. It was a better defence for them than any slit trench. Besides, if their assumptions were right they would have no time to dig any sort of defences.

Assumptions, Carter thought. Not a word the commandos normally allowed to be uttered. To *assume* made and ass out of you and me, the instructor had said at Achnacarry, writing the word on a backboard in chalk, before splitting it into three with chalk lines. But sometimes you just had to make assumptions and this was one of those times.

His ears pricked up; a new sound, different because it was still audible in between the crash and bang of discharging guns. It was louder already. Carter placed his hands behind his ears and twisted his head to the left, then the right. The sound was from the left, the side on which Kasserine Pass lay. There was the high revving notes of a petrol engine, but something else as well. Something metallic. As it grew in volume, Carter recognised the sound. Caterpillar tracks, metal clattering against sprocket wheels and grinding against the hard packed earth of the road’s surface. He looked towards the sound. There, right in the centre of the road, two tiny dots. Just enough illumination to show the drivers where the edge of the road lay, preventing them from steering off into the scrubland.

Carter estimated the vehicles to be about a quarter of a mile away. It had to be more than vehicle; the noise was too loud for it to be just one.

Reaching into his pocket, he pulled out his torch and switched it on, pointing it downwards so that a pool of light formed around his feet. There was a slight delay, but then the sound of the engine notes changed, whining as the gears were used to slow the vehicle. Carter remained in the centre of the road, but lifted the torch, pointing it towards the vehicles, raising and lowering the beam in a clear signal. Hidden behind the bright light, the vehicle's occupants wouldn't be able to tell that he wasn't one of them.

The vehicles continued forwards, the sound of the clattering tracks now louder than the engines, which were barely above idle revs. The lead vehicle ground to a halt.

"Che cosa c'é?" a voice called from the darkness.

Dann, they were Italian. It had been assumed that they would be German. That's what happened when you made assumptions. There was nothing to be done about it now. Carter had memorised his speech in German, so German it would be.

"Die Brücke ist zerstört." Carter said, the bridge is destroyed. He hoped his pronunciation was right.

"*Ho solo capito ' Brücke '.*" The Italian replied. It didn't matter. The conversation wouldn't be going any fuirther in any language. Carter's men, mvoing like wraiths through the darkness, surrounded the vehicles and the Italian crews found themselves staring into the barrels of a dozen or more point three-oh-three rifle barrels.

"Your next line should be *'Alza le mani.'*" Ernie Barraclough supplied.

"How do you know that?" Carter asked, after he had issued the order and the Italians had complied.

"My parents have a villa on the Amalfi coast. We used to go every summer before the war. I picked up a bit ogf the lingo. Enough to get by."

"What sort of things were you doing that required you to be able to say 'put your hands up'?" Carter chuckled.

"Just exptrapolating from basics, Lucky."

"Can you say 'get out of the trucks?"

"Try *'Esci dai camion.'*"

Carter tried it and the Italian drivers and their mates climbed down, being very careful to keep their hands above their heads except when they needed them for balance. Hands grabbed the men and started tying their prisoners up.

There were four trucks, Maultier half tracks of the type Carter had seen at Honfleur, though these were painted a sandy brown colour. The driver's door, Carter could see in the torchlight, bore the palm tree logo surmounted by a swastika, the symbol of the Afrika Korps.

"Ernie, have a chat with our eyetie friends and find out what you can about the fuel dump. Are the guards there Italian as well? How many are there, you know the drill."

Barraclough went off to find the prisoners while the rest of the troop set to work emptying the trucks. The cargo beds were stacked with the rectangular containers that the Britsh knew as Jerricans but the Germans called *Einheitskanister*. For the purposes of transporting fuel they were far superior to the British containers, known as 'flimsies' for good reason. These were built with rough handling in mind. Usually when any fell into British hands they were regarded as a valued prize, but not that night. Right then they were taking up space that the commandos would need for themselves, so the jerricans were thrown into the wadi, clattering and banging as they bounced off the ground and off each other. The echoing thumps told him the cans were empty.

It wasn't long before Barraclough returned. "They don't know much." He told Carter. "Until a couple of days ago they were part of a transport regiment based in Tunis. A dozen of them were sent out here to drive these trucks, delivering fuel to the front line. They've got a dozen or so pre-designated RV[1] points they deliver to. They don't know which one they've got to go to until they're in the cabs and ready to go. I think the front line is too fluid for anything more elaborate than that. They left the fuel dump shortly after six pm, as soon as it was too dark to fly. They dropped their load of fuel, loaded up with the empties from the last drop this morning and were on their way back to the dump again. The troops defending it are German but I got the impression that they're not Hitler's finest.

When you've got transport drivers referring to their allies as *'idioti'* then you can be sure that the quality of the troops isn't high."

"Thanks, Ernie."

"Lucky?" Carter turned as he heard a new voice behind him.

"Yes, Fred."

"The lorries are all empty. We can go as soon as you give the order."

"Thanks; start getting the men on board. Spread the men out between the lorries but make sure each one has a Bren in it. Put the all prisoners in the last truck. If the guards at the fuel dump start shooting, they'll be safest there. Give me a shout when everyone's aboard." The Geneva Convention again, Carter thought. Now that he had prisoners, he was responsible for their safety. Really he was in breach of the convention simply by taking them to the fuel dump, knowing that if the plan didn't work there would be fighting. But he couldn't just leave them sitting at the side of the road.

The first part of the plan had worked, at least. By intercepting the lorries they would now be able to approach close enough to the camp without raising the alarm. The guards would be expecting the lorries to return to pick up their next load and wouldn't suspect anything. Even the slight delay while they'd unloaded the empty jerricans wouldn't be remarked upon. Delays on a battlefield were to be expected.

It was the next part of the plan that was higher risk. The rest of the commando would already be creeping up to get as close to the dump's perimeter as possible without raising the alarm. With the sort of fieldcraft that the commandos had, that would be no more than a quarter of a mile, possibly less. Carter would drive the lorries right up to the gate and hope to overpower the guards before the alarm could be raised. Most of the guard would be in their tents, resting until it was their turn on duty. He doubted that there would be more than a dozen men actually out on the perimeter, patrolling in pairs or manning a weapons pit. If he and his men could get inside the dump, the chances were that they would be able to take it without a shot being fired. The choice was with the Germans, of course, but the news that the guard force wasn't of the highest calibre was good. Poorly trained soldiers were more likely to surrender than fight.

And if a fight did break out, there were nearly three hundred commandos lying in the dark ready to give the Germans what they asked for. Not for the first time, Carter was glad that he hadn't been born in Germany. Had he been, it might have been him commanding the fuel dump's guard and he wouldn't wish that on anyone tonight.

Waiting at the back of the short convoy was Arthur Murray, who had practically begged Carter for his part in the operation. Carter clapped him on the shoulder.

"OK, Arthur. You know what you have to do?"

"Yes. When I see or hear the ammunition dump blow, I have to blow the bridge, withdraw with my men and make my way to join up with you." Carter had assigned him Able and Baker sections for the task. Only one man was actually needed to lay and fire the explosive charges, but there was some safety in numbers.

"And if the Germans arrive here before we blow the dump?"

"I blow the bridge straight away and withdraw to re-join you."

"Good. No heroics though. I don't want you doing an 'Horatio at the bridge'[2]. Got it?"

"Got it, Lucky … and thanks."

"You may not be thanking me later. Withdrawing through enemy occupied territory, in the dark and with only handful of men isn't always as straightforward as it sounds.

"Don't worry, Lucky. I won't let you down."

Carter climbed into the second vehicle as Fred Chalk passed the word forward that all the commandos were on board. Carter had intended to be in the lead vehicle, but discovering Barraclough's language skills he decided on a change of plan. Sitting in the driver's seat was Paddy O'Driscoll.

"OK. Paddy, let's go." He said, keeping his voice low. The engine revs increased and O'Driscoll ground the gears. "Oops. Not used to this, sorr. We're more used to tractors in my part of the world."

“Now you tell me.” Carter muttered, as the halftrack lurched forward.

It wasn’t long before they saw the field hospital, lit up like a fairground. It was the only source of light, identifying its purpose so that it couldn’t be attacked by accident. The tents appeared to be white, which they might well be as it was a better colour to use in the North African heat. According to the reconnaissance photographs there would be a turning off this road which would take ambulances direct to it. The fuel dump was still hidden in the darkness beyond. It had its own access road. The road they were on continued to the small town of Gafsa before turning east towards the Sebkhet en Noual lake and then the coast.

Carter tried to keep his eyes turned away from the light to protect his night vision. Once destroyed it would take twenty minutes or more to return and he didn’t have that long. But the bright lights kept drawing him back. That was something else they had factored in, the arrival of ambulances filled with casualties. Despite the precaution of blowing the bridge over the wadi, a detachment of 6 Troop would set up a road block as soon as 4 Troop had passed, preventing any vehicles from approaching the hospital until the danger of fighting had passed and there was no further risk to already wounded men.

The elderly trucks with their modified *panzer* track units crawled along at twenty five miles an hour, forty kilometres an hour according to their speedometers, but the few miles between the bridge and the fuel dump was soon eaten up. They passed the turning for the hospital, marked by red and white striped poles set into the ground. They continued for the remaining half mile to the turning for the fuel dump. It wasn’t so easily identified and O’Driscoll had to slow to a crawl to make sure that they didn’t miss it.

“Stand by” Carter called through the rear window of the cab to the troops in the cargo hold. Someone near the tailgate of the truck would flash a signal back to the next truck and so on down the line. The men hunkered down behind the sides of the trucks so that the fuel’s dump’s guards wouldn’t see them until it was too late.

O'Driscoll swung the lorry into a hard left turn, missed the edge of the side road and the lorry lurched to one side before recovering as the front wheels found the load bearing surface again.

"Whoops." O'Driscoll said, between gritted teeth.

"Next time I'm going to get one of those Barbary apes to drive." Carter said, just loud enough for O'Driscoll to hear.

"Ach, sure, you wouldn't be good company for it." O'Driscoll chuckled. Back in the barracks he would have been given a dressing down for making such a remark, but out here such things helped to ease the tension. Carter suppressed a smile. Besides, he and O'Driscoll had been in enough tight spots together for a bit of good-humoured banter to be tolerated.

Somewhere in the darkness was the fuel dump, but it couldn't be seen. It was no more than stack after stack of two hundred litre drums, covered by camouflage netting to make them harder to identify from the air. From those drums the fuel would be decanted into the smaller twenty litre jerricans, for easier handling. Tents stood a short distance off to act as a mess hall, sleeping accommodation, ablutions and an office. During the day the lorries were parked up close to the fuel stacks and were also covered in camouflage netting. Having seen the photographs, Carter had to admit the dump wouldn't have ben easy to find from the air. If you saw the hospital first, which was very likely, the eye would be drawn to that, not to the mysterious humps a hundred yards to its south.

The fuel dump was probably kept re-supplied at night by convoys from the coastal depots, though they were also receiving attention from the Allied air forces. Now that the Allies had total air superiority in the region it was difficult for the Axis armies to do anything expect hide during daylight hours. At least it had been until they had decided to try to break through the Allied lines at Kasserine. Most of the Axis's own aircraft had already been withdrawn to Sicily and Italy. Only the fighters remained and few of them.

The backwash of light from the hospital provided enough illumination to put dim edges around objects. The fuel stacks themselves cast deeper black shadows, which helped to pick them out. Staring to see through the side window, Carter made out the hump of a sandbagged position. It appeared to be empty. With the steering wheel on the vehicle's left, Carter assumed that any sentries would be on that side so that they could speak to drivers as they approached.

The lead vehicle ground to a halt and Carter could hear Barraclough's voice above the muttering of the engines. Some sort of argument was taking place, with one of the sentries shouting in German while Barraclough shouted back in Italian. He had taken a jacket from one if the Italians to help with the deception, covering his British khaki with its revealing commando badges.

Using the distraction as cover, figures slipped over the lorry's tailgate and crept around the blind side of the vehicle, to reappear with their rifles levelled at the heads of the sentries, ending the argument.

Leaving a handful of commandos to secure the prisoners, Barraclough ordered his own vehicle forward and the others followed. They didn't steer towards the fuel dump, but towards the tents that housed the small garrison. Carter was able to pick out a thin sliver of light where a tent flap hadn't been secured properly. There was a row of eight larger tents. Four would house the platoons that made up the company, twenty four men to a tent. One would be home to the NCOs and another to the officers. The largest had already been identified as a mess tent because of the chimney that emerged from one end and the smallest, firthest away from the mess tent, was assumed to be the ablutions block, containing showers. Beyond that were narrow latrine tents, half a dozen arranged in isolation above holes dug in the ground.

The lorries ground to a halt and the men spilled over the sides, lining up facing the tents. The men inside should be asleep or relaxing, not suspecting anything. Two or three men appearing in the doorway, levelling rifles and Tommy guns, should be all that was needed to subdue them. Carter approached the smallest of the accommodation tents, the one assumed to house the officers. It was the one that showed the thin sliver of light. O'Driscoll fell in on one side of him and Danny Glass on the other.

At the doorway, Carter raised his hand, showing three fingers. Glass stretched his hand out so that it was hovering inches from the tent flap. Carter curled his fingers: three, two, one and the tent flap was pulled abruptly aside, allowing Carter to step over the threshold, his Tommy gun raised.

"*Hande hoch*." He barked, picking out a shirt sleeved figure sitting at a trestle table. He was reading a paperback novel by the light of smelly kerosene lamp. In the middle of the table sat a field telephone, next to it a half full bottle of schnapps and a tin mug.

The man dropped his book and obediently raised his hands.

"*Verstehen Sie Englishe*?" Carter asked.

"Having lived in England for many years, I speak very good English." The German replied, a sardonic curl to his lips. He wasn't wrong, either. There was hardly a trace of accent in his voice.

"OK. I have to tell you that this fuel dump is surrounded by three hundred and fifty commandos. If your men try to resist, it will end badly for them."

The man took in the commando flashes on Carter's uniform and the green beret on his head. "I do not doubt what would happen. Even here in Afrika we are familiar with the reputation of the Commandos. The Fuhrer refers to you as thugs and gangsters."

"It would be preferable if we didn't have to live up to our reputation." Carter replied. He had to admire the German officer's sangfroid. He doubted he would be so cool under these circumstances.

"I think I may be able to make things easier. I will give you my word of honour not to try to escape or interfere with your operation, if you would grant me a parole."

"I don't trust the word of a Nazi." Carter said with some contempt.

"Then it is a good job that I'm not a Nazi, Captain. Which, if you are interested, accounts in no small part for why I am here in the arse hole of the world and not enjoying myself in Berlin, putting my language skills to better use."

Carter noticed that the German wasn't wearing a side arm. Beyond the desk four camp beds sat in pairs on opposite sides of the tent. A uniform jacket lay on one, alongside a belt with a holstered pistol attached. "Who do the other beds belong to?"

"My second in command. Sadly he wasn't considerate enough of the local wildlife and managed to get himself stung by a scorpion. He is currently residing in the hospital."

"Only two officers for an entire company?"

"We were an entire company until yesterday, when I received orders to send two of my platoons to the front line. I fear things aren't going well for us, certainly if they need the services of the dross which I have to command."

"Your name?"

"I am Major Reinhardt." He pronounced it My-or. "Of the 121st Service Battalion. And who do I have the pleasure of addressing?"

"Carter, 15 Cdo." Carter threw up a cursory salute, a courtesy that was expected even between enemies. "Now, ideally I would like to disarm your guards, rather than have to kill them."

"I will order my *Feldwebel*[3] to go with your men and order the guards to surrender. They won't be a problem. If they were the sort who were prepared to die for their country they wouldn't be guarding a fuel dump in Libya."

"Tunisia, actually."

The German waved his hand dismissively, not really caring which African country he was in. "Come, let us go and stop our men from killing each other."

The rest of the tents, those that were still occupied, had been no more difficult to subdue than the officers' tent. By the light of oil lamps, the Germans and the British glowered at each other, but the Britons, with their rifles and Tommy guns held in steady hands, were securely in control. The Feldwebel was briefed in rapid German about what was expected and he went off with Fred Chalk and two sections of men to remove the sentries from their posts. The depletion of the guard force had reduced the number on duty to just ten at any time.

Over at the fuel dump, some fifty yards away, half a dozen Italians were working at re-filling jerricans ready to be loaded onto the next convoy, which would never now set out. They, too, were disarmed and taken into captivity.

The German re-took his seat at his trestle table and picked up the schnapps bottle. "May I offer you a drink, Captain Carter?"

"Thank you, but not right now. It's going to be a long night and alcohol won't help to make it shorter. But don't let me stop you."

The German poured himself a generous measure into his tin cup, replaced the bottle on the table without replacing the cap, then took a long drink, smacking his lips in appreciation of the fiery liquor.

"You seem to be very much in control." Lt Col Vernon said as he pushed his way through the tent flap.

"Major Rheinhardt has been very helpful, Sir." Carter introduced the two officers.

"A sensible approach, Major." Vernon pronounced.

"A pragmatic approach, *Herr Oberstleuenant*[4]. You do seem to have the upper hand. But I must ask, how you hope to destroy my fuel dump without breaching the Geneva Convention relating to hospitals."

"A fair question. We intend to move the hospital to a place of safety. At least, those bits of it that actually make it a hospital and not just a tented camp. It was Captain Carter's idea."

Rheinhardt nodded his head in understanding. "In that case, may I put my men at your disposal. It will be done quicker and then we can all get on with our lives."

"You propose collaborating with the enemy?" Vernon sounded quite shocked.

"I do. But I have a condition to make."

"I can't promise to grant it but go ahead."

"I assume that you don't wish to burden yourselves with prisoners when you leave. So you will dispose of our weapons and leave us behind. Am I right?"

"You are. In fact, seeing as we have your vehicles, we will load your weapons into them and take them with us."

"As I thought. In that case, all I ask is that you take me with you also. I am already in bad odour with the military and political authorities. Losing this command without a shot being fired will result in a court martial and there can be no doubt that I will be found guilty of something. My life expectancy can be measured in days, possibly hours. So, take me with you and put me in one of your prisoner of war camps. I will happily tell your intelligence officers everything I can, which actually isn't that much in terms of our tactical situation here." Rheinhardt saw the look that had formed on Vernon's face.

"You look at me with contempt, *Herr Oberstleuenant*, but please, be assured that I am actually a good soldier. On the breast of my jacket you will find the ribbon of the Knight's Cross, placed there by Hitler himself after our victory in France. But then I saw what was being done in Poland and I started to question my loyalties. Have you heard of *Auschwitz*, *Herr Oberstleuenant*?"

"I can't say I have." Vernon admitted.

"One day the whole world will hear of *Auschwitz* and they will be horrified, as I was when I saw it. I will tell your intelligence officers about *Auschwitz* and they will be horrified and they will tell *Herr* Churchill, who will also be horrified. It was my reaction to what I saw there that led to my being here. I questioned what I saw and that is not allowed. It is the 'Final Solution', the Fuhrer's personal vision of how to solve the Jewish problem once and for all time and cannot be questioned. I was supposed to have been sent to Stalingrad to suffer for my temerity, but an old friend in the *Bendlerstraße* switched the names on two sets of orders, so some other poor fool is now freezing to death while the Russians do their best to separate his head from his body. Which is why I cannot allow myself to face a court martial. It means certain death."

The three officers sat in silence, Carter not sure what he had just heard and Vernon taking it in. "We've heard about the camps." Vernon admitted. "But we assumed that the conditions were just a bit primitive, on the harsh side. Are you saying they're worse than that?"

"They are places where death has been turned into an industry, *Herr Oberstleutnant.* No man, woman or child who is sent to *Auschwitz* can ever hope to come out again. There are camps where people are sent for 're-education', but the Jews aren't sent to those. They are sent to Poland, where the good people of Germany don't have to witness what is being done in their name. So, you see why I have to ask you to take me with you."

At that point Fred Chalk and the German *Feldwebel* arrived to report that the German sentries had all been removed and replaced with commandos.

"I have to get on with evacuating the hospital." Vernon announced.

There was a rapid exchange of German between the Major and his NCO. "I have told *Feldwebel* Gruber that he is to assist you in any way he can." Reinhardt confirmed. The German NCO didn't seem to be put out by the order. Like most of his breed he did what he was told and let the officers get on with deciding what that should be. He wouldn't have made a good commando.

Vernon left, along with Fred Chalk and the German NCO.

"I thought that the SS ran the camps; you're army."

"They are called *Wachtbattalions,* Yes, technically they are SS, but in reality they are the sweepings of the gutters of half a dozen eastern European countries, including Russia. But the senior officers were from the *SS-Totenkopfverband*, the Death's Head Brigade. But it is the army who transports Russian prisoners to the camps. Because the Fürhrer considers the Russians to be *untermensch*, less than human, they aren't treated as normal prisoners of war. I was stationed in Berlin, but I made the mistake of sharing the affections of a woman with a General. He didn't like the competition, so I was posted to a transport battalion in Russia. It was a warning to others not to cross him.

Between the spring and autumn of last year I commanded several convoys of prisoners to *Auschwitz*. One day I was invited to have lunch with the commandant, Rudolf Höss. He got quite drunk and started boasting about what his camp was doing. The Russians were being used as forced labour to build another camp at a place called Birkenau, a couple of kilometres down the road. They were being worked to death because it was cheaper than feeding them and there were plenty more where they came from. But *Auschwitz B*, as he called it, was being built to exterminate Jews by the million.

He took me to see the building where they had tried it out. It was an old ammunition bunker, left over from when the Poles used *Auschwitz* as a barracks. He showed me the holes in the roof where they poured in the pellets that turned into gas when they came into contact with air. I can't remember the name of it, it started with Z though; you will understand that I was feeling quite ill by that time. Then he showed me the incinerator where they burned the bodies. The entire bunker was a working model of what they were building at Birkenau. It was already functioning, Höss told me, killing thousands of Jews a week."

Rheinhardt poured himself another schnapps, throwing it down his throat as though trying to wash away the taste of his words. "When I got back to my unit I made the mistake of expressing my feelings about what I had seen. I said it was dishonouring Germany. A few days later I was told that they were in need of officers at Stalingrad and my name had been put forward. Fortunately, I still had connections in the *Bendlerstraße* and I ended up here instead."

"I'm surprised you haven't tried to get back into favour by turning this into a crack unit." Carter said. It was what he would have done.

"Every army has units like this. Not everyone is cut out to be a soldier and it sends out the wrong message if they are allowed to go home. Also men get wounded, not just physically, but up here." He tapped his head. "We can't afford to just discharge them simply because they twitch a lot or they hold conversations with people who aren't there, so they send them to places like this. The best thing I can do is make life as easy as possible for us all." As easy as possible for yourself, Carter thought. But, then again, he hadn't seen

Auschwitz. He hadn't seen everything he believed in destroyed by a guided tour of a death factory.

"I have things to do." Carter decided to end the conversation. "May I remind you that you are on parole. If you do anything to interfere with what we are doing, I will have you restrained. I dare say the CO will decide to leave you behind as well."

Rheinhardt gave a bleak smile. "You need not worry, Captain Carter. I know where my best interests lie. Or, as you English would say, I know on which side my bread is buttered."

As Carter left the tent, The German officer was pouring the last of the schnapps into his tin mug. The telephone rang, stopping Carter in his tracks. He'd forgotten about that. Most remiss of him.

Before Carter could stop him, Rheinhardt had answered the phone. There was a brief exchange and the German scribbled something on a note pad, before returning the phone to its cradle. "The RV for the next fuel convoy." Rheinhardt reported.

"How does that work?" Carter asked.

"The divisional staff officer decides which units are to receive fuel next and directs them to the nearest RV, which is where we meet them. We drop the fuel and pick up any empty jerricans from the last drop. This one is about an hour distant. They will expect it at about …" he consulted his watch "… twenty two thirty hours. It is normal for me to phone back with an ETA when the convoy leaves."

Interesting, Carter thought. If the Allied artillery could be given the location of the RV, they could shell the units as they waited for their fuel. He picked up the pad. Written on it was some sort of code, 'TS7'.

"Where is that?"

Rheinhardt fished around in a satchel that sat under the table and drew out a map. He spread it out and pointed to cross on the map. It was also marked TS7. Carter's sharp eyes picked out several more spots, each marked with the letters TS and a number. "What does TS mean?"

"*Tankstelle*. It eans refuelling point."

Carter took the map and tucked it in his ammunition pouch. "What will happen when the refuelling convoy doesn't turn up?"

"First they will phone me to confirm that it departed on time. Then they will assume that something has happened on the road and a patrol will be sent to look for them."

Carter frowned. That was worrying. A patrol would be bound to reach the bridge where Arthur Murray and his two sections were waiting.

The field telephone rang again. Rheinhardt gave Carter a querying look. "Answer it." Carter instructed.

There was another short exchange before Rheinhardt replaced the handset once again. "A convoy has just left the coastal fuel depot." He informed Carter. "Six cargo trucks with two armoured cars and a platoon of infantry as an escort. The escort is Italian. It will take about three hours to get here."

Carter checked his watched. It was nine fifteen, so the convoy could be expected shortly after midnight. Well, at least they had been forewarned.

[1] RV - Rendezvous.

[2] Horatius at the Bridge – Generally referred to, incorrectly, as Horatio. A reference to the 19th century poem by Thomas Babbington, Lord Macaulay, written in the heroic style. It tells of the brave warrior Horatius, who defended a bridge alone against the might of the Etruscan army, thereby saving Rome. The final lines are: "With weeping and with laughter, Still is the story told, How well Horatius kept the bridge, In the brave days of old."

[3] Feldwebel – Sergeant Major.

[4] Oberstleutnant – Lieutenant Colonel.

8 – Bonfire Night

4 Troop had been replaced in the perimeter defences by 5 Troop and Carter found his men lounging in the German tents.

"Anyone know where the CO is?" He asked.

Fred Chalk was the one to reply. "He's over at the hospital as far as I know, chatting with the senior medic."

"Thanks. Don't get too comfortable, there're Jerries on their way here. Turn these lamps out." He indicated the kerosene lamps that were providing meagre illumination. "You're going to need your night vision before long."

After walking the hundred and fifty yards to the hospital area Carter found his CO standing in silence with a tall, thin man. He was wearing a white coat over his *Afrika Korps* uniform. The German's stiff body language and stony expression told how he felt about his hospital being disturbed in this fashion. Medics, German soldiers and British commandos were carrying stretchers towards the accommodation tents further away, visible in the backwash of the lights from the hospital. Others carried camp beds on which heavily bandaged men lay suffering the pain of their abrupt removal.

"Steven, may I introduce Colonel Stern, the medical officer in charge of this hospital." Carter saluted the man, who gave him a stiff-necked nod in return.

"If you will excuse me, *Oberstleutnant*," the doctor said, "I will go and start trying to repair the damage that your war crime is causing."

"He didn't sound too happy." Carter observed.

"I've already had to remind him that he had the choice of moving his hospital to a safer distance when the fuel dump was set up, but he chose not to. I also pointed out that I was doing the best I could to protect his patients from harm when I destroy a legitimate military target. It doesn't matter what I say, though, it's what the Red Cross says that matters. As we speak, Brigadier Duncan is delivering a briefing to the Red Cross in Algiers about this operation and how we are dealing with the hospital."

"I've got some news that may be of help to the Americans." Carter explained about the possibility of patrols setting out to look for what they would think of as a missing convoy and showed him the map and briefed him on the location of refuelling point TS7. Vernon called his radio operator, who was never far away, and took the headset and microphone from him.

"Hello Ginger, this is Fred." Vernon said into the microphone, trying to suppress a smile at the ludicrous call signs. For some reason they had all been chosen from the first names of American movie stars. The two Vernon had used were Fred Astaire and Ginger Rogers. Carter's troop callsign was Jimmy, for Jimmy Cagney, though his radio operator was at the bridge with Arthur Murtay, just in case he needed to call for help.

Vernon listed to the acknowledgement of his call and then continued. "Hello Ginger. I have a target in which you might be interested." He read a grid reference directly off his map, which he had identified by comparing it to the German version. "I suggest you commence firing at twenty two thirty, for fifteen, one fifer[2], minutes."

After the message had been acknowledged, Vernon returned the headset and microphone to his radio operator. The message would also be picked up by Carter's radio operator, Tpr Vardy and also by 6 Troop, who were further back along the road.

"Anything else useful?" He asked when he had finished the radio call.

"Yes, we can expect a platoon of Italians and two armoured cars in a couple of hours." He told Vernon about the re-supply convoy heading their way.

"It would have been too much to hope that we could get in and out without our presence being discovered. We cut the phone lines from the hospital as soon as we got here, but that doesn't mean they didn't get a message out as well. We'll do what we can to prevent the Germans getting here. If you were commanding that convoy and you saw the flames from this fuel dump, what would you do, Steven?"

"I'd halt the convoy at a safe distance, perhaps a mile or so away, and send the armoured cars forward to carry out a reconnaissance.

"Yes, that's what I'd do as well. I think that provides us with an opportunity. Now, a quick recap on where everyone is. 1 Troop are outside the perimeter, providing a protective screen and listening posts. 2 Troop are helping clear the hospital and packing up equipment to be moved along with the patients. 3 Troop are laying the demolitions. Your troop are resting, except for your two sections at the bridge. 5 Troop are manning the defences and 6 Troop are laying up behind the bridge because even if we blow it, infantry will still be able to cross and push towards us. Have I missed anyone?"

"I don't think so." Carter replied.

A fresh figure joined them, Andrew Fraser, the commander of 3 Troop. "The demolition charges are all laid." He reported.

"Good. I have another job for you now; you too Steven. "I'll want your men …"

He was interrupted by a shot ringing out through the night. There were voices raised in alarm from around the accommodation tents. Carter's stomach gave a lurch as a tent flap was opened and a figure was silhouetted in front of it. Carter had given orders for the kerosene lamps to be doused, so the only one that might now be lit was the one in the officer's tent.

"Sounds like a negligent discharge to me." Andrew Fraser commented.

"Find out who it was and make sure they learn a good lesson from it." Vernon growled.

"You were saying, Colonel." Fraser prompted his CO.

"Oh, yes. Steven has found out that there's a Jerry re-supply convoy on its way up from the coast, escorted by armoured cars and infantry. I want you to go forward and engage them when they get here. Steven, I want you to take two sections and four of the 2 inch mortars and provide cover for Andrew as he takes his men forward.

Leave your Bren guns behind. They'll be more use to us here. Your remaining four sections will stay here to act as my reserve."

"Happy to oblige." Fraser's lowland Scottish drawl made him sound bored, though Carter could sense the excitement emanating from him; the desire to be back in action once again.

"No problem."

Out of the darkness loomed the squat bulk of Fred Chalk. "May I interrupt?" he asked.

"Can't it wait, Mr[1] Chalk? The CO sounded distracted, examining his map, trying to identify any flaw in his plan.

"Just thought you'd like to know about that gunshot." The TSM said with as much dignity as he could muster. "The Jerry officer's topped 'iself." He offered his hand, palm upwards. A German military identity disc lay in it.

Lifting the disc from Chalk's hand, Carter felt sick. He had half suspected as much when he'd seen the light from the tent, but to have it confirmed was a blow."

"What did he want to go and do a thing like that for?" Although Vernon's question was rhetorical, Carter suspected that he might have been able to provide an answer. There are some burdens no man should have to bear and the total loss of belief in his cause was Rheinhardt's burden.

"That will complicate things." Fraser observed. "The Jerries'll say we shot him out of hand and it will be our word against theirs that we didn't." Prisoners dying in custody from anything other than natural causes or their wounds always attracted suspicion. "If we hide the body, is there any chance they won't suspect that he didn't go with us?"

"Not likely. There's blood and brains splattered all over the tent canvass." Carter winced at Chalk's no-nonsense description.

"There is something we can do though." Carter said. "Wrap his body in a blanket, Fred. Put it in the middle of the fuel drums, so it will be cremated when the demolition charges go off. If the officers' tent isn't burnt down by the fire, make sure that it catches fire later, before the Jerry prisoners come back. Boss, you'll need to tell Col Stern that we took Rheinhardt with us."

"How do we explain his absence when we get back to our lines?"

"My report will say that he was killed by enemy fire during the withdrawal from here. The lack of a body won't be questioned by our side and I think the Jerries will have other things on their minds."

"OK, I suppose it's the best we can do."

"Fred, on your way back, find Lt Barraclough and Sgt Carney. Ask them to come and find me here. Then get Easy and Fox sections ready to move. Get four mortars together and as many bombs as the men can carry in haversacks. The Bren gunners are to swap their weapons for rifles and hand over their extra ammunition for them as well."

"OK, Lucky."

"If you'll excuse me, I'll go and get my men ready as well." Fraser added, following Fred Calk back across the fuel dump."

"Was there any indication that Rheinhardt might kill himself?"

"He did seem pretty down. He'd been drinking heavily, so I put it down to that. I should have disarmed him."

"You'd given him parole; he's allowed to keep his sidearm under those circumstances. He won't be the first suicide that's been found with an empty bottle beside them and I guess he won't be the last. Damned inconsiderate of him though."

"Suicides rarely consider the consequences of their act. If you're in such a dark place that you want to kill yourself, then the problems of cleaning up after the event are unlikely to feature high on your list of priorities."

"You're wise beyond your years, young Steven." Vernon said, half mockingly. "Now, go and make a mess of that Jerry convoy. Oh, how are you going to deal with the armoured cars, by the way?"

"I'll leave that in Andrew's hands as he's got the explosives. He loves blowing things up. I'm sure he can find something around here that will let him stick an explosive device to the side of an armoured car."

[1] Warrant officers, especially those who are in specialist positions outside of the normal hierarchy, are sometimes addressed as "Mister" by officers. Within the military hierarchy they are neither commissioned officers nor senior non-commissioned officers (SNCOs), thought they will have progressed through the SNCO ranks. The origins of this of the use of 'Mr' are unclear but may date back to the early days of sail in the Royal Navy when specialists aboard ships were neither officers nor ordinary sailors. Many held the title of 'master': the ship's sailing master was the Captain's senior advisor on all matters to do with navigation and sailing the ship, the master gunner trained all the gun crews, the master-at-arms looked after on-board discipline and it is fairly clear what the master carpenter did. Technically, as Troop Sergeant Major, Fred Chalk should have been addressed by his abbreviated title of TSM, but no one would have corrected the CO on that minor slip of protocol.

[2] In the British army phonetic alphabet, the number 5 was always said as fife or fifer. Nowadays, in the NATO system, it is said as 'fiver'. Similarly, the number nine is always said as niner.

* * *

Carter and Fraser led their men on a compass bearing that would let them intercept the road about a mile from the fuel dump. Their assumption was that the Italian commander would halt his convoy about two kilometres from the fuel dump once he saw that it was on fire, before dispatching the armoured cars to carry out a reconnaissance. Once they reached the road Fraser would send a small demolition party back along it towards the fuel dump to wait for the armoured cars.

The crews of armoured cars, when they were all safely buttoned down inside, had very limited peripheral vision. That was bad enough during daylight hours but at night it gave the commandos a deadly advantage. They could lie close to the side of the road, to leap up and attach their improvised explosive devices to the metal flanks of the vehicles, before melting back into the darkness. Fraser had used a lot of explosives in the devices, so the crews would probably die without ever knowing what had happened to them.

The ground they crossed was rough and stony, but relatively flat. It was dotted with scrubby bushes and the occasional stunted palm tree. The commandos didn't exercise a lot of caution. The occasional night-time animal was heard to shuffle out of their path as they advanced. Wild dogs or foxes, Carter assumed, thought there were antelope in the area as well. There was no reason to suppose there were any enemy troops around and the convoy wasn't expected for at least another hour and a half by Carter's watch.

Vernon had originally planned to blow up the fuel dump at midnight but decided to advance that by thirty minutes so that the Italian convoy commander would be sure to see the explosion. He didn't want the convoy to approach too close and bypass the waiting commandos. They weren't setting up for an ambush, there wasn't enough cover for that. They would set up for a frontal attack, which depended on the convoy being parked on the road to their front. If, by some chance, the convoy passed them before stopping, the commandos would attack it from the rear instead. Seeing his two armoured cars exploding would be bound to weaken the resolve of the convoy's commander.

The night was ripped apart by the sound of a ferocious artillery bombardment. Carter checked his watch; twenty two thirty precisely. That would be TS7 being targeted. The attack rumbled on for fifteen minutes, the crump of artillery shells occasionally counterpointed by the boom of other explosions as some shells found a target. Eventually a stillness returned, at least for a short while, then there was the sound of detonations closer to them. Murray had blown the bridge across the wadi, which meant that a patrol had approached it. The lack of a bridge wouldn't stop the patrol. It would only force them out of their vehicles and onto their feet, crossing the wadi before returning to advance down the road where the lights of the hospital still shone brightly.

The hospital lights were powered by a generator mounted on a truck. The truck could be moved easily enough, but the electricity was supplied through hundreds of yards of cables strung through the ridges of the tents. Would Vernon try to disentangle them? Or would he just switch off the generator and move it to a safe distance? Probably the latter. They would need power for the fridge's that contained drugs. So, they couldn't delay the whole operation just for lighting. The Germans would have to sort that out for themselves in the morning, after they restored the field telephone connections that Vernon had ordered to be cut. And that would have to wait until after the commandos departed anyway.

They reached the road and Fraser deployed his men to either side. Carter positioned his troops well before the road, so that if a mortar bomb fell short, it wouldn't land amongst friendly troops as they advanced. A single red Very flare would signal that Fraser's men were about to make their final charge, which would tell both Carter and Fraser's own Bren gunners to cease firing to avoid hitting their own men.

Unlike its bigger brother, the three inch mortar, the two inch mortar used by the commandos didn't have a tripod. It sat on a small, hinged baseplate and had a handle fixed to the tube about a third of the way along its length, which the firer held and used to adjust the angle of elevation and the direction of fire. It meant that each bomb was liable to land in a different place, as the firer's hand wobbled as each bomb was launched. But the commandos were great adaptors. By lodging a pair of trenching tools into the ground they could tie the two handles together to form a crude bipod, on which the mortar's barrel could be rested. Range and bearing could then be adjusted by shifting the base plate.

The four mortars they had brought were soon set up, with a two man crew for each. The loader dropped the bomb down the tube and the firer pulled the trigger. The barrel's length was too short to allow the bomb to be fired automatically when it hit the bottom of the tube, as the loader's hands might not be out of the way. Instead the firer used a trigger to fire the weapon. This was another difference between the two and the three inch mortars.

They settled down to wait. It was the worst part of any operation. The mind played tricks with the darkness, turning bushes into moving figures. Each cry of a night bird or scuffle of a foraging animal caused the hairs on the back of the neck to rise. No amount of training could undo what a million years of evolution had bred into people to help them to protect themselves against predators.

The bombs for the two inch mortar didn't contain much explosive. Effectively it was more of a long-range grenade, fused to explode on impact and throw a lot of shrapnel around. But if it hit something vulnerable, such as a forty five gallon petrol drum[1], it would do a lot more damage. At least, that was what Carter hoped.

Things fell silent again after the blowing of the bridge, but the tension mounted as twenty three thirty grew closer. That would be the big one.

In the darkness someone whispered, "They'll hear the bloody explosion in Berlin when it goes off." This brought s few chuckles.

"Quiet there." Carter hissed. It wasn't that he feared that an enemy might hear, it was more that their focus would wander if general chatter was allowed to break out. "Sgt Carney, take that man's name."

Carter felt his face flush, glad that he was hidden by the darkness. His outburst was a mark of the strain he was feeling. On the surface this operation was no worse than any other he had been on; better in most ways as they had yet to come under enemy attack. But since his injury at Honfleur he had started to feel stress more frequently, even when circumstances didn't really warrant it, such as during training exercises. On the one hand he recognised the cause, but on the other hand it only made him feel worse, worrying that he might let himself down, or worse, let his men down. It was unthinkable.

On the dot of the half hour the skies above the fuel dump erupted into flame and roiling smoke as the fuel dump exploded. Even at that distance the blast washed over Carter and his men, its heat quite evident. It was followed by a series of smaller blasts as individual fuel containers cooked off, shooting upwards like rockets on Guy Fawkes night, sending streaks of light across the night. On and on it rumbled. Perhaps it might be heard Berlin, Carter thought, as his men gasped in amazement.

"Fuck me sideways." A voice said from the darkness. Thus time Carter didn't remonstrate. There was no point. But Sgt carney did.

"Look to your fronts." He barked, realising that most of the men had turned their eyes away from the road to watch the spectacle.

The flames were too bright to make out if the tentage had also caught fire, but Carter could hardly imagine them not going up as well. Burning fuel was spraying everywhere and smouldering camouflage netting was drifting on the breeze created by the fire, as hot air shot upwards, creating a vacuum that sucked in cooler air to feed the flames. The conflagration would certainly be seen from the enemy lines to the north, perhaps even the American lines further away.

It was only natural for the men to want to watch the display, it was what they had come here for, but the danger wasn't yet past. In fact, it was only just starting. Under any normal set of operating rules, they should now be stealing away into the night, making their way back to the safety of their own lines. But this operation was different. It always had been. The complication of the hospital had made sure of that.

They waited some more then, there on the horizon, Carter saw some pin pricks of light denoting the enemy. In peacetime they would have been bright against the darkness of the landscape, but they had been dimmed by paint and metal blinds into a series of tiny dots, too far away even to hear the sound of the engines, not that much could be heard against the background rumbling of exploding fuel drums. It wasn't even possible to tell what speed they were travelling at. Were they slowing already? Or were they travelling at the same speed. Without any reference points against which to make comparisons, it was hard to tell.

But they were still moving. As Carter watched, the leading set of lights resolved itself into a pair. The rest were the lights on the nearer sides of the vehicles. He started to become aware of the varying pitch of the engines, rising and falling as the drivers changed gear. Now they were slowing, the front vehicle setting the pace as it crept forward. Still no clue as to how far away they were. Bright lights a long way away – or dim lights closer to. Probably the latter, but how close? Carter couldn't afford to spring the trap by firing "star shell" in order to find out.

Finally, they came to a halt. One light on a following vehicle blinked out, then re-appeared as someone passed in front of it. The officer, going forward to talk to the commander of the armoured car.

A decision was reached and the front pair of lights started to move again. Just the one pair. Damn, that made things awkward. Rheinhardt had said there were two armoured cars. The other must be at the back. Would the convoy commander go back and send the vehicle to join its twin? He watched for the winking of lights that would tell him, but there were none, just the two blinks as he passed the lights on the vehicle, presumably a lorry, that was now at the front.

Carter watched the dots from the armoured car's lights as it headed towards the men hiding further down the road, waiting to blow up the vehicles. At least, he watched until the angle blocked the lights from his sight. That was far enough.

"Fire tube 1." He called into the darkness. Each tube had a bomb loaded and ready to fire. There was a muffled thump and whoosh as the missile shot skywards. At the zenith of its climb it exploded into bright light. Carter had his compass ready, taking a bearing on the middle of the convoy. "Bearing two one zero." He called. It was an approximation, all that it needed to be. The men could see the convoy now and could line up the white line that was painted on each mortar tube. "Range, four fifty." Carter estimated. "Tube two, fire for effect."

The second mortar fired its missile. The maximum range for the two inch mortar was five hundred yards. If they were too far away they'd have to dash forward to shorten the range and the enemy would have time to withdraw. The first bomb exploded on the far side of the truck. Not too short, too long. That could be fixed.

Using the bright light that was still drifting downwards, Fraser's Bren gun crews had opened fire on the trucks, pouring magazine after magazine of three oh three ammunition towards them from the flanks. But there was no sign of his men charging forward. Not yet. He was waiting for Carter to find the range.

"Shorten range, four hundred." Carter commanded. There was a shuffling as the mortars' base plates were pushed forward a fraction, which would send the bombs in a higher arc to land closer. "Tube three fire for effect."

The tube fired and they waited for the bomb to fall. This one was short. Carter estimated the correct range to be about the mid-way between the two explosions. "All mortars, new range four two five. All fire!"

The tubes coughed out a staccato salvo and the bombs started falling on and around the trucks. No two bombs from the same tube landed in the same place, as vibration shifted their point of aim slightly. The team had to keep adjusting them to prevent them from overshooting. As the illuminating bomb flickered out, Carter ordered another one to be fired. Keeping the target lit up gave Fraser and his men an enormous advantage. Carter imagined the men creeping forward under cover of the darkness that they still enjoyed until Fraser was ready to launch them on the enemy.

But the enemy wasn't just sitting there and taking the onslaught. Troops poured over the sides and tailgates of two of the trucks, one at the front and the other towards the rear. They fanned out into the scrub, taking up defensive positions and returning fire on the Bren guns. They hadn't yet worked out where the mortars were firing from, but it wouldn't take long.

The ground shook as another massive explosion ripped through the night. Carter turned and saw a fireball roiling skywards. It was the armoured car that had been sent forward, reduced to a heap of shattered metal and dead bodies. Carter gave an involuntary shudder.

Armour offered protection, but it could also turn vehicles into coffins.

Did the small demolition team know that the second armoured car wasn't coming? They and their explosive charges would be needed. Already Carter could see the other vehicle pulling off the road in order to get around the trucks that stood in its path. Moving forwards, its heavy machine gun spat fire as it went looking for the enemy.

One of the mortar bombs hit a fuel drum and it exploded with a whoof, sending burning fuel upwards and outwards. Some splattered onto the armoured car but it continued onward, undeterred.

The heat of the fire caused other drums to spontaneously combust, sending more explosions echoing through the night. Those soldiers who had stayed near the illusory safety of the trucks now understood their error and tried to run away, but for one at least it was too late. He ran like a human firebrand, smothered in flames, until he dropped. Carter hoped that he was dead because the pain of being alive would be too much for anyone to stand.

A red flare soared upwards from Carter's right. Fraser was going in. "Mortars, cease fire." Carter commanded.

Almost at the same moment tracer stitched its way across the sky towards them. Someone had worked out where they were and was directing automatic fire on them. Time to move.

The men hadn't waited for orders. Already the tubes were being strapped onto the backs of the four men who had carried them there by their loaders. The bags of bombs were being slung and the trenching tools recovered, their handles removed and the two parts strapped onto the small packs that the commandos wore. Carter led his men to the right, towards the road. He realised that the course he was taking would mean him bumping into the second armoured car.

He had seen it done once, just as a demonstration. Place the mortar tube on the ground, put your foot behind the base plate, tilt the weapon until it's almost horizontal and it could be used like a grenade launcher to fire directly at a target. It was worth a try against the armoured car. It was too big a target to miss from under a hundred yards. That wasn't the issue. The issue was whether the mortar bombs would damage the target or just send shrapnel buzzing uselessly around.

"Merchant, Tanner, On me!" Carter called, breaking into a jog. He only needed one mortar team and they were the closest to him. The men caught him up and matched him stride for stride as he increased the pace, despite their burdens. "You know what you have to do?"

"I do, Lucky." Merchant, the firer, replied. "I could fire it from the hip[2]. I've heard of it being done."

"No. We'll fire it from the ground. If you break a bone, someone will have to carry you and we can't afford unnecessary casualties." As soon as he said it Carter knew it didn't sound right. It made it sound as though there were such things as necessary casualties, but if Merchant noticed the slip he didn't comment.

The second armoured car had passed through the attackers but had now reversed its turret and was firing its heavy machine gun at them from behind, silhouetted against flames of the burning lorries. Those commandos who were most at risk had gone to ground, but that just meant that the attack was stalling.

When they were fifty yards away from the armoured car, at right angles to it, Carter brought his mortar party to a halt. He helped Frank Tanner, the loader, unstrap the tube from Merchant's pack and then loaded it for him as he placed the base plate on the ground. This was something they couldn't have done with a 3 inch mortar. That relied on the speed of the bomb as it was dropped into the tube, hitting a firing pin in the base to trigger the propellant cartridge. With the tube lying almost horizontally, there would be no speed. The 2 inch mortar, however, could have its bomb dropped into the tube then the angle adjusted until the firer was ready, then he pulled a trigger to fire the bomb.

The missile flew across the intervening space, glanced off the sloping armoured shell of the vehicle's turret and disappeared into the darkness. It must have landed on its side, because it didn't explode. "Lower man!" Carter snapped, at once regretting his harsh tone. It was hard enough firing the weapon when it was stable, let alone when the firer was breathing heavily after sprinting four hundred yards carrying a heavy pack.

The second bomb hit the vehicle in the middle of its metal side, exploding in a mini fireball and sending shrapnel buzzing through the air. The heavy machine gun kept firing. The armour must be thicker than it looked, Carter realised. "Keep firing." Carter ordered unnecessarily.

The other mortar teams were arriving now, setting up ready to add their firepower. If enough bombs hit the same general area, Carter hoped, the armour must be penetrated.

Three bombs hit in quick succession. The concussion inside the vehicle must be deafening, Carter thought. As if in confirmation, the heavy machine gun stopped firing and the hatch in the top of the turret started to open. A helmeted head appeared, then arms as the man levered himself up and over the coaming. He was halfway out when he slumped over, dead. Carter didn't know where the shot had come from, perhaps one of his men, perhaps one of Fraser's. It didn't matter.

"Cease firing" Carter snapped, rushing forward before he had time to find out if his order had been obeyed. It was now a race between himself and the rest of the armoured car's crew. If they got that body out of the way and closed the hatch, he would have to go back to trying to crack the armoured shell with the mortars once more. He pushed his Tommy gun around so that it hung at his back and wouldn't get in his way.

As he ran, he fumbled a grenade from a loop on his webbing and pushed it into his trouser pocket. He would need both hands free for the first part. He leapt upwards, grasping at the vehicle's smooth metal surfaces to try to get a hand hold. If he had approached from the rear he would have been able to use the footholds welded into the metal skin that allowed the crew to board. But he wasn't at the back, he was at the side. He felt his hands slipping and himself starting to slide down the side. Then hands grabbed at his ankles.

“Ups-a-daisy, Lucky” Prof Green’s voice shouted, propelling him upwards. Carter landed in a heap behind the turret, his head striking the barrel of the heavy machine gun, which was not enough to burn his forehead. He flinched backwards and narrowly avoided sliding off the vehicle, then clambered to his feet. Panicked voices could be heard from inside the vehicle, shouting in Italian. Too late, mate Carter said to himself, as he pulled the pin from the grenade and dropped it into the hatch behind the dead Italian. He heard it clatter against the metal interior and then he dropped from the vehicle and walked a few yards away from it. There was a muffled crack as the grenade exploded and some smoke drifted out from the turret.

“See if it’s driveable.” Carter instructed Prof Green and his helper, who turned out to be Danny Glass. So where was O’Driscoll? The three were normally inseparable. Of course, he had been one of the loaders for the mortars.

With the armoured car dealt with, Fraser’s attack was able to resume. “More illuminating rounds.” Carter shouted the order to his mortar teams. May as well give Fraser a clear view, he thought.

The fight didn’t last long after that. Seeing they were outnumbered, the Italian infantry started to withdraw. First it was a trickle of men, walking backwards, still firing their weapons. But then it became a rush, every man trying to escape. “Cease firing! Cease firing!” the voice of Andrew Fraser rose above the cacophony of small arms fire. Other voices took up the cry and the last few shots were fired before silence fell, broken only by the crackling of the flames from the burning trucks.

A Section of men rushed forward to try to reach the rear truck of the convoy, which wasn’t on fire. It would be useful but it was in danger. The front truck would be useless. By the light of the mortar shells that still lit up the sky Carter could see wisps of steam coiling up from the shattered radiator.

But the men were too slow. At least one Italian had reached it and now reversed it quickly away along the road. Some of the commandos raised their rifles and started shooting at it until Fraser ordered them to stop. It was only a waste of ammunition to shoot at men who were running away.

"Get the last two trucks away from the fire." Fraser shouted. They hadn't yet started to burn. If they dumped the fuel drums they would be of use to the commandos in the morning when they started their withdrawal.

Carter reached Fraser as the last of his NCOs reported in. "What's the damage?" He asked.

"One dead, three wounded. One of those is serious. We won't be able to take him back through the pass."

"What about the Italians?"

"Five dead, including their officer, another six with varying degrees of injury and half a dozen prisoners. The rest got away."

"We were told it was a platoon strength force, so that's twenty four, plus the drivers. That's pretty good going."

"I'd have liked that last truck though." Fraser grimaced. "Anyway, thanks for dealing with that armoured car."

"Couldn't let you have all the glory, old boy." Carter grinned.

[1] Forty five gallon drums, as they were referred to by the British, held 200 litres of liquid, which is how they became the international standard. The jerrican, or *Wehrmacht-Einheitskanister* as the Germans called it, had a capacity of 20 litres, or 10% of a fuel drum. The jerrican was far superior to its British counterpart, the "petrol, oil and water can" as it was designated, or flimsy as it was known by its users because of the ease with which it could be punctured or would start to leak. During the North Africa campaign, flimsies were known to leak as much 30% - 50% of their contents because of the weakness of their crimped joints and soldered seals. On one occasion a Quartermaster reported that his 70,000 gallons of fuel had been reduced to 30,000 gallons during transportation and was congratulated for losing so little. By comparison, there are World War II vintage jerricans still in use today in some parts of the world. Later in the war the flimsies were replaced by British jerricans manufactured to the German design, but in North Africa the capture

of a jerrican from the Germans was considered something to celebrate.

[2] There is at least one verified occasion on which a 2 inch mortar was fired from the hip. On 31st January 1945, in the Kangaw area of Burma, Lt George Knowland of 1 Cdo climbed out of a slit trench to fire a mortar at Japanese soldiers who were only yards from his position. He had previously exposed himself to fire a Bren gun into the enemy's ranks at close range when a Bren gun crew were killed and the replacement crew were injured trying to make their way forward. When the Bren ran out of ammunition he continued firing with his Tommy gun. Lt Knowland was awarded the Victoria Cross for his actions that day. It is unsurprising that the award was posthumous.

9 – The Hospital

The return to the hospital was made without incident, the wounded being transported in the two lorries once the fuel drums had been tipped over the tailgates and rolled off the side of the road. When they arrived, they were carried straight to the German medical team, who started to treat them immediately, not interested in which was an enemy and which was a friend.

On the return journey they heard the rattle of small arms fire from the area close to the bridge over the wadi, signalling an attempt by the German patrol to carry out a reconnaissance on the burning fuel dump on foot. The shooting didn't last long, which suggested that the patrol had withdrawn back across the wadi to wait for reinforcements.

Fraser and Carter found the CO and the other troop commanders, gathered near to the bright lights of the hospital for an O-Group[1]. Fraser reported on what had been achieved, including the capture of the two lorries. Carter added that they had inspected the armoured car and decided that it could be used, but it needed to be cleaned up first. He had left his two sections under the command of Sergeant Carney to do the necessary. The dead Italians would be buried by the roadside, but the dead commando had been brought in for burial at the hospital. Lt Col Vernon ordered a grave to be dug. They would hold a brief funeral service before dawn.

"We were just discussing what the enemy might do next." The CO continued. "Your opinion Andrew?"

"Well, the *Afrika Korps* are mainly daytime soldiers. They use the night to refuel, re-arm and refresh. According to the intelligence reports they only attack at night if they're sure of the dispositions of the forces in front of them. By now they'll know that we're a bit stronger than a small raiding party, but that won't tell them how strong we really are. Then they'll have to find a force big enough to tackle us. I don't think they'll pull troops out of the main battle, which means they'll have to use their reserves or bring uncommitted troops up from the coast. Either way, nothing will happen till morning."

"Steven?"

"I agree with Andrew. We can expect aerial reconnaissance as soon as it's light enough to see. A Fieisler or maybe a fighter aircraft if they have any left."

"That's pretty much the conclusion we had reached. Which means we'll have to fight off an attack at the same time as we re-assemble the hospital, then withdraw with the Jerries snapping at our heels. The good thing is that the Jerries daren't risk using artillery until we actually pull out, for fear of hitting their own hospital"

"We can use the prisoners to help with the assembly of the tents." The 2IC suggested. "Once we've shown them how to put up the first tent, they'll be able to do the rest themselves."

"We've got to work that bit out for ourselves first, Charlie, but you're right. The key thing will be to prevent the Jerries getting between us and the mountains. If they cut off our line of retreat we're really in trouble."

"Maybe we need to send a troop out on the southern flank then, to prevent that." The 2IC suggested.

"Good idea. Well, it can't be 3 Troop because they've just been in a fight …"

"We could manage." Fraser interjected.

"I'm sure you could, Andrew, but it isn't fair on your men. No, I'll send 2 Troop. 3 Troop can take over from 5 Troop in the perimeter defences and your four sections from 4 Troop, Steven, that were in reserve, can take over the outer screen from 1 Troop." He checked his watch. "I'll swap you back over at oh four hundred after 1 and 5 Troops have had a chance of a rest."

Carter nodded his head in understanding. If they were right about the Germans not attacking before dawn, the four sections of men would be enough to keep the listening posts manned for the rest of the night.

[1] O-Group – Orders group, an impromptu conference of the senior ranks present, to issue instruction on what was to happen next.

* * *

The rest of the night passed peacefully enough, with Carter moving from listening post to listening post to make sure the men were awake and alert. He didn't doubt them, but he had to make sure they knew he was awake as well. It wasn't enough to lead from the front, he had to be seen leading from the front and rumours started too easily.

The men in the listening posts were replaced at oh four hundred as promised by Vernon and Carter ordered them to relax as best they could. They found space near the German accommodation tents and lay themselves on the ground, taking off their webbing harnesses and laying their heads on their packs. It was cold now and the men had to wrap their ponchos around them to keep warm.

Carter was using the light from the accommodation tents to study the map when a thought struck him. He hurried to find Vernon.

"Paratroops, Sir." Carter blurted as he approached him, sitting alone with his thoughts.

"Where?" Vernon was on his feet immediately.

"Sorry. I didn't mean there are paratroops here. The Jerries, Sir. When they see the parachute drop from the C-47s in the morning, they'll assume we're paratroops."

"What makes you think that?"

"It's a matter of logic. They don't know how we got here. It would be natural for them to think that we dropped by parachute in the darkness. They'll think that what is being dropped is fresh supplies, meant to keep us in the field."

"I'm not sure what difference that will make."

"It will make a difference to their line of approach, Sir. They won't try to cut us off, because they'll think we're staying and that there will be a relief force coming to link up with us. That's the normal *modus operandi* for parachute troops. So, instead of trying to cut us off, they'll try to destroy us before the putative relief column gets here."

"And we've got two troops out on our flanks who won't be able to engage. I see what you mean. But we don't know which way they'll come."

"I think we do, Sir. If they want to bring armour they'll have to come from the east because the wadi cuts the road from the north and the mountains block the route from the west. Look at the terrain."

He showed the map. "A couple of miles further to the east from here there's an oasis. It's clearly marked. I guess that's where the wadi ends as the water coming down from the mountains empties out and soaks into the ground. Beyond that there's no natural barrier. They won't have to cross the wadi, which means they can bring tanks, lorries, half tracks ... whatever."

"I think you could be right. But if they realise we're commandos, not paras, they'll know we'll withdraw and the logical withdrawal route will be into the mountains. We can't guard against both."

"No, Sir. But if they come with tanks we'll need to be gone. We can't hope to fight off armour."

They were interrupted as the tall, gaunt figure of Col Stern approached. Vernon gestured for Carter to be silent.

"*Oberst* Stern, how can I help you?" Vernon asked, keeping his voice light.

"My engineer tells me that the generator is about to run out of fuel. If that happens, the refrigerators will lose power and the vaccines and other drugs stored in them will be useless. We'll also lose our electric lighting."

"There's fuel in the drums we left behind on the road." Carter said. "We could send a truck out to get some of it." It was ironic that perhaps a hundred thousand litres of fuel was still burning in the dump behind them.

"OK, arrange it." Vernon said. "Was there anything else, *Herr Oberst*?

“Yes. *Feldwebel* Gruber says that he is unable to locate *Major* Rhienhardt. Do you know where he is?”

“I sent an advance party to secure our withdrawal route.” Vernon lied smoothly. “The Major has gone with them.”

“Why? Why is he not here with his men?” Stern sounded genuinely surprised.

“We are taking Major Rheinhardt back with us for interrogation.” Vernon explained. “The rest of the prisoners will be left behind when we leave. We can’t be burdened with them.”

Stern looked dubious, not sure if he was being lied to but not having any evidence to suggest that he was.

“This is most irregular, *Oberstleutnant* Vernon. The Major is under the protection of the Geneva Convention.”

“The Major’s rights are being observed.” Vernon assured him. “There is nothing in the Geneva Convention that says we have to keep a prisoner here with the other men. He would be separated from them anyway, when he is sent to a PoW camp. The *Feldwebel* and the rest of the men can count themselves lucky. They will be returned to duty as soon as your army arrives.”

“Very well. But I will note the *Major’s* absence in my report.”

“As you wish, *Herr Oberst*.” Vernon bowed his head in apparent surrender.

The German turned on his heel and marched away towards his makeshift hospital in the accommodation tents.

“Well, we knew someone would notice Rheinhardt’s absence eventually. It could come back to haunt us.” Vernon observed.

“If it does, it does. We’ll report his death in the normal fashion. The lack of a body will cause a problem for any investigation. I doubt our own side will be interested and the Germans will have to be in control of this area if they want to go looking when the news reaches them. That will take weeks and the Germans will all be dead or in PoW camps.”

“But there’s always the Red Cross.”

“I think they would need stronger evidence of foul play bcforc they started an investigation, Sir. They’re thinly stretched as well. If necessary we'll have to fall back on the truth and hope that they believe us." Carter recognised what Vernon was doing. Getting himself to voice the answers to the questions allowed Vernon to test them. He did the same when they discussed operational plans, looking for flaws in his own thinking.

Vernon grunted. "The truth; yes, that's always believed. OK, well, I'll have a chat with the 2IC about your paratroops theory and see how we might re-arrange our defences. We'll know soon enough. It might help us if the Jerries attack form the east, seeing as our escape route is to the west. You'd better go and sort out that drum of fuel you promised the *Herr Doktor*."

* * *

Just before dawn they held a small ceremony to bury Tpr Coaker, Fraser's man who had been killed in the firefight with the Italian supply column. He was laid to rest in the small graveyard that the Germans had already established, the dates on the first crosses being 19th February. Hospitals and graveyards always went together in warzones.

Just as the sun rose above the eastern horizon, they heard the angry wasp buzzing of a Fieseler spotter plane. It flew north to south a safe distance from the fuel dump, though a couple of Bren gunners did try some shots until they were ordered to cease fire. There was no point in wasting ammunition.

The small, slow aircraft continued southwards before making a long, looping turn and coming back up on the western side of the dump. With the sun behind him, Carter raised his binoculars and followed the aircraft's progress. The observer, sitting on the side closest to him, held something to his face. A camera, of course, photographing all that he could see. No doubt the pilot was reporting back by radio at the same time.

A new sound started to emerge above that of the Fieseler's small engine. The howling note of a diving aircraft. Carter turned to locate the sound and saw the sleek body of a fighter descending from height to come in behind the spotter plane. For some reason Carter felt a desire to warn the crew of the German machine, even though he knew that the new arrival must be British or American.

The fighter levelled off at the same height as the German and tiny flames twinkled from the wings of the aircraft as the guns were fired. Bits started to fly from the Fieseler and it nose dived towards the ground, crashing and scattering debris across the dusty terrain. As the fighter passed, Carter could see what looked like a shark's toothy mouth painted on the large air intake below the engine[1]. Behind the cockpit the fuselage sported an RAF roundel in dark blue and red. The aircraft rose in an elegant climb, rolling through three hundred and sixty degrees to celebrate what wasn't so much a victory as an execution. Carter's eyes followed it upwards, then spotted two more shapes at a much higher altitude. The sandy brown coloured aircraft had friends up there.

The promised air cover seemed to have arrived, though Carter doubted that the aircraft would be able to take on tanks. He hadn't seen any bombs suspended beneath the wings.

"Over there." Prof Green arrived at Carter's elbow and pointed to the south. Larger dots appeared above the line of the mountains. It was difficult to judge their height, but they weren't low. As they grew in size Carter was able to make out distinguishing features. They were large, certainly and two engined. Carter hadn't seen their type before, even at Gibraltar where every conceivable type of aircraft seemed to have passed through while they were there. These must be the C-47s, the cargo planes that would drop the pre-packed field hospital to them. There were five aircraft, flying in a V formation. No, they were changing. The lead aircraft continued onwards while the other four turned to starboard, completing a slow circle to approach one behind the other.

Black dots began to drop from the open side door of the lead aircraft, before mushrooms of olive drab silk opened up to arrest their fall. Carter wondered why they had dropped the bundles of tentage such a long way from the hospital's position, until he realised that there must be wind up at their altitude that couldn't be felt where they were. The mushrooms drifted towards them before the bundles landed, bouncing and rolling along the ground before the mushrooms collapsed over them.

Trucks drove out from the other side of the still burning fuel dump, four men in each to load the tents and crates onto the back and bring them in. It had been proposed that some of the prisoners be used for that, but that had been vetoed. Prisoners in control of trucks might well decide to make a break for it and there was other work for them to do. Instead, 5 Troop had drawn the short straw.

The lead aircraft turned and headed back the way it had come as the second aircraft began its run. But it didn't disappear into the distance. Instead it made a leisurely turn to the east to fall in behind the fifth aircraft for a second approach. It couldn't possibly have more equipment on board, Carter thought. He didn't know how much a Dakota, as they were called by the British, could carry, but what had already dropped from it seemed to be a lot.

As the second aircraft flew away to the north, puffs of black smoke erupted around it and the sound of artillery fire could be heard. The Dakota climbed, leaving the altitude fused anti-aircraft rounds to explode beneath it. The third aircraft changed its route and made a tight turn to the west rather than risk the anti-aircraft gunfire. The fourth and fifth followed it.

But the lead aircraft was back, making its second run. A single tiny dot dropped from the side door, a parachute opening up as it fell. That was no cargo, Carter knew. That was a parachutist.

With the benefit of a man pulling on the shrouds, the parachutist was able to steer away from the cargo on the ground and towards the hospital site. He landed with his knees flexed, fell to one side, rolled and was back on his feet in one fluid movement, hauling the parachute's shrouds in, arm over arm and beating the billowing silk into submission. Once the air had been collapsed out of it, he dropped the oversized bundle on the ground and wriggled out of his harness.

Straightening up, the man removed his dome shamed helmet and replaced it with a maroon coloured beret. It was only as he approached the group of officers that had gathered to watch the parachute drop that Carter realised that the badge on the beret wasn't a silver winged parachute, but was the snake wrapped staff of the Royal Army Medical Corps.

The soldier came to a ramrod straight attention in front of Lt Col Vernon, pushed his Sten gun down to his left side and saluted with his right hand. "Warrant Officer O'Reilly, 1st Parachute Brigade, Sir."

"Can you stop saluting, Mr O'Reilly." Vernon warned. "I'd rather not attract the attention of a Jerry sniper.

"Jeez, he's from the Ould Country." O'Driscoll muttered, hearing the medic's Irish brogue.

"Not another bloody Paddy." Danny Glass mocked.

"Quiet, you two." Carter snapped. If they got started with what they regarded as banter it could soon escalate. "Haven't you got anything better to do?"

"Not right now, as it happens." Glass answered truthfully.

"Well, go and find something, the pair of you, before I decide to send you out to pick up the pieces of that Jerry spotter plane."

The two men hurried off, still bickering good naturedly.

Apologising, O'Reilly continued his introduction. "I'm here to help you assemble this field hospital, Sorr." The medic explained. "The Brigadier thought it might help things along, so to speak. Then I'm to come out with you."

"Will you be able to keep up with my men?" Carter knew that Vernon was only teasing. The Paras placed as much emphasis on physical fitness as the commandos. Indeed, the Paras had been born out of the commandos.

"'Twill be a cold day in Hell when I can't keep up with your men, Sorr." The warrant Officer grinned.

Vernon decided not to get further into the realms of commando versus paratrooper rivalries. "OK. Where do we start?"

"By showing me where you intend putting the tents, Sorr. Flat smooth ground is best, free from rocks and stones. But if you haven't got that, then as close as you can get to it."

Once the hospital tents had burnt out, the German and Italian prisoners had been set to work clearing the area of its debris. The work was almost complete and certainly left the area clear enough to make a start. "I'll be showing your men how to put up one tent. After that they'll be able to do it themselves. It's no big deal, as long as things are done in the right order."

"We're going to use the prisoners to do most of the work. As soon as they know what to do, we're getting out of here."

"A good idea, if I may make so bold, Sorr. The pilot of my aircraft sent a message. When he turned around after the first pass he saw quite a big column heading this way. They were throwing up a lot of dust, so he couldn't be sure, but he thinks there were maybe three tanks, eight armoured half trucks with another dozen trucks behind."

"In that case, we have no time to spare. Please carry on, Mr O'Reilly. I need to report this back to HQ."

Vernon called his radio operator across and started speaking into the set's microphone, while the 2IC took the Irishman towards Lt Barraclough, who was organising the Italian prisoners.

Carter thought about the force that was approaching them. If it included tanks rather than armoured cars, they would probably be Panzer IIIs. Not the best tank in the German army, but better than they needed to be against infantry that didn't have a single anti-tank weapon. Each of the armoured halftracks would carry ten men plus its two man crew, making three or four platoons in total. The trucks would carry a few more, perhaps five or six platoons. A battalion was usually made up of sixteen platoons divided into four companies, so ten platoons meant that there were some missing.

But it was a still a formidable force.

Carter raised his binoculars to his eyes again and faced east, then panned to the north. He was able to pick out a couple of taller palm trees that suggested there was more water there. That must be the oasis. He panned back right again and saw a haze of dust on the horizon. That would be the German force. He swung left again, further north, passing over the oasis. There it was, another haze of dust. That must be the missing company from the battalion. They were trying to outflank the hospital, probably on the nearer side of the wadi but it wasn't possible to tell at that distance.

"What do you make of the sums, Steven." Vernon arrived, accompanied by the 2IC.

"The Germans have spilt their force. The main attack will be from the east, with a flanking manoeuvre from the north, trying to surround us."

"Go to the top of the class. Yes, we suspect that the Jerries will try to surround the hospital in order to avoid a fight. They know that we can't use it for combat purposes, or we'll be in breach of the Geneva Convention. At the same time, they can't attack us for the same reason. But they don't have to attack. If they surround us we'll have no way of breaking out, so we'll have no choice but to surrender."

"So what are we going to do, Sir?"

"We're going to withdraw before the Jerries get here."

There was a lot of shouting from the men working on erecting the hospital tents and Carter saw the main canvass rising up on its poles, hauled by men on the guy ropes. Hammers rang out on metal tent pegs as they were driven into the ground to give the ropes something on which to anchor. Someone had found a medical orderly who spoke enough English to be able to translate O'Reilly's orders into German, and Ernie Barraclough was having a whale of a time shouting loudly in Italian and gesticulating with his arms, to the manner born.

Tents were tents in any army and the commandos could have worked out how to erect them. Small tents consisted of a canvass roof with side walls and doors already attached, while bigger tents had separate walls which were tied on with chords fed through brass rimmed holes. Carter had once attended a wedding in a marquee that had been very similar to what he was seeing being erected in front of him. The only real difference was the uniformly drab greenish brown colouring of the canvass and the large white painted disc on the roof with a red cross quartering it. It was how the tents connected together to form a whole that might present a mystery, but even that might have been solved with a diagram or two, but O'Reilly's presence certainly speeded things up.

"Once they've got one tent up, they'll know how to do them all." Vernon said, "So we can start pulling out. 5 Troop can start moving now, in the trucks we have available and they'll pick up 2 Troop as they pass them. I want them to set up defensive positions in the mouth of the pass which everyone else can fall back on. 1 and 3 troops can fall back on foot under Andrew Fraser's command. Once the 2IC has reached the pass he can send the trucks back for Fraser to use. I'm afraid that leaves you with the short straw, Steven. You'll be my rear-guard and I'll pick up 6 Troop and your other two sections as we withdraw. 6 Troop can stay out on the flank covering the wadi while the rest of us make a bee-line for the pass.

Rear-guard; so the prickling at Carter's neck hadn't played him false. With tanks behind them they were in for as tricky time. Traditionally rear-guards didn't fare well. Harried by a far larger enemy they were nibbled away at, mile after mile. The rear-guard at Dunkirk had accounted for most of the British prisoners of war taken by the Germans and also a fair percentage of the combat casualties.

A trooper trotted up and came to a standstill in front of Vernon. Carter didn't recognise him, so he must have been one of the new boys. "'Scuse me, Sir. Sentry reports movement to the east." He pointed in the general direction, just in case his CO didn't know where east was. Carter and Vernon raised their binoculars at the same time. About half a mile distant an armoured halftrack, a *Hanomag*[2] as the Germans called it, had just come to standstill, a haze of dust still settling around it. Figures poured out of the back and deployed to either side. They moved with a fluidity that spoke of practice. With the sun behind him, Carter couldn't see the commander of the vehicle, but he didn't need to in order to know what the officer was doing. He would be standing up in the cab, taking advantage of the additional height, looking at them through binoculars, just as they were looking at him.

“A reconnaissance.” Vernon grunted. “They’re being cautious. I wonder what they’ll make out of us putting up tents.”

“It will look like we’re settling in, Sir.”

“No, they’ll see the red crosses. What they won’t know is why we’re putting them up. It doesn’t matter though. From there they’ll probably be able to pick out our defensive positions, much good it will do them. By the time they get here we’ll be long gone, I hope.”

There was the growing howl of an aircraft engine from behind them and for a split second Carter wondered if the Germans intended to bomb their own hospital, but a dark shape flew above them directly towards the halftrack. Through his binoculars Carter could see spurts of dust gouting up as bullets struck around the vehicle. A machine gun on the German flank attempted retaliation but the aircraft was past them and continuing onwards before the gunner had the chance to get a proper aim. But the roaring of engines continued as two more aircraft flew over the hospital on either side. They bypassed the reconnaissance vehicle, heading directly for the main force.

Air raid drills would be set in motion as the German soldiers struggled to put distance between themselves and the larger targets offered by their transport. Vehicles would be damaged by the aerial onslaught and soldiers injured. It would delay the German advance for vital minutes.

Unfortunately, it would result in only damaged paintwork for the heavily armoured tanks. They would have had to have received direct hits from bombs for serious damage to be done and there were no reassuring crumps of explosions from in front of them. A pillar of smoke did rise up on the horizon, but it wasn’t enough to signify serious damage had been done to the enemy. A bombing raid was what was needed, but that didn’t seem to be forthcoming.

As Carter had suspected, now that the fuel dump had been destroyed the commandos were expendable. Any help that was forthcoming would be minimal as the American and Free French forces concentrated on winning the fight at Kasserine. The attack by the fighters had only been made because they were already in the area to cover the Dakotas as they had made their parachute drops. This attack would have used up most of their ammunition, so they would now return to their base. Carter suspected they wouldn't see them again.

"Oh, well done RAF." The 2IC said, as though the pilots could hear them.

"That may slow them, but it won't stop them." The CO echoed Carter's own thoughts. "Anyway, Steven, as I was saying, you'll be the rear-guard. You'll keep the armoured car with you, to give you a bit more oomph, so to speak."

"It will make a tasty target for the tanks, Sir." Carter made it sound like a comment than an objection.

"But it will also provide the men with some reassurance. That makes it a valuable asset."

Not for whoever was crewing the vehicle, Carter thought. For them it more likely to become their coffin. But the CO had made up his mind, so Carter's job was to follow his orders.

"Right, Charlie," Vernon said, rubbing his hands together in a manner that suggested finality. "You get your troops together and get on the road. As soon as Mr O'Reilly tells us the first tent is finished, the next group will start to follow."

As though hearing his name, the RAMC warrant officer approached the group.

"The first tent's almost finished, Sir." He reported. "I've just got to explain how the linking tents connect up and we can skedaddle."

"How many of the big ones are there?" Vernon asked.

"Four were sent. It's the most basic configuration. The first is for triage[3] and treating minor injuries, the second tent is the operating theatre, the third is post-op observation slash recovery and the fourth is recovery before discharge or evacuation. More tents can be added on to make the hospital bigger, but that's the basics. Each big tent is connected to the next by a smaller tent which forms a corridor.

"I see that you're carrying a weapon, Mr O'Reilly. Not really in keeping with the Geneva Convention." Carter observed.

"I'm also not wearing Red Cross arm bands, Sorr." O'Reilly gave a wry grin. "I'm not here as a medic, I'm just here because I know how to put up a field hospital. It doesn't even belong to the Paras. I'm more used to giving first aid under cover of a couple of ponchos. So I'll fight if I have to, if it's all right by you,"

"It's fine by me, Mr O'Reilly. If you'd like to head over that way," Carter pointed to where 4 Troop were lying around enjoying the sunshine, "and find Tpr O'Driscoll, he'll be glad to make you a brew and chat about the old country with you."

"Ah, a fellow Paddy, is it? Sure, I'd love to meet him. You know we're all related in some way; if not by blood then by marriage." Carter wasn't sure if he was joking but decided not to ask. Instead he went looking for Fred Chalk to get the men started on making their preparations for the withdrawal. It would be their job to take over the defensive positions from whoever was manning them currently. He wondered to whom he could give the job of crewing the armoured car. It was a task he wouldn't want to give to a mortal enemy, let alone a valued comrade.

[1] From the description given by Carter, this aircraft would most probably have been a Curtiss P40D, called a Kittyhawk in the RAF. It replaced the earlier P40C Tomahawk. It was slower and less manoeuvrable than a Messerschmidt Bf109, which was why it was side lined from the war in Europe. It was, however, considered to be superior to the Hawker Hurricane, which it replaced in North Africa. Kittyhawks were used by seven squadrons of the Desert Air Force from 1942 onwards and claimed a large number of victories over German and Italian aircraft in North Africa. Thc aircraft also served well as a fighter bomber, supporting ground forces.

Hanomag – named after the company that designed the vehicle, the *Hannoversche Maschinenbau AG*. Also referred to in day to day use as SPWs - *Schützenpanzerwagen*, or armoured infantry vehicle. Its official designation was Sd Kfz 251. It was the most widely used half-track vehicle, seeing service in all theatres where the Germans fought. Over 15,000 were built and they remained in use with some countries, who bought them at the end of the war, until 1995.

[3] Triage – assessing the casualty's condition in order to assign priorities for treatment. A casualty with little or no chance of recovery would be assigned the lowest priority and would just be treated with pain killers.

10 – Rear-Guard

Carter watched the lorries lurch away along the road. He felt sweat trickle down his back and realised that it was starting to feel warmer, yet it was barely eight in the morning. For so many weeks the weather had been coming out of the north; cool weather that had passed over the snow covered Alps, or the Pyrenees. While they had been in Gibraltar someone had said they could go skiing only a hundred miles away, in the mountains north east of Malaga. Carter had been dubious about that until someone told him they had also been skiing in Cyprus when they'd been stationed there before the war.

The wind was from the south now. The drift of the parachutes had shown that. Warm, dry air was coming up from the middle of Africa. There only seemed to be two seasons here; hot and not so hot. It would make fighting a war difficult. Tank engines didn't work too well in the sort of heat that could be expected. But Carter's mind was on more immediate matters. They would need to carry extra water if they wanted to avoid dehydration. The hospital had its own water bowser.

"Sgt Major Chalk, make sure everyone fills their water bottles before we leave. Anything else that can be found to carry water as well."

"The Jerries have got some jerricans we could use, load them on the back of that armoured car, Sir."

"OK, do that. Also organise a lottery and select a crew for it." It salved Carter's conscience not to have to pick men for that duty.

With the erection of the second large tent already underway, the CO dispatched the next wave of the commando, sending 1 and 3 troops westward on foot. Carter felt suddenly vulnerable, with so few men now guarding the fuel dump and the prisoners. Not that they were showing any signs of threat, but if they realised that the commandos were now a smaller number than themselves, they might try to turn the tables.

Time for him to consider organising some new defensive positions, where they wouldn't be at risk of becoming trapped inside the field hospital. The CO would want a head start, probably about half an hour, during which time they couldn't expect the Germans to stay where they were.

He checked the ground between the fuel dump and the road. It was flat and featureless. The road itself, however, stood a little bit above the surrounding terrain, allowing rain water to drain away sideways. If he put his men on the far side, they could scrape up some rudimentary parapets that would provide some basic cover. If they had enough mortars and Bren guns, they could keep the soft skinned Jerry vehicles at bay, at least.

With a bit of luck, the flanking force to the north wouldn't be in Hanomags. If they were, Carter had a problem.

He called Fred Chalk over to him and together they went to find the CO. Carter briefed him on his plan. Vernon checked the layout of the road and nodded his agreement. "Not exactly the Tower of London as far as defences are concerned, but it's better than being stuck in the open. I'll give you all the mortars and bombs that we still have. Give me thirty minutes after I've passed through your positions, then you can withdraw.

"I'll do my best, Sir."

"I know you will, Steven. That's why I gave you the job." Vernon turned away and started calling men towards him, readying them for the withdrawal.

"OK, Sgt Major. Get the men back to the road and get them digging like their lives depend on it, because they probably do."

* * *

Carter surveyed his defences, looking for anything he could improve. There wasn't much. He had six sections which equalled forty-eight men, one officer, a Sergeant and Sergeant Major. For weaponry he had four two inch mortars, a dozen bombs for each one, six Bren guns, rifles, seven Thompson sub machine guns, not including his own, and about a hundred rounds of ammunition per man plus a few grenades.

Oh, and an armoured car which was probably more of a liability than an asset.

He had split his force in two, half the men prepared to engage the northern advance and half looking southwards. Neither force was strong enough to repel a serious attack. The best they could do was slow them down.

Half an hour, that was all Vernon had asked him to hold. Carter looked at his watch. Still fifteen minutes to go. Plenty of time for a determined enemy to roll right over them.

The good news was that one of their own patrols had identified the vehicles on the northern flank as being half track trucks, not *Hanomags*. At least that was something. It allowed him to put three mortars on his southern flank, where the greater risk was likely to appear. The armoured car he put on the northern side. Its heavy machine gun would keep the trucks at bay, forcing the Germans onto their feet where the mortar and Bren guns could do their deadly work. With a bit of luck, he could keep them back about half a mile, trying to avoid his rifles. The .303 weapons weren't much threat at that range - unless they were in the hands of a commando. His men were excellent shots and on a long rifle range could score far more than the average number of hits for that distance.

On the other hand, the Germans would be bound to deploy light machine guns, their favoured weapon for infantry attacks. He hoped the hastily erected dirt parapets would protect his men.

On the other flank he was dependent on pure luck. Nothing he had would stop a tank, but a lucky mortar bomb might land inside the open top of the rear of a *Hanomag*, wreaking havoc amongst the troops inside. It was a faint hope though.

The Germans would know by now that they were no longer inside the hospital perimeter. Despite dire warnings of retribution to both the medical staff and the prisoners, it would be too much to hope that someone hadn't sneaked out on the far side, making their way to the recce *Hanomag* where it still sat about half a mile to the east.

Dust rose to the south of the fuel dump, signalling the German advance on that side. Carter raised his binoculars and tried to penetrate the haze. There was a tank in the lead, no doubt about that. The short barrel of its 5 cm gun jutted through the dust, pointing the way towards them. Behind, the dark shape of three *Hanomags* were visible from time to time, travelling in line abreast, about thirty yards between each vehicle.

But it was to the north that the fighting started. The armoured car had moved forward into the gap between his men and the Germans and engaged the soft skinned trucks, just as he had agreed with Ernie Barraclough. The further the vehicle was from the tank, the happier Carter was.

On the far side of the hospital and the burnt out fuel dump, Carter could just make out the rest of the German force. They were spread out in an extended line, apparently waiting to see what their comrades could achieve.

Why had the Germans committed so few troops? Carter wondered. No doubt they were aware they were only facing a rear guard, but that didn't mean it didn't have teeth. It suggested that the Jerries still didn't realise they were facing commandos, so they expected an easy victory.

The German tank fired a round from its main armament, but it flew well behind Carter's men, sending up a harmless gout of sand and rock. More worrying was the stream of bullets from its secondary armament, a machine gun. The bullets stitched a line across the front of the defences, making his men duck. Carter realised how exposed he was and hurried to take up his position in fox hole he had dug in the centre of the defensive line.

The four enemy vehicles turned in formation, moving into the gap between the burnt-out fuel dump and the area where 3 and 4 Troops had ambushed the Italian re-supply convoy the previous night. They were now no more than half a mile distant. The two outer *Hanomags* started firing their machine guns, the third being unsighted by the bulk of the tank to their front.

Carter ordered the mortars to open fire at extreme range. The only chance they had was to reduce the odds by inflicting damage on the armoured half tracks. A spurt of sand and fire showed where the mortar bomb landed, close to the right hand vehicle, but not close enough to do any damage. The second and the third bombs were no closer. It was like throwing a pebble into a millrace in the hope of hitting a fish.

An increasing noise caused Carter to look up and behind him. It was the sound of aero engines, transcending the chatter of small arms fire and the distant crump of mortar bombs. The three fighter aircraft were back. Carter muttered silent thanks to the senior officer who had decided that Carter and his men shouldn't be abandoned.

The fist aircraft streaked low over their positions, low enough for Carter to see three small objects detach themselves from the underside of the aircraft and streak downwards. They hit the ground just in front of the tank, covering it in debris. But the vehicle emerged seconds later, unscathed.

The *Hanomags*, however, came to a sudden standstill. Although they were armoured, with their passenger compartments open to the sky they were far more vulnerable to shrapnel and debris. Troops spilled out of the back, streaming away to either side, trying to put as much distance between themselves and the vehicles that would surely be the next target for the aircraft.

The first aircraft climbed and turned, leaving the attack zone clear for the next in line. Again Carter saw the bombs drop from beneath the wings and fuselage. The tank seemed to disappear in a ball of flame and smoke as one bomb struck. The other two exploded harmlessly to one side.

When the smoke cleared, Carter used his binoculars to try to assess the damage. Where once there had been a tank turret with a 50 mm gun extending from it, there was now just a gaping hole in the tank's fuselage, flames flickering up from it as something inside burned. The barrel of the tank's main armament lay on the ground nearly fifty feet away, flung there by the bomb's blast. The rest of the turret lay in several large lumps, scattered around the vehicle.

The third aircraft began its attack. The furthest *Hanomag* started to move again, but away from Carter's position. It turned, making a run for safety. The aircraft, however, was more intent on the vehicle in the middle, releasing its bombs as it passed the wreckage of the tank, so they continued forward under their own momentum. None of the three bombs seemed to do any damage, until Carter saw a tendril of smoke rising from the *Hanomag's* engine compartment. The tendril became a puff, the puff became a stream and then smoke was pouring from the engine compartment in great waves. The driver and gunner abandoned their crippled vehicle and ran to join their colleagues taking refuge some distance away.

But the three aircraft weren't yet finished with the Germans. The lead aircraft lined itself up again and started its second diving attack, flickers of flame at the leading edges of its wings as it started to machinegun the troops on the ground. Completing its run, it made a tight turn and flew west over Carter's positions, waggling its wings before climbing away to turn back ready for another strafing[1] run.

The message was clear enough. 'Time for you to go; we've got your back.'

"Sgt Major Chalk." Carter bellowed to make himself heard above the roar of aircraft engines. "Double these two sections back half a mile and dig fresh positions."

He didn't wait to see if his orders would be obeyed; there was no need. Instead he ran across to Ernie Barraclough's sections.

"Your two sections are going to do a fighting retreat." He told him. It was a standard manoeuvre. One section would remain facing the enemy, ready to engage, while the other withdrew fifty yards. Then they would take up defensive positions while the first section withdrew, the two sections leapfrogging past each other until they reached safety, or until ... Carter stopped himself before he could complete the thought.

He searched for the armoured car, spotting it moving back towards them, its turret turned rearwards, towards the enemy and firing the occasional machine gun burst to keep the enemy's heads down. He waved his hands frantically, trying to attract the driver's attention.

The vehicle speeded up and in less than a minute it pulled up alongside Carter. Prof Green's head appeared above the top of the turret.

"What are you doing in there?" Carter snapped, then chided himself for asking a stupid question. When danger was around, Green was usually to be found close by. "Don't tell me! Glass and O'Driscoll are in there with you."

"We are that, Sorr." Paddy O'Driscoll's cheery face appeared alongside Green's.

Carter let out an exasperated sigh, but he had no time to pursue the matter right then. "I want this armoured car to keep pace with the rearmost section at all times. You are to keep the enemy at a safe distance while we withdraw. Got that?"

"Keep the enemy at a safe distance." "Green replied in a monotone.

"Would that be a safe distance for them, or a safe distance for us, Sorr?" O'Driscoll beamed.

"Shut it, Paddy!" Green advised, pushing the Irishman's head back down inside the turret. "We'll cover your backs, Boss." Green said. "I take it you'll be with the rearmost section as well?"

"I will Prof. And if another tank turns up, I want the three of you out of there and running like hell as soon as I give the word."

"We won't need telling twice." His head ducked back inside the armoured car and its engine revved as the driver, presumably Danny Glass, steered the vehicle out onto the northern flank. German infantry could be seen in the distance, making darting runs from meagre cover to meagre cover as they sought to close the gap on the commandos. A burst of machinegun fire from the vehicle sent them diving for cover.

The two sections under Ernie Barraclough were Charlie and Delta. Carter gave Barraclough command of Charlie while he took control of Delta. As they climbed out of their shallow defences, Carter saw one man lying still. He walked over and prodded the man with his toe. He didn't move. Carter turned him onto his back, reeling back in horror as he saw that the man no longer had a face. A bullet had shattered against a rock in the hastily constructed parapet, smashing the missile apart, the fragments flailing the man's face. One larger piece must have penetrated his skull to kill him. Carter hoped it was a quick death.

He reached inside the man's shirt and snapped the fibreboard identity disc from the chord on which it hung. Taking the man's rifle he unlocked the bolt and withdrew it from the weapon and slid it into his pocket. There was no way he was going to leave a working British weapon for the Germans to use. He planted the barrel deep into the soil to mark the man's position, then turned and trotted to catch up with the men who were already heading towards Charlie section fifty yards to their rear. They walked backwards, never letting their eyes leave the enemy. They could drop into firing positions in a split second if need be.

[1]Strafing – Ironically, this word is of German origin '*straffen*', meaning to punish. It took on its present meaning during the First World War when troops first came under aerial attack from machine guns mounted on aircraft.

11 – Dingoes

The morning wore on, with Carter's men withdrawing yard by yard towards the head of the wadi and the safety of the ravine. For a while the three aircraft continued to harass the enemy but, finally, out of ammunition and short on fuel, they had to return to base. Carter didn't expect to see them again.

The Germans took the opportunity to advance more swiftly, calling up another tank to replace the casualty. Still Carter wondered why they didn't commit their full force. It didn't make any sense.

The armoured car made swift forays forward to send the infantry to ground once again, before withdrawing. The newly arrived tank peppered it with 50 mm shells but failed to score a direct hit. Tanks were great against static or slow-moving targets, like other tanks, but against a more nimble opponent the gun was less effective and if the tank itself was moving the gun was almost useless. It could only be a matter of time, though, before the tank landed a killing shot.

Once again, the skirmish line drew level with the two sections that had been sent ahead to dig in. Carter sought out Ernie Barraclough, who had withdrawn with the two sections who had prepared the positions.

"We lost another man." Carter said, his mood sombre. "Trooper Whitham."

"Machine gun?"

"No. It was a single shot. I think they've got a sniper deployed."

"Not much we can do about that right now."

That was true enough. The normal counter to a sniper was to deploy your own snipers to try and locate and kill him. That wasn't an option for a force that was withdrawing. Carter checked his map. Behind them there was a gentle rise, no more than a few feet high but a hill all the same, when compared with the surrounding terrain. Beyond that was more flat ground for about a mile until they reached the wadi. Then they had another two miles to go to reach the foothills, and another mile or so before they would be inside the embracing arms of the ravine. The Germans could chase them in there if they wanted, but the commandos would pick them off like flies if they tried.

Carter examine the slope, wondering why Ernie Barraclough hadn't dug his new positions at the top. Always take the high ground. It was golden rule, but Ernie seemed to have forgotten it. He'd have to have a word when this was all over.

But for the moment, he tried to work out if it offered enough of a height advantage to be worth defending. As his eyes scanned the low ridge they opened wide, not believing what they were seeing.

It was the unmistakable angular shape of a turret. Too small to be that of a tank, he thought, but definitely large enough to be that of an armoured car, lying 'hull down' as the tankies called it. The bulk of the vehicle was lying below the summit of the hill, like an iceberg concealed beneath the sea, making it harder for an enemy to spot it.

There was the unmistakable sound of revving engines, one from either end of the hill. Around the flanks came two armoured cars, one on each side, their large wheels churning up clouds of dust. They raced in an arc to get around the commandos' positions and hem them in. Anyone trying to escape would be cut down by one or other of the three vehicles.

But when the two vehicles stopped they didn't aim their weapons at the commandos. They aimed east, towards the advancing Germans. Carter rose from his cover and trotted forward until he was standing beside the nearest vehicle. It wasn't unfamiliar to him. He had seen several just like it on the dockside in Algiers. Dingoes, they were called, manufactured in Coventry by the Daimler company.

The roof of the turret folded back and a figure rose, climbing out to stand on the hull. The soldier removed a pair of headphones, laid them on the top of the turret and jumped the short distance to the ground. He extended his hand.

"Tony Gossard, 1st Derbyshire Yeomanry." He introduced himself. He wore Lieutenant's 'pips' on his shoulders. His educated tones didn't quite cover up his East Midlands accent.

"Steven Carter." Carter answered, taking the offered hand and shaking it. "15 Commando. Where on earth did you spring from?"

"We've been sent to keep an eye on this area to make sure that the Jerries don't try to outflank the Yanks. But I could ask the same question of you. That fireball last night; was that your work?"

"It was. We were sent to blow up a fuel dump and that explosion was us doing the job. Have you seen our main force? They should have passed through here a short while ago."

"We saw some trucks heading west. They looked like Eyeties, but they were too far away for us to engage. Besides, we could hear fighting from this direction and we thought we had better take a look."

"I'm glad you did. We're being chased by a Jerry tank and a whole load of mechanised infantry. At least three *Hanomags*."

"That Italian armoured car, is it with you?" Gossard nodded in the direction of the vehicle, which was parked next to the defensive positions, its engine burbling as it idled.

"It is."

"You're lucky. My lads wanted to take it out. But I could see that you were British, so I made them hold their fire until we could find out what was going on."

"You have armour piercing weapons?" Carter's voice soared with hope.

"Don't get excited. They're only Boys[1] rifles. They could take out your armoured car, but they won't stop a tank, as we've found out in the past, to our cost."

"Pity."

"Is that all that's behind you? One tank and some mech infantry?

"There's more a bit further back, on the other side of the field hospital. Another tank and we estimate a battalion strength of infantry all told. They may have moved forward now. I've been puzzling as to why they haven't committed the whole force. If they had, we'd be dead by now."

"Fuel, old chap. You blew up the only dump in this area. If they use up the stocks they have with them, they'll run out and won't be able to get back to their own lines. From the report I got this morning, the battle's nearly over. The Yanks and the Free French have retaken the pass and are pushing Rommel's men back towards their start line[2]. If that tank and those *Hanomags* run out of fuel the Jerries'll get cut off and they'll end up in a PoW camp, so they have to conserve their fuel stocks. Lucky for you, eh?"

"They call me Lucky." Carter grinned. "Are you able to help us at all?"

"I think we can make some contribution, seeing as we're here. If I take my boys out onto the flank, we can get in behind the infantry and cause some trouble. The tank will have to stop and try to deal with us. If we can do enough damage, the Jerries will be forced to break off their pursuit of you while they bring up reinforcements. At the very least it will slow them down and give you some respite."

"Look, while I'm very grateful for any help we can get, don't risk your men's lives for us. Don't mix it with that tank."

"I have no plans on dying out here, Steven. If it start's getting hairy, we'll withdraw to a safe distance. We can play tag with them all day that way."

"Just as a matter of interest, how did you get your armoured cars across the wadi. We blew up the bridge last night."

"That was you, was it? We thought it was the Jerries. Anyway, we guessed the bridge was blown so we did it the hard way. We found a low spot, where the wadi wasn't quite so deep, then dug ramps on both sides. It took us most of the night."

"I think we owe you blokes a drink when we get back to Algiers."

"I think it will be more than one Steven. But you have to get back first, so best you get moving."

[1]Boys – Rifle, Anti-tank, .55 in, Boys; also known as a Boys Anti-tank Rifle and, incorrectly, as a 'Boyes'. Nicknamed 'the elephant gun', its explosive ammunition was capable of piercing light armour, but was no match for the heavy armour of a tank.

[2] The positions attacking troops are in at the start of a battle is known as the 'start line'.

* * *

Carter took them around the side of the low hill, which avoided them being 'skylined'. On the reverse slope they picked out the wide tracks left by the Dingoes, heading back towards the crossing point the men of Derbyshire had made in the wadi. It wasn't long before they heard the sound of battle once more; the slow heavy thump of the Boys rifles interspersed with the lighter sound of machine guns and the occasional crump of the tank's heavier artillery.

Carter looked over his shoulder and saw a plume of smoke heading skywards, whether it was from a friend or an enemy there was no way of knowing. He kept the men moving at a fast pace, leading from the front.

They reached the artificial ramp, cut in the side of the wadi, a short while later. The ramp had been cut from the top downwards, the spoil being thrown into the bottom of the wadi to raise its level and reduce the amount of digging required. Still, it had been a mighty effort. The Dingo only had a drew of two, so six men had cut those ramps, unless there was another troop of them somewhere out in the desert. Gossard hadn't mentioned them if they were.

Carter had hoped to continue using the armoured car to cover their rear, but the boulders strewn along the bottom of the wadi, deposited over the eons by heavy rain, told Carter that it wasn't an option. The Armoured car would end up moving at a slower pace than his men could manage, until it eventually fell victim to damage by a boulder.

The Jerricans of water, already depleted as the men topped up their water bottles, were unloaded and the men told to drink as much as they could. What was left of the water was decanted into two cans, which were hoisted onto the backs of two men. Carter promised they would be swapped around every fifteen minutes, to share the load. Twenty litres of water weighed twnety kilograms, about forty four pounds. It was a heavy load to carry for any distance.

Green wanted to boobytrap the armoured car, but Carter vetoed the idea. “There’s friendly forces in the area.” He advised. “If they come across it we could end up killing our own.”

Instead he soaked a rag in petrol and stuffed it into the armoured car’s refuelling pipe, before setting it alight. As he made his way down the wadi Carter heard the crump of the explosion as the flames lit the vapour escaping from the fuel tank. The armoured car wouldn’t burn out, the fuel tank was too well protected by armour for that to happen, but it could no longer be refuelled, so it was useless to the enemy if they stumbled across it. Green had already disabled the machine guns by the simple expedient of removing the firing blocks and throwing them out into the desert.

With Carter on the left and Barraclough on the right, they led the way down either side of the bottom of the wadi. From time to time Carter climbed the side to scan the ground in front of them through his binoculars, but he couldn’t make out any threat. Neither could see any trace of the rest of the commando.

Carter checked the map from time to time, taking compass bearings on the peaks of the mountains towards which they were heading. He was able to plot their position with a high degree of accuracy, even without the evidence of the foothills rising in front of them. He wasn’t concerned about their direction of travel, the wadi gave him that. He was concerned about how long they were taking. Every minute that passed gave the Germans time to catch them up and get past them.

After half an hour Carter called a halt. They’d had a busy morning and a rest was deserved. Even though they couldn’t spare the time, he couldn’t let exhaustion win the day. The men had to have time to catch their breath, even if it was only for a few minutes.

The men needed no second bidding to get their ‘hexi’ stoves out and make a brew. They opened tins of bully beef and packets of hard tack[1] biscuits to make a rudimentary lunch. Carter sent pickets up to lie on the parapet of the wadi and keep guard.

Prof Green handed Carter a mug of tea. They always 'buddied up' at mealtimes. Carter waved away the offered biscuit with a slab of gelatinous bully beef perched on top. "No appetite right now, thanks Prof." He'd had no appetite since he'd seen the dead soldier's missing face back at the road.

"You need to eat boss. You're not going to get through those mountains without something in your belly." Green's tone was light, but his concern for his officer shone through.

"Later, maybe. I've still got plenty of food in my pack."

"You're the boss, boss." Green said, taking a large bite out of the bully beef, the biscuit beneath it proving a challenge to his teeth, as it usually did. They weren't called 'tooth dullers' for nothing.

After twenty minutes Carter called the Troop Sgt Major across to him. "Get the pickets in. We'll move on in two minutes."

"No problem." Fred let out a low whistle and beckoned to the four soldiers who had been detailed to the task, two facing each way along either side of the wadi. Their 'buddies' had made sure they got tea and food.

Three of the men slid backwards towards the bottom, controlling their descent with their elbows and feet. One, however, decided he needed to make a call of nature before returning. He straightened up and stepped above the parapet, struggling with his fly buttons as he went.

Fred Chalk started to shout a rebuke for the man's stupidity, but it was already too late. The man started to fall before Carter heard the crack of the rifle that had fired the shot. He tumbled and rolled his way to the bottom, his arms and legs getting tangled in the sling of his rifle. Then he lay still.

"Sniper!" Barraclough called, the first to react. The men scattered to the sides of the wadi, where the steep walls provided some cover.

Carter ran to the dead man, turning him over. There were two holes in the man's neck, one for the entry of the killing bullet and the second, a far larger one, for its exit. It had either been a lucky shot, or a very good one. Carter suspected the latter.

Barraclough arrived beside him and examined the wound. "Shit. The bullet came from the left. That means the sniper is in front of us."

Carter looked up to the to the top of the wadi and imagined how the man had been standing when he left the safety of the sloping ground. The only way the bullet could have hit him from that side was if it had come from the west, the direction in which they had to travel to reach safety, Barraclough was correct. But how had the enemy got in front of them?

Maybe it wasn't the enemy. Maybe it was a nervous commando from the main force who had seen the man and mistaken him for a German. Or it might even be someone from another unit, such as the Derbyshires they had encountered earlier.

Well, there was no way of solving the mystery from the bottom of the wadi. Carter took out his binoculars, slung his Thompson over his shoulder and crawled up the steep incline. Keeping his head as low as he could, he raised the binoculars and made a careful examination of the ground between themselves and the not too distant foothills. Nothing, just a jumble of loose rocks and other debris.

A whip cracked beside his ear, then he heard the bang of a rifle. The whip crack had been the supersonic passage of a bullet. He had been seen and the sniper had taken a pot shot at him. Not such a good shot this time, though, with him presenting a much smaller target than the dead soldier.

But he had seen the tell-tale puff of smoke from the sniper's weapon and it had been from that jumble of rocks. He raised his binoculars again, examining the line more closely. Maybe it wasn't the haphazard natural feature he had thought it was. Maybe it was the parapet of defensive positions, similar to those that his own men had been digging off and on all morning.

A movement caught his eye and he adjusted his position to take a closer look. What he saw, he was pretty sure, was the rounded dome of a helmet. It was difficult to make out, as its sandy brown colour blended with the background. If it wasn't a helmet, then it was a very smooth round rock. It wasn't the sniper, however; he had been further to the right, which meant that there was more than one person out there.

What it didn't tell him was who they were or how they got there. There wasn't enough of the helmet visible to determine its overall shape. It could be the familiar 'soup bowl' of a British helmet or the more rounded shape of a S*talhelm* of the *Afrika Korps*.

Ideally, he would have liked to have a sniper up here, but all his snipers were in Alpha Section, as they were in the other troops. If the withdrawal had gone to plan, they would now be dug in at the entrance to the ravine, waiting for his men to arrive.

The thought of his snipers triggered a memory though. Arthur Murray, along with Able and Baker sections, had blown the bridge over the wadi when he had heard a German patrol approaching. What had happened to that patrol afterwards? Had they stayed opposite Murray's two sections, waiting for daylight so they could assess the situation? Had they withdrawn to their own lines? Or had they moved along the side of the wadi looking for another place to cross? In their vehicles they would have had to withdraw quite a distance to avoid the noise of their engines being heard. So, they could have parked their vehicles and returned on foot.

At which point they might have heard the Derbyshires digging their ramps. Not knowing their strength and assuming they were part of the same force as Murray's men, they would have given them a wide berth.

Then they would have heard the sound of the ambush of the re-supply convoy, followed by the explosion and fireball from the fuel dump. It would have given them pause for thought. When dawn broke they would have seen the Dakotas and the fighters and … what might he, Carter have assumed? He might have assumed that a major offensive was in progress. The leader of a small patrol might decide that discretion was the better part of valour and order his men to dig in.

He would have seen the commando withdrawing to the foothills, over three hundred men on the far side of the wadi and that would have confirmed his decision to stay concealed. Right up until Carter's much smaller force arrived along the bottom of the wadi, threatening to discover the patrol. Rather than let that happen, the enemy officer decided to keep Carter's men at bay by using his sniper to pin them down. No doubt he was already positioning a machine gun further along the wadi, turning its narrow breadth into a killing ground.

"Glass, O'Driscoll! Get up here but keep your heads down." Glass was the best shot he had available. His skills were what was needed now.

The two men scrambled up the slope and slid into cover alongside him.

"Three fingers to the right of the wadi, in amongst some rocks." Carter directed Glass towards the dome of the helmet, which was still visible. It moved slightly, as the though the wearer was turning his head, perhaps engaged in a conversation with his nearest neighbour. "Do you see a domed shape?"

"Got it."

"I'm pretty sure that's a Jerry. But he isn't the sniper. He's further to the right. Maybe one finger further north."

"Can't see anything there."

"No, but he's somewhere around there. I want you and Paddy to try to get him to fire again, then see if you can take him out, or at least force him to withdraw."

Once a sniper's position had been discovered, they always withdrew before the opposition could counter them. There was probably nowhere for him to withdraw to, but they could make him change position and that would disrupt his activities for a while. Glass might even get a lucky shot in and silence him for good.

"How am I supposed to get him to fire?" O'Driscoll asked, already knowing the answer.

"I'm sure a clever bloke like you can work that out." Carter clapped him on the shoulder and slid down the side of the wadi to re-join the rest of the troop.

Barraclough hadn't been idle. He had two of the mortars already in position, the crew collecting the remaining bombs from the commandos around them and stacking them in the space between the two weapons.

Carter showed Barraclough the map and indicated the approximate position of the Germans defences. "I think that's about three hundred yards."

"I'll go up and spot the fall of shot." Barraclough offered. Carter was about to countermand him, when he realised that he himself would be better employed leading the attack on the German position when the time came.

"OK. I'm going to site a third mortar to fire along the length of the wadi. If I was in command of that patrol, I'd cover the length of the wadi with a machine gun. It will be a tough fight."

"We could withdraw back to the ramps, then head down the far side of the wadi, out of range and make it to the ravine that way."

"It will take too long. The Dingoes can slow up the Germans that are behind us, but they can't stop them. We could end up between a rock and a hard place, as our American cousins say."

"Wasn't that the Ancient Greeks?" Barraclough asked with a smile.

"Probably, but this isn't the time to debate the matter. Besides, we have no way of knowing if there's more of them on the other side, just lying in wait for us to do just what you suggested."

Carter heard the distant crack of the sniper's rifle, followed shortly afterwards by the reply of Danny Glass's Lee Enfield. "Better get up top. I'll be sending the first bomb over in a couple of minutes."

Using his compass, Carter lined the two hand-held mortars up on the target and gave them an approximate range. Using their trenching tools as support for the mortar barrels, the crew adjusted the angle of elevation, experience telling them roughly how high they should be aiming. The loader slid a bomb down the tube of the right hand mortar.

Lying on the side of the wadi a few yards behind Glass and O'Driscoll, Ernie Barraclough waved to show that he was ready.

"Fire!" Carter shouted. The operator pressed the trigger at the base of the tube and the weapon coughed as the charge fired.

They listened, waiting for the crump of the explosion as the bomb hit the ground. They didn't have to wait long.

"Thirty short." Barraclough shouted, telling them by how much they had missed the target. The crewman lying on the ground made a slight adjustment to the angle of elevation. The loader dropped another bomb down the tube.

"Fire" Carter called again.

Away went the second bomb.

"Spot on." Barraclough announced. The second crew responded by making small adjustments to their weapon before firing their first bomb.

Satisfied that the mortars were ranged correctly, he called another crew over to him and started setting them up to fire along the wadi.

An explosion erupted behind Carter, showering him with loose dirt and pebbles. Damn, the Germans had mortars of their own. This was going to be a difficult fight. But they had gone long and they wouldn't necessarily know that. Being at the bottom of the wadi gave them some concealment.

"Fred!" Carter called to get the attention of his Sgt Major. "Move the men forward a bit, away from where the Jerry mortars are falling."

The Sgt Major began shouting orders and the men crawled forward along the floor of the wadi, using whatever cover they could find. Most of them had worked out what an enemy machine gun could do in the confined space.

Carter pulled his whistle from the top pocket of his shirt and showed it to the mortar crew. "Two whistle blasts means fire. One blast after that means you're dropping short and three blasts that your going long. Four blasts means cease fire. Make sure you do. No last minute shot so you don't have to carry the bomb, because we're going to be right in amongst the Jerries a couple of seconds later." It was always worth reminding mortar crews of the risks of them killing their own friends by being a little bit slow to stop firing.

"Not much risk of that, boss." the firer said. "We've only got three bombs left."

"Is that all, amongst the lot of you?"

"Yes. We fired most of them at those *Hanomags* when we were withdrawing."

"In that case, make sure you hit the target with the first one." Carter chuckled, letting them know it was a joke. There was no way the handheld mortar could find the target first time. There were too many variables.

[1]Hard tack biscuits – descended from the ships biscuits of the Napoleonic era (and earlier), these had hardly changed in one and a half centuries and formed one of the main ingredients of the field rations issued to British soldiers, known as 'compo (composite) rations'. The biscuits were unsalted, hard and dry and were difficult to bite through. Most soldiers soaked them in water or tea before attempting to take a bite (perhaps the origin of the practice of dipping biscuits in tea that has come down to us today). The main change to the biscuits was the way they were stored. From the First World War onwards they were sealed in airtight tins to keep out vermin and insects. In modern 'compo rations' the hard tack biscuit has been replaced by an oatmeal block and fruit biscuits similar to those that can be bought in supermarkets. As a young airman serving in the RAF in the late 1960s and the 1970s, the author was issued with compo rations containing hard tack biscuits. While most soldiers will still complain about the quality of compo rations (now called Operational Ration Packs, or ORPs), they have improved a lot since World War II – and since the 1970s.

* * *

They had barely moved a dozen yards when the machine gun opened fire. Carter could see the plume of smoke from its discharge, hanging in the still air at the bottom of the wadi. Carter blew two short blasts on his whistle and heard the cough of the mortar firing. The bomb fell short but was still close enough to pepper the machinegun's crew with debris. There was no point in calling for the aim to be changed. The weapon just didn't have that sort of capability for fine tuning.

Carter used the diversion to leapfrog ahead of the most forward men and take the lead. There was cover in front of him, but he and his men would be exposed as they tried to get to it. But he couldn't afford for them to get pinned down. If that happened the Germans would move forward out of their defensive positions and line up along the edge of the wadi to fire down into them. It would be a massacre.

He signalled for a Bren gun crew and sent them to the far side of the wadi. From behind an outcropping of rock they would be able to return fire on the German position and keep their heads down. However experienced the Germans might be, they weren't suicidal. At least Carter hoped they weren't.

Once the Bren was firing, he began moving from rock to rock, making short, sharp dashes. The sounds of footsteps and equipment rattling told him that at least some of his men were following him. A second Bren gun opened fire. It sounded like it was coming from above him and Carter hoped that the crew hadn't gone so high up the side of the wadi that they had left themselves exposed to the sniper.

Carter dived behind a larger rock and almost had the air knocked from his lungs as Prof Green landed on top of him.

"Sorry Boss." Green apologised. "Fox section are right behind you." He re-assured his officer. They had been the leading section as the Troop moved along the before their rest break.

Another mortar bomb dropped onto the machine gun's position, but this one was long.

But the machine gun stopped firing. The bomb may have fallen long, but it may have blasted shrapnel into the rear of the position, if the machine gun crew had put all their efforts into protecting their front. It wouldn't be the first time that a crew had made that mistake in their haste to get into a firing position.

Carter used the break to dash forward another ten vital yards, Green right on his shoulder. The place Carter had chosen was too small for the both of them and Green had to run a few more yards to find cover of his own.

The machine gun opened fire again just as Green dived behind a boulder.

They still had a hundred yards to go. It was too far to attempt to throw grenades and the mortar was down to its last bomb. They would have to take the machine gun post the hard way, the way they had done it during the last war. Carter's heart sank. He would lose men, he knew.

"Fix bayonets!" Carter yelled over his shoulder. Even above the clatter of the machine gun and the crump of the mortar bombs he heard the scrape of metal on metal and the soft clicks as the long spikes were locked into place.

"Bren Guns! Cover fire!" The words were screamed as he got to his feet and dashed forward. Ten yards and he hadn't been hit. Something plucked at the sleeve of his shirt. Another ten yards and he was still uninjured. The third mortar bomb threw up a gout of soil and the machine gun fell silent again, but only for a moment. Another ten yards and he was still running. He groped at the front of his webbing, looking for a grenade. He would be close enough soon.

But his dashing forward meant he couldn't take care of where he was putting his feet. He tripped on something and fell heavily, both his hands occupied with other tasks. He rolled over, feeling pain in his ribs. But he hadn't been hit, he was sure of that. Bury the pain! He told himself. He climbed back to his feet and resumed his careering run, zig zagging to put the machine gunner off his aim. An officer, a statistician in civilian life, had once told him that he was as likely to run into the stream of bullets as to avoid them, but that was the way they had been trained to do it, so that was the way he did it. Puffs of dust erupted around his feet, but he kept running.

Fifty yards, he reckoned. Close enough to have a go with a grenade. He dived for cover once more, then pulled the pin. His closed fist around the grenade to hold the safety arm in place as he rose once again, drew back his arm and threw. In his mind's eye he was at Lords, throwing the ball that would snatch the bails off the stumps to dismiss Don Bradman and win the Ashes for England.

The grenade had barely left his hand when he dropped back into cover again. As he hit the ground he felt something tearing at his back pack, but he didn't feel the slam of a bullet hitting his body. Still alive.

The grenade exploded and Carter got to his feet once more. Bodies flew past him. While he had paused to throw his grenade, other men had kept running. He couldn't have that. He had to be first into the machine gun pit. He grasped his Thomson and his thumb felt for the safety catch, sliding it down, ready to fire the weapon. Twenty five yards to go. He held the weapon firm against his hip and opened fire. He could see the barrel of the machine gun now, two terrified looking faces behind it as the crew saw their enemy close on them.

The loader started to rise to his feet, but he didn't make it. He was dead before he got half way up. Had he been going to surrender? They would never know. Carter aimed his weapon at the gunner, lying prone behind his weapon, and opened fire. Rounds sprayed from left to right as the weapon bucked in his hand. The gunner's head dropped onto his arms and his right arm dropped from the trigger. Red stains started to spread across his back where Carter's bullets had struck him.

The gun fell silent as Carter and his men dashed through the position and out the other side.

There was no time to celebrate. Above them was the German defensive line. If they were quick they could rake it from end to end before the Germans had time to turn and reorganise their defence. Carter pulled the pin on another grenade and lobbed it over the edge of the wadi.

"Up there, now!" Carter grabbed the man nearest to him and propelled him towards the side of the wadi. He scrambled up after him, the grenade exploding just before they reached the top, peppering them with dirt.

Carter raised his Thompson and as he breasted the top of the slope he started firing, aimlessly at first, but then picking out targets. Close to him a German crawled on his hands and knees, blood pouring from his arm, the sleeve of his uniform shredded by shrapnel. A few yards away the German defence line stretched away from them. Carter raised his sights to avoid hitting the wounded German and shot the man beyond him instead. The commando that Carter had propelled up the slope ran past him, his rifle extended to spear the man with his bayonet. Other feet pounded past.

A German threw his rifle to one side and lay face down, his hands extended in front of him in surrender. It was the trickle that started a flood. Weapons clattered to the ground, the Germans rising to their feet with their hands above their heads.

"Cease fire!" Carter screamed. "Cease fire!" He knew that soldiers were capable of just about anything when their blood was up. He had no desire to preside over a war crime. Prof Green barged a commando to one side, just before he speared a prisoner with his bayonet. Fred Chalk started issuing commands in crisp, calm tones, the soldiers responding automatically to his authority.

Spotting an officer in the middle of the line, Carter sauntered towards him, trying to display a greater degree of calm than he felt. Adrenalin still coursed through his veins and his vision was blurred at the edges.

The officer wore the single pip of a an *Oberstleutnant,* or 1st Lieutenant, on his shoulder. He drew his pistol from his holster and offered it to Carter. It would have been normal to allow the officer to keep his sidearm as a token of respect, but it was a Luger and Carter had always fancied one of the distinctive weapons as a souvenir. Instead he took the pistol and stuffed it into his webbing belt.

"*Oberstleutnant* Shäfer." The German clicked the heels of his desert boots and made a small bow.

"Captain Carter." Carter replied. "Do you speak English?"

"*Nein. Ich spreche kein English.*"

Carter turned and shouted along the line of defeated German soldiers, still standing with their hands up. "Do any of you speak English?"

A short figure poked his head from the line. "I speak a little."

"Good. Tell your officer that you are all prisoners of war. You will be treated in accordance with the Geneva Convention."

The soldier repeated Carter's words. At least, Carter assumed that he did. The officer said only a few words in reply.

"*Oberstleutnant* Shäfer says he understands. He will co-operate."

"Good. Now, tell all your friends that my men will search them. They will remove anything that can be used as a weapon and any military documents, but you will be allowed to keep any personal possessions. Once that has been done, you will be put to work digging graves for both our dead and your own."

Glass and O'Driscoll ran up, breathing heavily. "Did we get him?" Glass asked.

Carter pointed to a long barrelled rifle lying with the other discarded weapons. It had a telescopic sight mounted at the rear of the barrel. "I have no idea. I didn't see who was holding that." He replied. He noticed a shine of bright metal on the top of O'Driscoll's steel helmet.

"Are you OK, O'Driscoll?" Carter never called him Paddy in front of the rest of the troop, to avoid accusations of favouritism.

"Just a bit of a headache, Sorr." O Driscoll grinned in reply.

"I told the idiot to raise it on his rifle butt, but would he listen? Would he fuck!"

"Dat wouldn't fool no one." O'Driscoll replied scornfully. "Besides, I'm still here, aren't I?"

"Get out of here, the pair of you." Carter said, trying to hide his relief to see them both still alive.

Fred Chalk arrived, his face grim. Carter didn't have to ask what he wanted. The first action to be taken after securing a position was to establish the number of casualties suffered.

"How bad is it Fred?"

“As you know, we lost Trooper Taplow to the sniper. We lost two men to that machine gun; Nevis and Sutcliffe. In addition we’ve got two men with minor wounds and two more seriously injured. Proctor should be OK, but Gore has a severed artery in his leg. We’ve put a tourniquet around his thigh, but I doubt he’ll make it.

“All from Fox Section. Better split the others up between the remaining sections. The four remaining men won’t be effective as a combat section now.

“Already done. By the way, the contents of your backpack are scattered all along the wadi.”

Carter shrugged his way out of his webbing and examined what was left of his pack. He’d felt something hit it but hadn’t realised how badly it had been damaged – or how close he had been to death. There hadn’t been much of value in it, but it had contained his shaving kit. He couldn’t leave that behind.

Fred Chalk gave a cheery smile. “Don’t worry, boss. One of the men volunteered to go down and gather your stuff together. I’ll get you a pack from one of the dead. He won’t be needing it anymore.”

How Fred Chalk could be so matter of fact, Carter couldn’t fathom. But it was a practical solution and Fred Chalk was good at those. Perhaps his focus on the practical allowed him to block out the pain of the deaths.

Carter felt a tug on his sleeve and found a soldier pointing towards the east. “Vehicles, Sir.”

For a moment Carter’s heart sank. Out of the frying pan, he thought. But through his binoculars he saw the now familiar shapes of the three Dingo armoured cars, travelling in line abreast and at their maximum speed of about fifty miles an hour. They were kicking up quite a cloud of dust.

As they drew closer Carter waved his arms above his head to show they were friendly and the vehicles started to slow, then drew to a stop just short of what had been the German defensive line. Lieutenant Gossard climbed down from his vehicle and clambered over the rocks to shake Carter’s hand once again.

"Steven!" Gossard greeted him as though they had just met outside a pub. "I had a feeling it might be you again. We heard the firing and I thought we'd best come and investigate. Who are this lot?"

"I'm not certain. I haven't had time to question them, but I think they're a patrol that crossed our path last night, trying to use the bridge across the wadi. I suspect they were looking for somewhere to get their vehicles across and ended up here. Hearing all the action last night and this morning, they decided to stay until they could find out what was going on, then we pitched up."

"Yes, we avoided the bridge because we thought the Jerries might be defending it."

"Funnily enough, it was unguarded. Not that it matters because my men blew it up when this lot tried to get across."

"I hate to be a wet blanket, old boy, but that Jerry tank is going to catch up within the next hour, maybe less. I think you and your men need to get moving again. I've had orders to re-join my squadron, so we were already on our way back when we heard the kerfuffle up here, so we'll be on the move as well."

"We'll get going as soon as we've buried the dead. I wonder, could you do me a favour? We've two seriously injured men. Could you take them with you? They're not likely to survive the route we're taking."

"It will be a tight squeeze, but we'll fit them in somehow. So, you're going back through the mountains."

"I think we have to. If we stay with you we'll slow you down. We can't disguise thirty sets of footprints, so the Jerries will know which way we've gone. If that tank catches us up, as you say it will, then they'll sit back and pick off your armoured cars one by one. I'm not going to risk that and without your armoured cars, we're finished anyway. The one place we know that tank or the *Hanomags* can't go is through the ravine. If they try to follow us on foot, we'll have the advantage, so I'll doubt they'll do that.

"Makes sense. OK, get your men to bring your casualties over and we'll see how best to fit them in."

The shallow graves had been dug. They would be covered with boulders to prevent scavengers from digging up the bodies. The Germans were allowed to bury their dead first and Carter ordered that their weapons be returned to them with one bullet for each, so that they could fire a volley over their dead comrades.

Afterwards, the Commandos formed a square around the three graves containing their own comrades and said their own farewell, before firing a volley of their own.

As Carter watched the Dingoes disappearing in their cloud of dust, he called their interpreter over.

"You can tell your officer that we're letting you all go." Carter instructed. "We can't take you with us." He explained.

"You shoot us for escaping." The German said, quite clearly believing that was what the commandos had in store for them.

"No, we won't." Carter said firmly. "About two miles that way you will find German soldiers." Carter pointed eastwards.

Carter's men had already rendered the German's weapons unusable and now they were filing away along the bottom of the wadi once more, Ernie Barraclough leading the way. Only Carter and Fred Chalk remained. "You see. Only two of us." Carter pointed to himself and Fred Chalk.

"Yes, but you have Tommy Gun." The German pointed at the offending weapons. "rat-tat-tat." He imitated the sound of them firing on automatic.

"Oh, suit yourselves. You can stay here until you rot for all I care." He turned and headed for the edge of the wadi. "Come on, Fred. There's nothing more for us here."

12- Tebessa

The last couple of miles passed without incident. If the Germans were closing on them, there was no visible sign. Not even a distant haze of dust thrown up by caterpillar tracks.

As the wadi passed into the foothills it began to narrow, tilting gently upwards to enter the ravine. At the mouth there were two pillars of rock forming a perfect gateway. Even with his binoculars Carter could see no sign of the main force of 15 Commando. Had they gone ahead without the rear guard? Had they already been written-off as dead or prisoners?

But, then again, they were commandos. He shouldn't be able to see them until it was too late.

Carter joined Barraclough at the front of the column. The wadi was now too narrow to allow the passage of two files of men.

"Almost there, Ernie."

"And not a moment too soon."

"You did well. This is your first combat operation, isn't it?"

"Yes. Can't say it was fun, but I wouldn't have missed it for the world."

Movement between the two pillars of rock caught Carter's eye. A figure appeared and stood exactly in the centre of the space. Carter recognised the tall, angular frame of the CO, Lt Col Vernon. He was joined by the 2IC and then by the QM.

"Quite a reception committee." Barraclough observed.

"Probably can't believe we're still alive." Carter grunted.

More figures appeared behind the senior officers, then along the sides of the ravine and above the two pillars. It wasn't the whole commando, Carter could estimate that it was no more than half, but they all wanted to witness the return of the rear-guard.

Clapping broke out. First one pair of hands, then a few, then all of them. It wasn't the rapid applause that might be used to acclaim a famous singer, more the measured rhythm that might be heard on a cricket pitch or rugby field as one team applauded the efforts of their opponents after a hard-fought game.

"Wait." Carter whispered into Barraclough's ear, stepping to one side to allow his soldiers to pass him. "Let the men go first. They've earned it."

The men's backs stiffened, their heads coming up, making it look like they were growing by several inches. As they reached the CO he greeted each one, most of them by name, before shaking their hand and letting them pass into the mouth of the ravine.

As the last man had his hand shaken, Carter nudged Barraclough ahead of him to accept his plaudits, before coming to attention before Vernon himself. "Rear-guard reporting back." He said. He didn't salute, just in case there was an enemy sniper around. Salutes were for parade grounds.

"Well done, Steven." Vernon grasped Carter's hand in both of his and pumped it like he was trying to extract water from the ground. "I knew you could do it."

"We very nearly didn't."

"Much as I'd like to hear the story, there's no time now. No time for your men to rest either. I've organised tea, which they can drink on the march, but I want to get as far into this ravine as we can before dark. I've sent 1, 2 and 6 troops ahead. 3 Troop will act as our advance guard and you'll be pleased to know that 5 Troop will take over as rear-guard, though I don't expect them to have much to do. Your other two sections are still here, waiting for you to resume command."

Carter checked his watch. It said four pm. He could hardly believe that they were still on the same day as when they had left the field hospital to take up their positions on the road.

As they walked towards the men forming up Vernon spoke again. "How bad was it?" He asked.

Carter knew he was asking about casualties. They tried not to use the words, but everyone understood the euphemisms.

"Five dead all told. We managed to bury three but had to leave two where they lay. A few men with minor scrapes and scratches,

We had two very seriously injured and we sent them off with an armoured car unit we ran into."

"Armoured cars? I didn't know there were any friendly forces in this area."

"No and they didn't know about us, either. But they came in damned useful. They're part of the story though, so I'll save that for later."

"Yes, you must dine with me tonight and tell me all about it."

By dine, Carter knew, Vernon was referring to tea served with the ubiquitous bully beef on biscuits. He chuckled. "I'd be delighted, Sir. Is it black tie?"

"No, my dinner jacket is at the cleaners, so we'll go with informal. I'll see you later."

Vernon broke off to head towards the front of the column of commandos waiting to move off. Carter's men sat holding mugs of steaming tea.

"Come on you lot." He jollied them to their feet. "No time for sitting around. You'll have plenty of time to rest when you're dead."

"I feel like I'm dead now." Carter recognised O'Driscoll's voice, even thought it was muted.

"If you don't get to your feet, O'Driscoll, you'll wish you were dead." Fred Chalk barked. The men groaned and muttered but obeyed the order. Much as he knew his men needed rest, Carter also knew they had to put as much distance between themselves and possible pursuit as they could. The good news was that the two remaining troops would have to move at the speed of Carter's men, which meant that they controlled the pace.

One foot in front of the other. You can do that in your sleep, Carter told himself.

* * *

As the sun sank behind the mountains, Vernon gave the command to stop for the night. They couldn't navigate the ravines in the dark in safety, so they had no option but to halt. Carter's men didn't start brewing up, as they usually would. Instead they removed their webbing, laid down using their packs as pillows, wrapped their ponchos around themselves and were asleep within seconds. Carter had already assured them they wouldn't be required to stand guard that night.

Seeking Vernon out as the shadows lengthened, Carter felt mildly jealous of his men, now fast asleep. He and his CO shared a can of bully beef and some tinned peaches, but Carter struggled to keep his eyelids from drooping. Vernon also produced a hip flask containing whisky, from which he allowed them just one mouthful. The burn of the neat spirit served to wake Carter up, if only briefly.

"Can't afford to be getting tipsy." Vernon counselled. "We're not of the woods until we're safely back at Fort-de-l'Eau. Not that there are any woods around here, of course."

Carter chuckled dutifully, then started to tell the story of their experiences during their withdrawal from the field hospital and how each of their fatalities had occurred. Vernon would want to know, so that he could include some details in his letters to the next of kin. Nothing traumatic, of course, but it was important for families to have some context for their loved one's death. Carter, too would write, as he always did.

"Bit of good fortune running into that armoured reconnaissance patrol." Vernon commented.

"More than just a bit, Sir. I doubt we'd have made it without them. I must remember to send a few cases of beer down to them when we get back."

"Quite right. They earned it." It was a small courtesy, but one often respected.

"You know, I don't think I'll ever get used to losing men." Carter admitted to Vernon.

"And I hope you never will. We must never forget that every man's life is precious. They rely on us, their officers, to look after them. It's an unwritten contract. We must never squander their lives. If the generals had taken that view in the last war, the casualty rates might not have been so horrendous."

"You think the High Command was profligate with our soldiers' lives?" It was unusual for Vernon to be critical of more senior officers, even though most of the ones he was referring to were now retired or dead.

"Perhaps not deliberately, but certainly by not giving the matter due consideration. A sin of omission, rather than commission, perhaps. But the men ended up just as dead. It wasn't just our generals, of course. The Germans and the French were just as cavalier when it came to throwing men in front of the guns."

"From what I've heard, both Hitler and Stalin have repeated history at Stalingrad." News of the end of the great battle had come through just days before they started out on their own operation.

"So I've heard as well." Vernon replied "It's thought that both sides committed over a million men to the battle, perhaps two and half million in total. That's far more than the Battle of the Somme at its height."

"Any word on casualties?"

"Neither side are saying. Both sides are claiming victory, but it's the Germans that are withdrawing. I think it will probably be the end of Hitler's war in Russia."

"He obviously never read the accounts of other military leaders who tried to invade Russia." Despite his fatigue, Carter was interested in Vernon's take on Allied relations with the Soviet Union.

"Yes, fighting in Russia is a whole different sort of combat. Not only are the distances vast, but the weather makes it all but impossible except for a few months of the year."

"And Stalin, so I've heard, isn't too careful about preserving the lives of his people."

"I wouldn't say that to the wrong people right now. He is our ally, after all." Vernon cautioned.

"What's the old saying? 'Politics makes strange bedfellows.'"[1]

"Yes. And 'my enemy's enemy is my friend.'"[2]

"I wonder how that will work out when the war ends."

"I'm no expert." Vernon admitted. "But I suspect that Stalin has an agenda that doesn't match ours. Once he crosses the border into Poland and Germany, he may not be too keen to withdraw again. We've already seen some evidence of that with the Molotov – Ribbentrop Pact[3]. Russia and Germany carved Poland up between them, until Hitler decided he wanted Russia as well."

Carter failed to suppress a yawn, apologising as he did so.

"I'm sorry, Steven. Most inconsiderate of me. You must be exhausted. Go and get some sleep now. We'll be moving out at first light and you'll need to be on your toes to avoid accidents in these mountains."

Carter took his opportunity to leave, wishing his CO goodnight as he yawned his way back to his men. He was asleep so quickly that in the morning he couldn't remember actually laying down.

[1] Charles Dudley Warner, 19th century American essayist and friend of Mark Twain.

[2] From a Sanskrit work of the 4th century BC entitled the Arthashastra, a work on statecraft. Probably not the work of a single author, its first recorded English use was in 1884 and it was semi-official policy during World War II, when many alliances were formed on the basis of mutual convenience.

[3] More correctly known as the" Treaty of Non-aggression between Germany and the Union of Soviet Socialist Republics", as well as guaranteeing non-aggression between the two countries it also divided up certain territories between them, including Poland, Estonia, Latvia, Lithuania and northern Romania. Hitler broke the treaty when he attacked Russia on 22nd June 1941.

* * *

Dawn brought dark clouds scudding across the sky, mutterings of thunder echoing through the ravine. The men ate a hasty breakfast and then prepared to move out. It may have been warmer, but winter wasn't quite finished with North Africa.

Carter found that much of his food had failed to find its way into his new pack. For breakfast
He had to make do with a tin of sardines smeared onto biscuits. There was no point in challenging the commando who had collected his possessions from the ravine. Whatever food he had found he had considered to be his reward. Carter decided to let him have his little victory. There would be something that needed painting or digging or carrying at some time in the man's future and they would both know why the man had been given the job. A mess tin of porridge and some tinned pears would seem like a poor price to pay when the time came.

Fred Chalk made his morning report. "A few blistered feet, but nothing major. The two men with injuries are managing OK and the wounds seem to be healing fine. The men seem to be in good spirits after a night's sleep."

"Good. With a bit of luck we should make it out of the ravine by midday. Let's hope someone remembered to send the trucks. It's still a long walk back to Algiers."

They set off along the ravine, with 3 Troop still leading and 5 Troop bringing up the rear. After half an hour the heavens opened, bringing rain down on them in sheets. There was nothing the men could do but hunker down under their ponchos and wait it out. As before, the rainwater quickly filled the floor of the ravine, rushing past their feet in a mini tsunami. The men scrambled to gain some height, wanting to avoid having to walk in soaked boots. But water also streamed off the ravine's flanks, so there was no real respite.

As suddenly as it had started the rain stopped. The sky cleared and the rocks steamed in the morning sun. It dried clothes, but wet leather wasn't so easily dealt with. The men marched on stoically, trained not to curse the things they couldn't control.

They rested when they reached the plateau, taking time to make some tea and eat whatever rations they still had. Seeing Carter not eating, Green came over and offered him a wedge of bully beef.

Carter accepted it with good grace. “I thought you had plenty of food left.” Green observed.

“So did I.” Carter said, chewing on the cold meat.

“Do you want me to …”

“No. I’ll deal with it in my own time.”

“Not really the commando way, nicking your comrade’s food.”

“No, but I’m guessing he was hungry as well. We’ll be well enough fed when we get back to Algiers. I can wait till then.”

“Here’s something to chew on while we walk, then.” Green offered him two hard tack biscuits.

Carter put one in the pocket of his shirt then snapped a bit off the other, putting it in his mouth and following it with a mouthful of tea, waiting for it to soften enough to chew. “Thanks.”

Vernon called them to form up again and they began the slow descent back down to Algeria’s coastal plain and the road where they hoped to find the lorries waiting for them.

It was late afternoon when the advance party finally stepped out of the narrow gorge and onto the flatter ground that separated the mountains from the road. Their nostrils were at once assaulted by the smell of food cooking. Ahead of them stood a line of trucks, as hoped for, but beside them a field kitchen had been erected and a pair of khaki clad cooks bustled around kerosene fuelled cookers.

The voice of a sentry challenged them.

“Who goes there? Friend or foe?”

“Friend.” The leading commando replied, coming to a halt.

“What’s the first line of the second verse of the National Anthem?” The sentry challenged.

“No idea!” the commando replied.

“Pass friend.”

It was an old joke, but it always got a laugh. The sentry was from 1 Troop and had recognised the new arrivals easily enough.

An officer appeared from behind the trucks and made his way to meet the commandos, who were now streaming down the gentle slope.

The leading commando snapped to attention as he recognised the Brigadier's rank badges. "Where's your CO, young man?" He asked.

"Still in the ravine, Sir." The soldier stammered. Facing the enemy he would have been as cool as a cucumber, but faced with a senior officer he suddenly became tongue tied.

"Wait here and ask him to join me at my Jeep." The brigadier instructed. "The rest of you men, form a line at the cookhouse and get some hot food inside you. You've earned it."

The men needed no second bidding and hurried forward, pulling their mess tins from their packs as they went. It was probably "anonymous stew"[1], as the soldiers called it, but it smelt delicious after the best part of three days of living on tinned bully beef and tea.

[1]The ingredients of stews served up by field kitchens were often not easy to identify. Several catering sized tins of food were usually mixed together in "dixies' (large multi-purpose cooking vessels) and very often no one had read the labels to make sure they were all the same type of food. It wouldn't be unusual for beef, chicken and sausages to be mixed together along with vegetables and even fruit. Seasoned soldiers never asked what was in the stew, because the answer from the cooks was usually "not a clue". Hence the name, anonymous stew. For more information on Army catering, please see the Historical Notes at the end of the book.

* * *

A file of trucks bumped their way across the tracks of the freight yard and drew to a halt. Troops clambered down, hauling their packs, webbing and weapons down after them, stretching their backs and necks to remove the knots from their muscles.

"Where's the train then? A trooper asked.

"I think that might be it." Another replied, nodding towards what was in front of them.

"You've got to be kidding."

Technically it was a train. A long line of carriages sat on a pair of railway tracks. The carriages were old when Lawrence had been in

Arabia. Now they were ancient. One in the middle of the set sagged visibly on its suspension. There were no windows, just dark gaping rectangles; if there was any paint left on the exteriors then it wasn't visible to the naked eye. At the front stood a locomotive that was shrouded in steam that seemed to leak from around every rivet. Thick black smoke belched from its funnel. An engineer was hammering at something underneath the driver's cab. He looked to be in the same sort of condition as his charge.

"What did you expect?" Sgt Maj Finch bellowed. "The fuckin' Orient Express? Get your kit on board, jaldi! Then come back and start loading the supplies."

The soldiers jumped to obey, each troop heading for one of the two carriages designated for them. The insides of the carriages were no better than the outsides had promised. The heat from the early May sunshine was oppressive and the lack of windows did nothing to cool the interiors. The seats were hard wooden slatted benches spaced two feet apart along both sides and most of the luggage racks were broken. As they entered the carriages the soldiers passed evil smelling cubicles that were probably toilets, but none of them wanted to find out for sure.

There was one upside. They were finally leaving Algeria. Not that there was anything wrong with Algeria, of course, but the commando had felt under-employed and this move held the promise of action.

Since the success of Operation Carthage and the obligatory visits by senior officers all intent on associating themselves with the event, the commando had done very little except train. They had trained on the beach; they had trained at sea; they had trained in the mountains and they had trained in the desert. They were sick of training.

Twice they had been put on standby to mount landings ahead of the American forces in their attempts to capture the city of Tunis and on both occasions the operations had been cancelled at the last minute; the second one when they had actually been at sea. No reason had been given, but the general feeling was that the Americans didn't want to share any credit with the British that they didn't have to. General George Patton had taken command of the American II Corps after the Battle of Kasserine and he wasn't known for his willingness to share glory.

But now Tunis had finally fallen, the *Afrika Korps* and their Italian allies had surrendered and the war in North Africa was over. From the Atlantic to the Indian Ocean the Allies were in control. Everyone knew what must come next. Worried about flapping ears, the CO hadn't said where the train was taking them. But anywhere that offered the commandos the chance to fight was alright by them.

"Where are we going, boss?" Green asked Carter as they climbed aboard the creaking train.

"You know I can't tell you that." Carter replied. "But I can tell you it isn't where everyone thinks. We won't be going there for a few weeks yet and we've more training to do before we get there."

"Very cryptic. Go on, give us a clue."

"We're going to re-join the British Army. The 8th Army to be specific."

It was no more than the men were already speculating. "Egypt then."

"I didn't say that."

"But that's where Monty's HQ is."

"But the Army itself is spread across Egypt, Libya and Tunisia, so don't jump to conclusions."

"It's a long way to Cairo by train." Green fished.

Carter grinned. "Who mentioned Cairo? This train is going to Tebessa, which is still just about inside Algeria. After that we don't know how we will be travelling. The CO expects orders when we arrive there."

"Wasn't that near where we were during Carthage?"

"Not far away. A bit to the north west."

"Blimey. We're not going that far then."

"You can remind me of that after we've spent a few hours in this." Carter stamped his foot on the floor of the carriage, raising a cloud of dust.

"Why don't we just go by lorry?"

“Because the Americans have worked out that we are no longer on a special mission for Eisenhauer and they want their vehicles back.”

“Why? They haven’t needed them up till now.”

“Well, they want them back anyway. So we’re going by train, at least as far as Tebessa.”

“And then?”

“And then we find out where we’re going next.”

This ends the fourth story in the “Carter’s Commandos” series.

Historical Notes

At the beginning of this book I have tried to portray something of the mundane nature of the war in Britain from 1941 until the invasion of France in 1944.

For the first nine months of the war it had been referred to as a 'phoney war' because not much had happened; very little land combat and only occasional air and sea encounters. That changed in May 1940 with the *Blitzkrieg* advance of German troops through Belgium and Luxembourg, the invasion of France and the evacuation of the British Expeditionary Force from Dunkirk. This was followed by the Battle of Britain and the very real threat of invasion. After that, however, another sort of phoney war descended with a similar pattern for the troops based 'on the home front', ie in mainland Britain. The war here was being fought mainly by the RAF and the Royal Navy and its main effects were being suffered by the civilian population in the form of nightly bombing raids and food shortages.

The RAF was defending our skies or bombing Germany, while the Royal Navy was locked in a deadly battle with the German U-Boats in the North Atlantic, escorting the vulnerable convoys that were carrying the food needed to feed the population. The only soldiers that were regularly involved in fighting were the commandos who raided across the English Channel and the North Sea.

The main fighting on the ground was happening far away in North Africa and, from December 1941 onwards, in the Far East. The hundreds of thousands of British, Canadian and US Army soldiers stationed in Britain were largely unemployed.

This left commanders with a major headache as far as keeping the soldiers occupied was concerned. Day time was taken up with a variety of training activities, but the evenings left the soldiers with lots of time on their hands and, as the old saying goes, the Devil makes work for idle hands. Many a young officer would have had the same problems as Carter, trying to keep the men occupied in the evening, rather than roaming the streets of local towns, drinking and getting into fights.

My father recalled commandos being mobbed in the streets of Worthing and Weymouth by young women, much as young women mob the pop stars of today. The commandos really were hero worshipped. This did bring about resentment from other branches of the armed forces and from the male civilian population and that resentment did, on occasions, spill over into violence.

Sporting contests, film shows, dances and concert parties were some of the ways that commanding officers occupied their men in their spare time. I haven't mentioned my mother in these books until now, but this is where she comes into the story, though only in a 'walk on' capacity. Her name in 1942 was Kitty (a pet name based on her real name, Katherine) Sutherland and she was a member of a concert party. This is not the same as ENSA (Entertainment National Service Association, more colloquially known as Every Night Something Awful). ENSA was made up mainly of professional entertainers and some very big names, Vera Lynn, George Formby and Gracie Fields being the best known, appeared in their shows, as well as some acts who were so bad that they had struggled to find work before the war! The concert parties were strictly part time amateurs drawn from within the ranks of the armed forces.

In 1940, after a year in the Women's Land Army, my mother volunteered for the Auxiliary Territorial Service (ATS), the women's army, where she trained as a telephonist. Her first posting was to Brighton, where she was just a few miles away from my father, first in Bishopstone and later in Worthing, though they were destined not to meet for another 8 years and on the far side of the world. She did have a Canadian boyfriend, but never saw him again after Operation Jubilee in August 1942. She never found out what happened to him. She was later posted to Dover Castle, which is when she became involved in concert parties.

My mother had a good singing voice and specialised in the traditional songs of her native Scotland, such as *Bonnie Annie Laurie* and *The Skye Boat Song*. Being based in Dover my mother wouldn't have performed as far afield as Weymouth, so that is a fiction to allow me to shoehorn her into the story.

Units that wanted the concert parties to perform had to provide transport for them and my mother, whose Soldier's Service and Pay Book (Army Book 64) gives her height as 5ft 1in (155cm) in her stocking feet, recalled having to be lifted bodily into the back of 3 ton trucks to travel to the venues at which the concert party performed. She also remembered the regular air raids and shelling from the French coast that Dover Castle suffered. It wasn't called "Hellfire Corner" for nothing.

Although it wasn't encouraged, it wasn't unusual for the women in the concert parties to be invited out on dates after they had performed. It gave my mother a more active social life than the one she'd had down on the farm while in the Land Army. It also led to her marriage and early discharge from the ATS in 1944, followed by the birth of my stepsister on New Year's Day 1945.

Later in life, at a 3 Cdo reunion, my mother was persuaded to recreate her concert party performance for the benefit of the former members who attended.

While at Weymouth, my father's unit, 3 Cdo, was asked to assist the police in re-capturing two escaped prisoners from Portland Prison, which they succeeded in doing. I have no first-hand account of how the search was carried out, so the account with which I start this book is entirely fictional.

3 Cdo had been sent to Weymouth with a view to carrying out an operation on the Cherbourg peninsula, but Lt Col Durnford-Slater, 3 Cdo's CO, didn't like the plan and it was shelved. So, in between the relentless training, 3 Cdo spent its time testing the defences of various naval establishments and airfields in the South West of England, much as I described 15 Cdo doing at Prestwick in Operation Dagger.

They also spent a lot of their time in various sporting contests with their great rivals 4 Cdo, who were based 65 miles away in Winchester. At one football match, 3 Cdo's 'team' greeted the 4 Cdo team off the train and took them on a pub crawl around Weymouth.

When it came to the start of the match, the tipsy 4 Cdo players found themselves facing a team of totally sober footballers who had stayed in barracks. Unsurprisingly, 4 Cdo lost the match, though they did get their own back at a subsequent meeting of the two teams. 3 and 4 Cdos served side by side several times during the war, starting at the Lofoten islands in 1941 and continuing through to Dieppe, D-Day and onwards. Their rivalry, on and off the sports field, was legendary.

It was on 13th October 1942 that the wearing of the green beret was authorised for the Army commandos. Partly this was due to the lobbying of the CO of 1 Cdo, but partly an acknowledgement that as the Parachute Regiment had been authorised to wear a maroon beret, a similar accolade should be awarded to the much longer established commandos. 1 Cdo was the first unit to be issued with the berets, partly because of their CO's lobbying, but partly because they were due to depart for North Africa to take part in the Operation Torch landings in Algeria (8th November 1942).

If you watch old World War II newsreel footage, especially that taken on D-Day, you can always spot the commandos because, such was their pride in their units, they preferred wearing their green berets to wearing their steel helmets.

The British were as paranoid about a possible invasion of Gibraltar as I have described and with good reason. If either the Spanish or the Germans had succeeded in an attempt, they would have closed off British access to the Mediterranean Sea from the west, forcing all movements of troops and supplies to make the lengthy voyage around the Cape of Good Hope, through waters patrolled by German U-Boat packs. Resupply of the strategically important island of Malta, with its large Naval base and airfield, would have been all but impossible and without that the possibility of Rommel completing the conquest of Egypt might well have become a reality, providing the Germans with an oil supply route from the Persian Gulf through waters totally under their control.

There was at least one German plan, Operation Felix, which aimed to invade the colony with the connivance of the Spanish. Due to the German invasion of Russia, the plan was first postponed and then shelved. Given the critical impact of oil supplies on the German war effort later in the war, the abandonment of Operation Felix can only be seen as a strategic blunder.

The Royal Navy did have Spanish ports under blockade, controlling the flow of oil and food into a country that was starved of both. The people were hungry, especially in the cities and unemployment was endemic, so a new revolution was a real threat. Spain was also short of currency, Spain's gold reserves having been moved to Moscow at the "suggestion" of Stalin during the Civil War to prevent it falling into Franco's hands. That made Spain heavily reliant on foreign loans and British influence also played a part in those being granted. So, there are reasons why Franco had to stay out of the war, even if he would rather have joined it on the side of the Axis. The gold was never returned.

Throughout the war, espionage was rife on both sides of the border between Spain and Gibraltar. The security services estimated that there were as many as 150 Spanish and Gibraltarian spies working on the Rock at any one time and acts of sabotage were carried out. For their part, both MI6 and military intelligence employed agents on the Spanish side of the border, trying to gather intelligence on Spanish intentions and also to keep an eye on the *Abwehr*, the German military intelligence organisation, who were spying on the British and running the agents in Gibraltar. No Allied ship could enter or leave the Mediterranean without it being noted by Spanish or German observers, and the same applied to air movements through Gibraltar's airfield.

Much of the diplomatic effort put in by the British Ambassador to Spain, Sir Samuel Hoare, was aimed at keeping Franco from siding with the Germans, to whom he owed a significant debt for their support of the Nationalist cause during the Spanish Civil War (1936-1939).

From the time Gibraltar was first captured from Spain, in 1704, British army engineers started burrowing into the rock in order to provide protection against bombardment. But it was during World

War II that the Royal Engineers carried out a lot of the work, constructing underground barracks, offices, workshops and even a fully equipped hospital complete with operating theatres. When my son was in the army, serving with the Royal Engineers in the late 1990s, he was part of a working party sent to the Rock to block up many of the Napoleonic era tunnels to prevent tourists wandering into them and getting lost. Most of the materials the working party used had to be carried up the Rock on foot because there are only footpaths leading to some of the tunnel entrances, which makes the original tunnelling operations even more remarkable. The hundreds of tons of soil and rock that was removed at various times was used to extend and strengthen the harbour walls. Some of the World War II tunnels are still being used by the military.

The commandos did spend periods varying between 3 and 6 months on the Rock, with the aim of discouraging Spanish ambitions to take control of it. It also allowed time for them to acclimatise to the Mediterranean conditions. 1 and 6 Cdos had been based there in the weeks prior to their involvement in Operation Torch. My father's unit, 3 Cdo, spent about 3 months there before moving to Algeria and then onwards to the Gulf of Suez to prepare for the invasion of Sicily. They were replaced, in their turn, by 2 Cdo.

The activities in which the commandos engaged were much as I described, with the exception of Carter's operation in Spain. I needed something dangerous for Carter to do while he was on the Rock, so I created that fictional adventure.

At the time of writing, Gibraltar is still home to both a Royal Navy dockyard and an RAF airfield, which is also the colony's commercial airport. The peninsula still retains a lot of old colonial charm and if you happen to be on holiday on the Spanish side of the border, it is worth a day trip, if only for the duty-free shopping. On a clear day the views from the top of the Rock are stunning, with the African coast visible. If you go up the Rock in the cable car, women are advised to remove earrings and necklaces, as the resident Barbary apes do love to try and steal shiny objects.

Fort-de-l'Eau is a genuine place and 3 Cdo were based there for several weeks before moving to Egypt. However, it wasn't a former Foreign Legion fort, it was a transit camp consisting mainly of tents. I wished to add a little romance to my story, so the fort is my invention. The suburbs of Algiers have spread to encompass the area where the original Fort-de-l'Eau stood and it is assumed that it no longer exists. The commando's stay was unremarkable except for one incident which I have borrowed for this book.

Unable to obtain any transport from the British military authorities, the Second in Command, Maj Charlie Head, blagged some brand new vehicles from the US Army by pretending that the commando was about to undertake a secret mission on behalf of General Eisenhower and needed vehicles in order to train in the Atlas Mountains. The story was never checked and when the commando departed by rail for Tunisia the vehicles were left at the railway station.

The Battle of Kasserine started on 19th February 1943 with the Germans making a surprise attack on the pass with the intention of cutting the American coastal supply lines and surrounding the troops already threatening Tunisia. Rommel wasn't in favour of this approach, preferring to attack due west to capture the major rail head at Tébessa before turning north, but he was overruled by Field Marshall Kesselring, his commander in Rome. Initially the American and Free French forces defending the pass were dislodged by the suddenness of the attack but the rapid advance of the depleted American 1st Armoured Division (nicknamed "Old Ironsides") pushed the Germans back again. Suffering supply problems as well as being on the retreat, Rommel called off the offensive on 24th February, incurring the displeasure of Kesselring.

This battle was a turning point in the war in North Africa. From then on, the Germans would be on the defensive. Not only was it a defeat for the Germans, but it was also the first major land battle in which the American Army had been engaged in the European theatre (even though it was actually in Africa). Their performance demonstrated their durability, their adaptability and their fighting spirit. The remaining units of the *Afrika Korps* and their Italian allies surrendered to the Allies on 13th May 1943. The city of Tunis was the last bit of Africa that the Germans held.

I have borrowed one genuine unit from the Allied Order of Battle (organisational chart of units deployed) for Kasserine, the 1st Derbyshire Yeomanry. Equipped with Daimler Dingo armoured cars, they were deployed to the south of the battlefield to act as forward reconnaissance to provide warning should the Germans attempt a flanking manoeuvre. As such they were operating in the same area I have placed 15 Commando, so I feel it is legitimate to engineer an encounter between the two units for the purpose of my story. The Derbyshire Yeomanry (founded in 1794) was amalgamated into The Leicestershire and Derbyshire (Prince Albert's Own) Yeomanry in 1957. They remain part of Britain's Reserve Army.

3 Cdo weren't involved in the fighting to liberate Tunisia. In the spring of 1943 they transferred by rail and sea to the Suez Canal, where they took up residence at a place called El Ataka, which has now been absorbed into the city of Suez. By coincidence it is where I have sent 15 Cdo at the end of this book. We will pick up their story again in Book 5 of the Carter's Commandos series, entitled "Operation Leonardo".

For those who may think I have been rather unkind about Army catering, I offer no apologies – I've eaten it. It wasn't until quite late in the war that the Army managed to get a solid grip on the feeding of its troops.

The provision of food for the army had largely been left in civilian hands until the formation of the Commissariat and Transport Department in 1880. This department would eventually become the Royal Army Service Corps, then the Royal Corps of Transport and finally the Royal Logistics Corps. However, the actual cooking of the food was left in the hands of the units themselves.

In barracks this job was often handed over to locally employed civilians, but in the field the soldiers still had to look after themselves. No training was provided for cooks until the formation of the Army School of Catering in 1913, however, the personnel who attended were still drawn from their own units, with little thought given to aptitude or motivation. In some units, being sent to train as a cook was seen as a black mark or punishment. The most talented cooks tended to end up in the Sergeants Mess, as it was the RSM who decided on the placement of the staff, the next best went to the Officers' Mess, with the remainder going to the Other Ranks Mess, or 'cookhouse' as it was known colloquially.

My father, an infantryman, was sent on a cookery course in March/April 1941 and spent the next 4 months being sent to cook for engineer and pioneer units in the London area who were employed on the construction of defences. One of the reasons he volunteered for the commandos was to get away from the tedium of that duty. He had joined the army to fight, not to cook porridge. And yes, before you ask, he was sent on his cook's course after a spot of disciplinary bother. He did, however, become a very good cook, as my family could testify after many a Sunday lunch.

The Army Catering Corps (ACC) was formed in March 1941 with the aim of improving standards of catering across the Army. However, it took time for the newly trained ACC personnel to have an impact and catering in the field continued to be a somewhat haphazard affair as many an old soldier could testify. The Army Catering Corps was absorbed into the newly formed Royal Logistics Corps in 1996 but catering within barracks is once again back in civilian hands in many UK garrisons, with civilian catering companies operating under contract to the MoD. The focus of Army catering is now on feeding soldiers in the field.

Operation Carthage is entirely fictional but is the sort of operation that the commandos might undertake. I took the name from the ancient city of Carthage, which was built on the north eastern corner of Tunisia, close to the modern city of Tunis. It was originally a Phoenician colony before growing into a nation in its own right. It dominated the eastern end of the Mediterranean Sea for several centuries, including the colonisation of both Sicily and Sardinia. As the new Republic of Rome started to emerge, the two cities became rivals and then enemies, fighting three major wars that spanned a period of 120 years, known as the Punic Wars (referring to the Carthaginians' Phoenician origins). In the end it was Rome that won the final battle. After laying siege to the city they captured it. The population were killed or enslaved and the city was destroyed to prevent it from rising again. The whole area was then colonised and became an important source of grain to feed the people of Rome. The remains of the city have been excavated and may be visited. It is a flimsy excuse for choosing the name of a book, but what can I tell you? I'm a history geek.

Rudolf Höss was a real person and, as the Commandant at Auschwitz from 1940 to 1943, he is the most reliable witness for what happened at the three Auschwitz concertation camps (there was an *Auschwitz C* but it is less well known than the larger A and B camps). He returned there again in 1944 to supervise the murder of 430,000 Hungarian Jews in a period of just 56 days. After being arrested in 1946 Höss eventually made a full confession. He was condemned to death at the Nuremburg war crimes trials for his part in the Holocaust, was taken back to *Auschwitz* and was hanged there on 16th April 1947.

The treatment of Russian prisoners of war was as I had Rheinhardt describe it. They were worked to death, died from the summer heat and the winter cold, they died from disease, starved or were beaten to death on a whim. Of the 10,000 Russian PoWs transferred to build the Birkenau camp in January 1942, none were still alive in May. Similar treatment was meted out to the first inmates, the Polish military, political and intellectual leaders arrested after the defeat of Poland in 1940.

I have been inside the former ammunition bunker at *Auschwitz A*, which was turned into the first gas chamber and it is a chilling place. I have also been inside the former camp at *Birkenau* (*Auschwitz B*) and seen what was left of the gas chambers and crematoria, which the Germans tried to destroy as the Russian army advanced towards them in 1945. It is a place that makes strong men weep. I don't believe in ghosts, but on that sunny spring day in 2018 I felt as though I was surrounded by a million of them.

I include reference to Auschwitz in this story because, as I write this book, we have just had the commemorations for the 75th anniversary of D-Day and it seemed like a good time to remind readers of what the Second World War was about. It wasn't just a war between the Allies and the Axis over who ruled Europe or who controlled South East Asia and the Pacific Ocean, it was about good vs evil. It may not have been about that when it started, but it certainly was by the end.

Today, far right groups are once again springing up across Europe and their views on race are no different from those of the Nazis back in the 1930s and 40s. There is also a major split in the British Labour Party regarding the anti-Semitic views expressed by some party members. It is critical that we remember what humanity can do to itself when it follows the wrong leaders or when it looks away from what is being done in the name of the people. Within that sentiment I include what the State of Israel is doing to the Palestinians in the name of the Israeli people.

* * *

It was a Royal Artillery officer, Lt Col Dudley Clarke, who had first suggested the establishment of a specialist raiding force to attack German occupied France. This suggestion reached the ears of Winston Churchill, who embraced the idea with typical enthusiasm.

The Army commandos were established in June 1940 on the direct orders of Winston Churchill. It was he who recognised that to maintain the war effort until victory could be achieved, he needed to maintain the morale of the British people following the disaster that had been the evacuation from Dunkirk. The skilful use of propaganda had turned that defeat into a sort of victory, but genuine victories, however small, would be needed if he was to convince the British people that the war could be won.

It would be the commandos that would provide those small victories. Often the targets of their raids were insignificant in military terms but, on occasions, they had a far greater impact than could ever have been imagined. For example, following successive raids on Norway, Adolf Hitler became convinced that they were the prelude to an invasion of that country as a steppingstone for invading Denmark and then Germany itself. No such plan existed, but Hitler ordered 300,000 additional troops to be sent to Norway, where they remained for the rest of the war, along with additional Luftwaffe and naval units. The fact that the invasion of Norway never came about was proof to Hitler that his strategy had worked. Had those troops been available at Stalingrad, El Alamein or in Normandy in 1944, who knows how the outcomes of those battles might have been affected.

15 Commando is a fictitious unit. The Army commandos were numbered 1 to 14 (excluding 13). 50, 51 and 52 commandos were formed in North Africa. The Royal Marine Commandos weren't formed until 1942 and took the numbers 40 to 48. Unlike the Army commandos, only 40 (RM) Cdo was made up of volunteers. The rest were just Royal Marine battalions that were ordered to convert to the commando role. For this reason the Army commandos tended to look down on them, but once they had proved themselves in combat they became part of the commando family.

No 10 (Inter Allied) Commando was made up of members of the armed forces from occupied countries in Europe who had escaped. There were two French troops, one Norwegian, one Dutch, one Belgian, one Polish, one Yugoslavian and a troop of German speakers, many of whom were Jewish. They often accompanied other commandos on raids to act as guides and interpreters, as well as carrying out raids of their own.

If you wish to find out more about the Army commandos there are a number of books on the subject, including my own, which details my father's wartime service; it's called "A Commando's Story". I have provided the titles of some of these books at the end of these notes. These also provided the sources for much of my research for this book.

Achnacarry House is the ancestral home of Clan Cameron and it was taken over by the War Office to become the Commando Training Centre. The original occupants of the house moved into cottages in the grounds. During the course of World War II over 25,000 commandos were trained there, plus their American counterparts, the Rangers, who were modelled on the commandos. Originally each commando was responsible for providing their own training, before the first training centres were set up at Inveraray and Lochailort, in late 1940, before moving to Achnacarry.

Although in use from 1940 onwards, Achnacarry House was a holding centre for volunteers for special service before becoming a formal training school in March 1942.

Should you ever travel to that part of Scotland you will find a small museum to the Commandos at the Spean Bridge Hotel. At least, it was there the last time I visited. If you continue to drive north along the A82 for a couple of more miles you will come across the Commando Memorial, unveiled in 1950. You can't miss it, it's 17 ft high. If you have time, please stop for a moment to remember the men who trained in that rugged countryside. Some of them, including my father, have memorial plaques lodged there in the small memorial garden.

In the fictional world, Captain Carter and Cpl Green, LCpl Glass and Tpr O'Driscoll are destined, like my father, to have many more adventures before the war comes to an end.

Further Reading.

For first-hand accounts of Commando operations and training at Achnacarry, try the following:

Cubitt, Robert; A Commando's Story; Ex-L-Ence Publishing; 2018.
Durnford-Slater, John, Brigadier: Commando: Memoirs of a Fighting Commando in World War 2; Greenhill Books; new edition 2002.

Gilchrist, Donald: Castle Commando; The Highland Council; 3rd revised edition, 1993.
Scott, Stan; Fighting With The Commandos; Pen and Sword Military; 2008.
Young, Peter, Brigadier; Storm from the Sea; Greenhill Books; new edition 2002.

For a more general overview of the commandos and their operations:

Saunders, Hilary St George; The Green Beret; YBS The Book Service Ltd; new edition 1972.

Preview – Operation Leonardo

1 – El Ataka

Even after nearly two weeks of travel, the camp was a less than welcoming sight. Rows of dun coloured tents stretched away in parallel lines, a larger tent with a chimney sticking up behind it indicating where the mess tent was. A wooden hut that looked as though it might have been made from packing cases, served as a guardroom, a wooden pole, striped red and white, resting across a couple of white painted oil drums was the sole barrier against intruders.

Behind the camp, at a distance of about three miles across a flat plain, some low rocky hills rose to form a backdrop. The intervening ground, Carter was to discover, was called the El Ataka Plain.

A sentry snapped to attention as the commando was called to a halt on the road. His shoulder tabs bore the legend 'South Africa'. He was from one of the African Auxiliary Pioneer Corps[1] (AAPC) units that were raised from the tribal lands. Carter had seen them several times on their journey south from Port Said.

Standing next to the nearest sentry was a Captain, wearing the shoulder flashes of the Royal Army Service Corps, acting as a one-man reception committee. The sentry raised the pole and the officer marched out to salute the 2IC, who was leading the commando in the absence of the CO.

After a short conversation, accompanied by some pointing, the commando was permitted to enter the camp. At this point the NCOs took over, detailing the commandos to their tents. Twelve men to a tent, five tents per troop. Senior NCOs had their own shared tents, as did the officers. Slightly less crowded, but not by much. There was no haste. It would be a while before the rear party arrived with the trucks carrying their kit bags, ammunition and other stores.

The 2IC and Quarter Master were closeted with the RASC Captain for some while, being briefed on the arrangements for the supply of food, water and other essential consumables. The rest of the officers would be briefed later.

The heat was oppressive, the humidity worse. Sunshine glistened off the Gulf of Suez, a short distance from the camp gate. It looked welcoming but the troops knew that there were jellyfish in there that could inflict a nasty sting. Someone had suggested there were sharks as well, but that hadn't been confirmed. Out in the gulf, a dozen merchant ships sat at anchor, waiting their turn to make the one hundred and twenty mile journey through the Suez Canal to the Mediterranean Sea at Port Said. An Ack-Ack[2] ship bristled with guns, standing guard against air attack.

As the sun set over southern Egypt, a metallic clanging summoned the soldiers to their first hot meal in a week. It was 'anonymous stew', but after so much bully beef they welcomed it. The AAPC cooks also made a pretty good cup of tea, they discovered.

Fed and watered, the men stretched out on their camp beds, resting as the heat of the day ebbed away.

15 Commando had arrived at El Ataka.

[1] African Auxiliary Pioneer Corps (AAPC) – When World War II broke out, the Kings of the High Commission Territories in South Africa, the self-governing tribal lands, wished to show their loyalty to Britain. They allowed their men to volunteer for service with the British Army. In some cases the volunteering part was a little more compulsory than in others. Men from Swaziland (also called Eswatini), Basutoland (now Lesotho) and Bechuanaland (now Botswana) formed labour pools which were employed in Egypt to replace Cypriots and Palestinians who had been killed in the defence of Greece. Their main work was as labour for building roads and airfields, but they also provided guards for stores depots and tented camps. Later in the war, manpower shortages led to them being used to man coastal artillery and ant-aircraft batteries. They also followed

the British 8th Army into Sicily and Italy. The AAPC grew to approximately 36,000 strong before being demobilised in 1946. They suffered 816 casualties during the war, including 600 men of the 618th Basoto Pioneer Company that were killed when the SS Erinpura was sunk by German bombers off Benghazi..

[2] Ack-Ack – anti-aircraft. The words are taken from the word assigned for the letter A in a form of phonetic alphabet used during World War I.

* * *

"In terms of security," The 2IC said, "Our greatest risk is theft. As we discovered in Algiers, anything not nailed down is liable to go walkies. Apparently, it's even worse here. The average Egyptian is an honest, hardworking sort, but Suez is a port city and they always attract the wrong types, looking for easy pickings.

"You can say that again." One of the other officers said. "I'm from Liverpool and half the houses in our street were kept fed by stuff that had fallen off the back of a lorry leaving the docks." That brought a laugh from the assembled officers.

"Precisely. We can expect thieves to try to get through the perimeter fence at night, according to Captain Reynolds." Carter assumed that Reynolds was the RASC Captain. "The AAPC guards do carry out patrols, but there's too few of them to protect the whole perimeter twenty four hours a day. So we will do what we did in Algiers and mount our own patrols outside the wire. It worked in Algiers so I dare say it will work here. Word will soon get out not to mess with us." There was a threat implied by the words and Carter knew what injuries could be inflicted with the wooden handle of a trenching tool. He didn't approve of the action but knew that telling commandos to exercise restraint would fall on deaf ears.

One of the Tilley lamps[1] guttered as the pressure started to drop and someone gave it a couple of pumps to restore it.

A hand went up. "Any idea how long we'll be here, Sir?"

“Not a clue. Hopefully the CO will get some indication while he’s in Cairo. He’s due here at the end of the week.

“We seem to be a long way from anywhere we’re likely to be needed.” Someone else commented.

“We were a long way away when we were in Scotland” The 2IC reminded them, “but that didn’t stop us doing our jobs. Even though the war in North Africa is over, the airborne threat still exists. The Luftwaffe are only a couple of hours flying time away in Crete, so the powers that be are keen to keep the army spread out, so we make a harder target. I’m sure that you saw some of the other camps as we came down here.”

There had, indeed, been plenty of camps to be seen. The whole approach into the city of Suez seemed to be one vast sea of dun coloured tents. Much of the 8th Army had been withdrawn back into Egypt to shorten their supply lines, leaving garrison troops to protect the towns and cities of Libya and Tunisia.

“The men want to know if they can go into town, Sir.” Carter chipped in.

“Not yet, Steven. First, we have to get the camp organised, then I want us to do some navigation exercises to get to know the area. We’re here to train for our next operation, so we’ve got to find the right sort of locations for landing and assaults. The CO will tell us more about that when he gets here, I’m sure.

[1] Tilley lamp – A paraffin fuelled camping lamp that uses air pressure to force a fine mist of paraffin through a heated element to provide a much brighter light than could be produced by burning a wick. The lamp needed ‘pumping up’ from time to time to maintain the air pressure. Largely replaced by bottled gas fuelled or battery powered lamps these days. The Tilley company still exists and still manufactures its eponymous lamps.

* * *

The Officers’ Club was busy even in the middle of the week. Junior officers jostled for space around the bar, while more senior figures made us of the tables for games of cards or backgammon. Carter squeezed himself into a gap that opened up briefly next to a Royal Navy Lieutenant Commander who sat nursing his drink at the bar.

The buzz of dozens of conversations was such that Carter had to raise his voice to order a glass of whisky. When the Egyptian barman went to drop ice into the drink, Carter held his hand over the top of his glass and said 'no thanks'.

"It's OK to take the ice, old chap." The naval officer said. "The water's from a safe source."

When they had arrived at the transit camp in Port Said they had been given lectures on health and hygiene by a Royal Army Medical Corps doctor. "I can't stress this enough, gentlemen." He had said. "Don't drink the water unless it has been boiled for at least five minutes or has been treated with water purifying tablets. Your weak British tummies just can't handle the local bacteria. The most common mistake people make is to put ice in their drinks or eat salad vegetables that have been washed in untreated water. You'll end up with gyppie tummy[1]. It won't kill you, but it will probably make you wish you were dead." He said, as his audience gave an appreciative chuckle.

It was a hard lesson to get across to some of the men, who thought they were strong enough to resist a few bacteria. They were wrong, of course. Two men had to be left behind in Port Said because they were unfit to travel and another had to be taken off the train as they travelled south.

"If you're sure." Carter said.

The man raised his glass and gave it a swirl, the ice cubes clinking against the side. "It's good enough for my G&T."

Carter removed his hand and nodded to the barman. Two cubes splashed into the glass and the barman retired to the far end of the bar where empty glasses were being waved to try to attract his attention.

"Peter Curshaw." The man offered his hand.

"Steven Carter, Sir." Carter replied.

"First names only in the club, old chap. Unless there's braid on the peak of the cap." Gold braid on the peak of the cap indicated an officer of senior rank. It would be unseemly for a junior officer to address anyone of that seniority by their first name, even in a social setting such as this.

"Thanks for the tip."

Curshaw spotted the Commando flashes on the sleeves of Carter's shirt. "You lot are new in town."

"Yes, just arrived last week." Having been Duty Officer the night before, Carter had been granted 'shore leave' to visit the Officer's Club, along with the men who had just finished a week of night patrols around the camp. They had travelled in a three ton truck, the men being dropped outside the Salvation Army Club, with warnings not to stray too far. Carter knew the warning was a waste of time. The men were keen to explore the dubious delights of Suez and no warnings would be heeded, no matter how strongly worded. Carter just hoped that they would remember the other warning they had been given, to stay in groups of four. Those and the dire warnings of the medical officer in Port Said.

The truck had dropped Carter off at the Officers' Club, agreeing to return at twenty two hundred hours to collect him and however many of the men that made it back to the Sally Army.

"I won't ask what you're doing here. I know you can't say."

"It's probably the worst kept secret in Egypt." Carter replied with a grin. "You'll see us around a lot. We've got landing craft arriving in a few days and it's a bit hard to miss them. Presumably you're on convoy escort duties."

"No, actually. I've got command of a flotilla of fast Motor Launches. We're on anti-pirate patrols."

"What, 'yo-ho-ho and a bottle of rum' and all that? Sounds a bit old fashioned."

"You'd be surprised. It's a big problem."

"You mean against convoys guarded by destroyers and corvettes." Carter sounded dubious.

"Oh no. They're too well armed to be bothered. No, these are locals looking for easy pickings. They attack trading dhows."

"There can't be much money in that."

"You'd be surprised. That coffee you had for breakfast was probably made from beans grown in Ethiopia and brought up the Red Sea in dhows. The spices that hide the fact that the meat in the stew is on the turn, are traded in Aden and Muscat. Going the other way is cotton, either in bales or as made up cloth. Also there's manufactured goods from Europe, most of it's channelled through Turkey these days so it can't be traced back to the German occupied countries, but once it arrives in Suez it's shipped on in dhows, just as it always has been. Your average dhow will carry a cargo worth tens of thousands of pounds. Then there's the people doing the pilgrimage to Mecca, travelling from Sudan, Ethiopia, Egypt and along the coast from Yemen and further afield; they're ripe to be robbed. Some are taken as slaves, especially the women."

"Slavery as well. Who'd have thought it." Carter finished his drink and signalled to the barman for another. He nodded at the Navy man's empty glass and it was pushed across for a refill.

"It never really went away in this part of the world. It's just better hidden."

"But what's this got to do with us?"

"His Majesty, King Farouk's[2] Navy is quite small and is too stretched in the Red Sea and they're not well equipped for inshore work, so we're helping out as a favour. We carry Egyptian police officers who actually make any arrests, just to keep things legitimate."

"Are you having much success?"

"Not really. We have to be very lucky to intercept any of their boats. Most of the dhows don't carry radios, so they can't call for help if they're attacked. We think the pirates are based on the Saudi Arabian Peninsula and we can't encroach into their waters without risking a serious diplomatic incident. His Majesty King Saud is too busy with his internal political problems to pay much attention to a few pirates at the extreme northern end of his Kingdom. He does get a bit upset when pilgrims are kidnapped, so most of his naval activity is centred around Jiddah, which is the port nearest to Mecca.

"So where do the local pirates hide?"

"On the far side of the Gulf of Aqaba. That's the waterway that leads from the Red Sea up to Transjordan and Palestine[3]. The Saudi coastline is very sparsely populated. Mainly small fishing villages and a few palm groves where there's water. We think they may be using one of those as a base."

"Can't you lie off shore and wait for them."

"We've tried that, but they seem to have good intelligence. They always seem to know we're coming and don't venture out, or they sneak past us in the dark, or they send their boats out before we even arrive. I've got three boats and they have to be refuelled and re-victualled at regular intervals. I can't cover the amount of sea that needs to be patrolled."

"I know what I'd do." Carter said.

"I'd welcome any suggestions."

"First set a trap. Train your men to sail a dhow and then go out and wait to be attacked. I'd put a few commandos on board, maybe a dozen, just to make sure that there was enough firepower."

"What we call a Q Ship[4]." Curshaw said, looking thoughtful. "A lion dressed up like a lamb. But they never all attack at once. Some would be bound to get away and warn the others."

"You follow them. Find out where they go. Then you mount a commando raid to clean out their nest. Commandos could get in and out without anyone even knowing they'd been there."

"Sounds intriguing. Do you really think that the Saudi's would never be any the wiser?"

"Only if they actually saw you with their own eyes. Given what you've said that's probably unlikely. But any competent commando would do a recce first, just to make sure there weren't any army, navy or police around. Do the Saudi's have an air force?"

"I've never seen any planes other than ours and Jerry's. I have to say it's an intriguing idea. It certainly beats cruising around in circles hoping to stumble across them at sea."

"What sort of boats do they use?"

"Quite modern now. When they first started up they used old fishing boats or dhows of their own, but they were slow and clumsy. Since then they've stolen enough cargoes to be able to trade up to skiffs powered by outboard motors. Each boat holds four or five men. They're still not fast enough to get away from my boats, but they can outpace the dhows they attack."

"What do they do when they capture a dhow. Do they unload the cargo?"

"No. According to the ones we've arrested, they take the dhow to a safe location and let it be known they have it, what the cargo is and what price they're looking for. Potential buyers come along, view the cargo and make them an offer. Once a price has been agreed the new owner takes it to one of the ports that's not too fussy about checking ownership. There's plenty of those along the African coast and in the Persian Gulf. They sell the cargo then sell the dhow and a few weeks later it's probably back in Suez with a fresh coat of paint and a new name. It's very hard to prove ownership of a dhow."

"OK, as I see it, you have two different problems. The first is to take the pirates prisoner, the second is to find out where their base is so it can be attacked. The first part we've already covered. The second part means letting one or more of the boats escape, then follow them ashore with a boat of your own. You'd have to have a boat in the water already, something small but also capable of keeping up with them."

"I think they'd rumble us if they saw a boat in the water. It wouldn't look right to them and they'd break off the attack. I think we'd have to capture one of their boats, but that might be possible if we're using a Q boat."

"How well are they armed?"

"At first all they had was World War I vintage rifles and handguns left behind by the Turks. But they've got more modern weapons now, mainly Lee Enfields stolen from us and Italian rifles left behind after the Abyssinian campaign. There's an extensive black market for weaponry in the region. The police interrogate the prisoners we catch and we've heard tell of automatic weapons, but we haven't seen any direct evidence of those yet."

"How do they find about about the dhows they're going to attack?"

"We suspect that they've got informers in the native port, where the dhows tie up. Let's face it, the Jerries are running plenty of local agents, so it's no stretch to presume that the pirates can do the same. For north bound traffic they probably have spotters along the coast. The dhows tend to keep inshore. It's easier to navigate that way and they can find shelter quicker if the weather turns nasty."

"You'd need to put a story round the port about your dhow then. Make it sound like a nice juicy target."

"You make it sound like we're actually going to do it." Curshaw laughed.

"It's worth giving some serious consideration. The only thing stopping you, really, is the diplomatic ramifications of mounting an operation on Saudi Arabian soil. The part with the dhow you could do tomorrow if you had the resources."

"True. That itself would be success and we've had damn few of those."

Curshaw bought Carter 'one for the road' and they chatted some more, then Carter had to leave to catch his truck. Curshaw rose from his bar stool as well.

"Good luck." Carter said as he left the club, Curshaw climbing into a taxi to take him back to his boats. "If you go ahead with the idea, let me know how you get on."

[1] Gyppie tummy – a corruption of 'Egyptian tummy', an illness that had been suffered by British soldiers in Egypt since before the days of Kitchener. Differences between the way water is treated in northern Europe and elsewhere results in bacteria remaining in the water that visitors can't tolerate. In India it was referred to as 'Delhi belly'. For the most part the water isn't dirty, it's just different. British and other European travellers still suffer from these ailments today, which is why bottled water is so popular in hot climates.

[2] King Farouk was the hereditary king of Egypt from 1936 to 1952. It is fair to say that he was kept in power by a strong British military presence, ostensibly protecting the Suez Canal. Farouk was known as something of a dissolute character and cared more for his own pleasures than the proper governance of the Egyptian people. He was deposed in a coup by Colonel Gamal Abdel Nasser, the leader of a group of likeminded army officers, called the Association of Free Officers. This coup and the subsequent nationalisation of the Suez Canal provoked the 'Suez Crisis' of 1956 which led to the downfall of the British Prime Minister, Sir Anthony Eden.

[3] These were the names given to the British protectorates that we now know as the countries Jordan and Israel. The port city of Aqaba gives its name to the gulf that gives Jordan it's only access to the sea. On one side it shares a border with Saudi Arabia and on the other a border with Israel at the neighbouring city of Eilat.

[4] A Q Ship could be a naval vessel disguised as a merchant ship to fool the enemy, or a merchant ship which carried concealed armaments. They were used to lull enemy vessels into a false sense of security before attacking them. The first recorded use of a Q Ship or boat was in the 1670s when a specially designed Royal Navy cutter, HMS Kingfisher, was used against Algerian pirates. In World War II the Germans used 13 Q Ships. The Atlantis, an auxiliary cruiser (a naval vessel that looked like a merchant ship) named *Goldenfels* which was disguised as a Dutch merchant vessel, was responsible for the sinking of 145,000 tons of Allied shipping. Britain used nine Q ships with the intention of entrapping German U Boats, all but one of which were converted merchantmen. HMS Chatsgrove was a converted Royal Navy P-class sloop built in 1918. Two of those Q Ships were sunk in 1940 and the remainder were decommissioned in 1941 without having recorded any successes.

* * *

The arrival of the landing ship Prince Leopold, a former Belgian cross channel steamer, signalled the start of the commando's more intensive training. They still had no idea what their objective was to be. All they knew was that it was in the Mediterranean Sea and the landings would take place in high summer, probably July.

"To be honest with you." Lt Col Vernon had told them on his arrival from Cairo, "I'm not sure Monty knows what to do with us. Colonel Bob Laycock[1] is on his planning staff and, as you know, he's an experienced commando, but the planners don't seem to be listening to him that well. I'm sure they'll find us a suitable objective but, in the meantime, we just have to train for any eventuality."

So, the commandos built simulated defences along the rocky shore of the Gulf of Suez and started attacking them from the sea, both by day and by night. They then built strongpoints further inland and simulated raids deeper into enemy territory. All the attacks started before dawn, meaning they had to board the Prince Leopold the night before, steam out into the gulf and then turn back to board their landing craft before the assaults. It was tiring work and the three months between their operation in Tunis and their arrival in Suez had left them with lower fitness standards than those in which they took such great pride. So they now worked extra hard to regain that edge that made them, in their not so humble opinion, the best soldiers in the world.

Out on the plain beyond their camp they constructed a firing range and all day and often into the night, the crack and rattle of small arms fire echoed over the tents. Ammunition trucks, manned by more of the AAPC, were frequent arrivals at the camp gates to replace the thousands of bullets that the commandos expended on the range. As for the native population, after a few night-time encounters with the commando patrols, they learned to give the camp a wide berth.

Each afternoon, between three and five pm, the commandos took refuge in their tents, the side walls lowered and the flaps tied down as tightly as physically possible. Not only was it the hottest part of the day, but a vicious wind blew up across the plain, sending dust flying through the camp to coat anything that wasn't covered up. It got into the food and water supplies, it got into men's eyes, mouths and up their noses. It caked their weapons that they kept so scrupulously clean. It attacked their stomachs when it was ingested and, all in all, made life a misery. The men's only defence was to wrap their neck clothes around their faces and hope to get a little sleep inside the heat and darkness of their tents. After the wind died away the men were allowed to swim, all thoughts of jellyfish or sharks forgotten as they tried to clean the thick dust off their bodies, before they headed into the port to board the Prince Leopold for yet another assault on the shores of the Gulf of Suez.

Lt Col Vernon disappeared up to Cairo again and when he returned the mocked up installations they were attacking were modified. A new installation was built some distance inland, made to look like an artillery battery, using lengths of metal scaffolding pole to represent the guns. Troops took turns acting as defenders while the remainder of the commando carried out the assaults, the sounds of blank ammunition and pyrotechnics shattering the dawn. Barriers were erected for them to negotiate. They were told they were drystone walls, though a lack of materials made them appear more like heaps of brown desert soil topped with some of the smaller boulders taken from the beach.

For recreation, games of football and rugby were organised against neighbouring units but the commando's competitiveness and physical aggression soon meant opponents were hard to find. The RAF refused to play them on reputation alone, the CO of the nearest RAF base having encountered the commandos once before back in England. His technicians and aircrew were too valuable for him to risk broken limbs playing sports against the commandos. If there was no unit that would play them, the troops played against each other, making the rivalry even more intense.

Carter was making his way back from the firing ranges, wiping grime from his face with his neck cloth. He hadn't had a good morning, having hit the static targets with only half his shots and missing the moving targets completely. Although he usually carried a Tommy gun when on operations, all the officers kept their hand in with three-oh-threes as well.

One of the Headquarters clerks intercepted him on the way to the officers' tents. "CO's compliments, Sir. Could you join him in his office." Carter suppressed a smile; the CO's 'office' was a curtained off end of the HQ tent.

"Thank you, Ecclestone. Tell the CO I'll be there as soon as I've cleaned myself up a bit."

Carter entered his tent and grabbed his washing kit. No time for a shower; etiquette dictated that he refilled the elevated water tank for the next person who wanted to use the facility and he didn't have time for that. A lick and a promise, to remove the worst of the grime, would have to do. Fortunately, the laundry truck hadn't delivered that week so he wouldn't be expected to be in a completely clean uniform. He sorted out the cleanest of his already used shirts and shorts and smartened himself up as best he could.

Still hot and bothered, he hurried to the HQ tent, coughed loudly in front of the CO's curtain to announce his presence and stuck his head around the open end.

"Ah, Steven. I understand you've met Lt Cdr Curshaw."

[1] In 1941 Col Robert Laycock took a force of three commandos, 7, 8 and 11, to the Mediterranean for the purpose of carrying out harassing and disrupting operations against the Germans and the Italians. On arrival he absorbed the three small Middle East commandos, 50, 51 and 52, into his command. As he wasn't a Brigadier, his force couldn't be called a Brigade, so it was referred to as Layforce. They provided men for the siege of Tobruk, carried out an operation on the Litani river in in Syria, a major raid on Bardia in Libya and aided in the defence of Crete, where they suffered heavy losses. A small force from 11 Cdo also carried out an audacious raid to try to kidnap General Erwin Rommel, but it failed as he wasn't at his reported location. He had left there several weeks before the raid. Suffering heavy losses and a lack of reinforcements, Layforce was eventually forced to disband. With the remaining commandos being

absorbed into organisations such as the Long Range Desert Group. One of 8 Cdo's officers, Major David Sterling, formed the unit that would one day become famous as the Special Air Service Regiment. Laycock was later promoted to Brigadier and given command of 2nd Special Service Brigade, which would evolve into 2nd Commando Brigade, operating in Italy, Yugoslavia and Albania.

And Now

Both the author Robert Cubitt and Selfishgenie Publishing hope that you have enjoyed reading this story.
Please tell people about this eBook, write a review on Amazon or mention it on your favourite social networking site. Word of mouth is an author's best friend and is much appreciated. Thank you.
Find Robert Cubitt on Facebook at **https://www.facebook.com/robertocubitt** and 'like' his page; follow him on Twitter @**Robert_Cubitt**

For further titles that may be of interest to you please visit our website at **selfishgenie.com** where you can optionally join our information list.

Printed in Great Britain
by Amazon

62575405R00147